DEGENERATE, REGENERATE

The Sequel to
Fairytales Don't Come True
and Volume 2 of the
Criminal Conversation trilogy.

Laura Lyndhurst

As flies to wanton boys are we to th' gods:
They kill us for their sport.

- William Shakespeare,
King Lear, 4:1, 37 – 38

CONTENTS

1: ARRIVAL

The island was dying, and that wasn't an issue as far as Lieutenant Stephanos Stephanidou was concerned; what really irked him was that he had been selected to share its demise. Selected? Manoeuvred, more like, outflanked, set-up and then sent down, to this desolate and almost-deserted island, this remote region about as far away from the bustle and business and busy-ness of the city, of the capital, of Athens, as it was possible to be. The arsehole of empire; he remembered reading that somewhere, in regard to Burma and the British Empire. Go back to the Ancient civilizations, Greece followed by Rome, at that time Armenia, Assyria and Mesopotamia took the title; too far from the capital to be governed effectively and too alien to assimilate Western culture. OK, so this island wasn't that far away, just a few miles off the coast of Turkey, but in today's terms it had to be right at the edge of modern Greece, by anybody's reckoning.

He'd arrived on what was laughably called the ferry, a small and dilapidated vessel from a neighbouring island at which he'd arrived by a similar vessel, having flown into the biggest island nearby to boast an airport. Even the hardiest of tourists in search of what they were pleased to call 'The Real Greece' would be sorely tried at having to make such a journey, he reckoned, so there were few if any tourists; which was of course why the island was dying. And here he was back at the beginning of this chain of thought.

The beginning? No, not here, this was the end, more like. Go back to Athens and his old self, an intelligent and well-educated lieutenant of police, in the course of a

1

promising career. Sent to work under a far-from-ideal superior officer, paranoid and jealous of his own post, sweetened as it was, Lieutenant Stephanidou had no doubt, by many perks, small and not-so-small, the bribes and bungs earned through looking the other way on numerous occasions over many years. The senior officer sensed a threat and a rival in the junior, a man already noted for his integrity and determination to discharge his duty honestly and not troubling to hide his contempt for the superior whom he despised. Not too difficult for the junior to make mischief, make waves, cast doubt on the conduct of the senior in the right places, the right ears. Have him discharged, at the very least, dishonourably and without pension, and then step easily into his shoes? The senior couldn't have that, so he made the mischief, whispered supposed worries regarding the junior into the right ears. A set-up arranged, the blame for certain mistakes placed squarely on the shoulders of the innocent junior, with so-called brother officers ready to support the senior, for the correct consideration, of course, and the junior cautioned, disciplined and destined to end his career on this God-forsaken island, much as those who fell foul of the Roman emperors were wont to do. He'd read that somewhere, or seen it on TV; which? Immaterial, really, but wherever it was from he remembered hearing that the Emperor Augustus, banishing his daughter Julia for scandalous sexual antics, had sent her to an island which measured only eight miles from one end to the other; or was it that one could walk from one end to the other in eight minutes? Tiny, anyway, enough so to drive the occupant mad, and looking at the island which awaited him, Stephanidou tried to comfort himself with the obvious fact that this island was bigger than that to which poor Julia was sent; by how much he was yet to find out.

The main town of Ayios Andreas itself was nothing; a small harbour, into which he was unceremoniously put ashore with his belongings, few as they were because he wouldn't need much here. A few buildings, all in a dilapidated state of repair and in need of renovation, although knocking them down and starting again might be the easier option, Lieutenant Stephanidou thought. Shops and houses in the main, he noted, and, at the far right-hand end of the harbour-front, a church. He scowled at the sight of this particular edifice; despite his upbringing in the Orthodox church, his faith in God had suffered as a result of his recent injustices at the hands of Man. Where was the place for a merciful God in all of that, he had asked himself, over and over again, where the justice? He was an ordinary man, trying to live a good life, not asking a lot, but this evil had come upon him anyway; so he wavered on a thin line between belief and disbelief and came down firmly on the side of the latter.

He dragged his attention back to the harbour-front and noted the regulation kafenion with a couple of old men sitting outside, immobile as if they were permanent fixtures, which they probably were. It was far too quiet, though; where were the children? They were noticeable by their absence, at this time of day; where was the regulation group of little girls, sitting on the pavement giggling and speaking secrets to each other? Where the small boys with bicycles, chasing each other loudly around and being shooed away by irate waiters when they got too close to the outside tables and the paying customers sitting there? No girls, no boys, no tavernas, no waiters and no customers either, for that matter; just a place marked by a piece of waste ground to the other side of the harbour, covered with concrete and garbage, plus a group of crumbling buildings that looked as though one of the non-existent children could push them over with one finger.

Lieutenant Stephanidou resisted the urge to try pushing them himself, for fear of the consequences, and contented himself with asking directions to the Police Station from

3

the old men; they pointed, and gave brief directions; so not statues then. He found his way, to yet another decaying building in the back street behind the harbour front; a street of sorts, anyway, if not particularly long, with few buildings interspersed by patches of waste ground, decorated with refuse including a rusting bicycle and overgrown with weeds which in one case were being slowly and methodically consumed by a tired and world-weary-looking donkey which appeared as ready to fall over as the building to which it was lackadaisically tethered.

He made his way into the police station, marked as such by the rather ragged blue and white national flag which hung wearily from the tarnished pole which stuck out at right-angles from the wall over the doorway. It was rather too dark inside, the air heavy and humid despite the efforts of an old and creaking ceiling fan which rotated slowly and noisily over his head. A figure moved behind the front desk, pushing backwards the revolving chair on which he sat by dint of pushing against the desk with his feet, which had been resting thereupon. Stephanidou duly introduced himself, receiving a desultory handshake and greeting in return; "Yes", he was indeed the Captain in charge, assuming there was anyone else working there of whom he might be in charge, and "Yes, I was expecting you". After polite enquiries as to whether Lieutenant Stephanidou had had a good journey, he got down to business. "You're posted to Palliohorio; I'll take you there myself, now, do you want coffee, water, to freshen up, first?" The Lieutenant took advantage of all these offers as he covered his dismay; where was Palliohorio? He'd assumed he'd be working here, where the action was, he thought ironically; could it get any worse?

It could. After a drive of about thirty minutes, in a police car that rivalled both so-called ferries for dilapidation and lack of speed, Captain Petrides parked up in a tiny village, if it were big enough to deserve that classification, and ushered his new subordinate into one of the damp and derelict-seeming buildings which lined the square, along with the regulation church and kafenion, the usual couple of old men sitting outside looking like clones of those seen in Ayios Andreas. They were outside both church and kafenion, he noted, because the latter was positioned right next to the former, with anyone attending church obliged to pass through the forecourt of the kafenion to get there. The captain followed his eyes, and his thought; "The church owns the building and the land, and rents it to Giorgos for his coffee shop; it makes them some money, and the men don't have to walk too far to get into the church, so everybody benefits". He didn't add, Lieutenant Stephanidou thought, that given the apparent average age of the population here, should the men happen to die whilst sitting in the kafenion, or walking the short distance from there to the church door, it wouldn't be too much trouble to get them to their own funerals.

The police station-house consisted of a one-storey building, opposite the church and kafenion, apparently falling down like everything else around it; the whitewash of the old brick walls and the blue of the door and shutters were faded and dirtied with time and long-overdue in needing to be renewed. Inside, an unprepossessing office area, painted at about the same time as the outside, Stephanidou reckoned, consisted of dirty off-white (very far off) walls, furnished indifferently with a rusting and creaky ceiling fan to match that seen in the office at Ayios Andreas and shabby yet still functional (just about) metal-framed and laminate desk, chair and filing cabinets. A door at the back of the room led to the living accommodation, shabby yet mercifully functional, like the office area. A small kitchen, bathroom and bedroom, all leading off of an only-slightly bigger living room at the back which, however, boasted what must be the height of modern living here; a television, antiquated and black-and-white (which

5

became apparent when Captain Petrides switched it on with an air of pride) but at least in working order. A door from this room led onto a terrace to one side of the building which was shaded by unkempt grapevines growing over a rusting metal structure of poles, facing onto an overgrown and wilting mess which may once have been a garden. The outer boundaries of this consisted of yet another crumbling brick wall, low enough to scale easily to reach what would be Lieutenant Stephanidou's mode of transport; a beat-up old banger with 'POLICE' embossed upon it, the word recognisable despite patches of paint having flaked off of the letters in places, which sat drunkenly on the uneven road surface outside the wall. It must have been a new car in about the early twentieth century, Stephanidou thought ironically.

Captain Petrides was fulsome in his praise of these official and domestic arrangements; his whole air was of one who has single-handedly recovered the Parthenon Marbles from the British and is returning them to their rightful home in Athens. "Everything under one roof, you see, convenient and comfortable; no spending hours stuck in the traffic whilst getting to work. Sofia, Giorgo's wife at the kafenion, will cook for you if you wish, and do laundry and housework too, and she won't charge you much. There's a small shop over the way, run by Stelios, you can't miss it, but you can always pick up stuff when you come into town to see me. Everything's there in the office, files and so forth, car keys in the desk drawer and the car is parked round opposite the terrace, as you can see. I suggest you get some rest now, have a good sleep and familiarise yourself with it all in the morning; but don't rush, you've plenty of time, nothing ever happens around here anyway. Give me a call when you're up and about."

So he departed, leaving the Lieutenant to a late meal at the kafenion, courtesy of Sofia; there wasn't much available but cold food, bread and cheese and sour village

6

wine, and Stephanidou wondered if there ever would be
anything cooked, given that Sofia and her husband Giorgos
were clearly on the wrong side of eighty and apparently not
up to much by way of strenuous physical activity. But they
were welcoming and friendly, generous with the wine and
ouzo and interested in anything he could tell them of the
latest goings-on in Athens, the extent of their outside world,
it seemed. But the food they gave him was much better
than nothing, given that Stephanidou hadn't eaten since
before his lengthy ferry journey, and the alcohol helped
him to whatever sleep he found possible in what followed,
a hot night in a hard bed with no air-conditioning, but
unsurprisingly he hadn't expected any. There was an old
ceiling fan, but it had only two settings, off and on, and
went around so slowly and creaked so alarmingly when in
the latter mode that the Lieutenant feared that, even should
he get to sleep despite the noise, it might just fall down and
decapitate him with one of the blades while he slept. So he
turned it off altogether and slept fitfully, dreaming of his
life; his old life, as he had thought earlier, except that life
for him felt over, by now. Ironically he thought, for irony
was rapidly becoming his default mode of thinking, that it
wouldn't be much trouble to get him to his own funeral at
the nearby church either; because from here on in he was a
dead man.

2: PREMATURE DEATH

He didn't feel much more alive the next morning, after his ablutions in the old-fashioned bathroom; but at least there was water in good supply. He had to get used to the antiquated toilet facilities common on the remoter islands, however; *Paper in the bucket, not the pan, or I'll be in the shit in every sense,* he thought with an attempt at humour which raised his spirits a little. They were lowered again, however, when he unpacked his few things, including his iPad, with all the latest technology. *My God! Will there be internet coverage in a place like this?,* he thought, in a panic; if there wasn't, he might just as well put a bullet through his head right now. Amazingly, however, after some time spent setting up the equipment, he got a connection; not superfast, but not bad, so he wasn't totally cut off from the world outside. It must be the proximity of the Turkish mainland, he decided, the populated coastal areas with all those tourists wanting to keep in touch with home via their iPads and smartphones. He made a call to Captain Petrides but his superior did not pick up; probably forgotten to turn his mobile on and over at the kafenion for want of much else to do. The Lieutenant decided to try again later, because now he was very hungry, having eaten little on the previous day, so made his way to try his luck at the kafenion with Sofia's cooking.

Stephanidou's emergence from the station-house was greeted by the local priest, seated outside the kafenion opposite. A large man, almost as wide as he was tall and ageing, apparently like everyone else here, he wore his greying beard and hair long, the latter tied back under his black hat. His office was recognisable by his black cloth even before he semi-rose from his seat and raised his hand in salute. Father Lambros, for that was his name, was expansive in his welcome; an amiable soul, he promised the best that the place had to offer by way of company and conversation. He lamented that Lieutenant Stephanidou had in actuality inherited a dead man's shoes, Lieutenant Polycarpou his predecessor having recently and unexpectedly died; cirrhosis of the liver from which he hadn't realised he was suffering. Probably drank himself to death, Stephanidou thought, through nothing to do; and I'll probably go the same way. As he ruminated on drink, Giorgos brought him food, a breakfast of bread, cheese, olives, yoghourt and so forth, the standard morning fare countrywide; Stephanidou reflected that he'd had cold food last night, and hoped that lunchtime wouldn't be long in coming so that he could have something hot apart from coffee.

The priest regaled him with talk as he ate his breakfast. "So, you'll not have a difficult time here, there are few of us now and we're all quite law-abiding, I assure you, if you ignore our consumption of ouzo. Even with too much of that in us, I fear, we're all too old to cause any trouble." He laughed at his own gentle humour, and proceeded to name the inhabitants of the village to Stephanidou, which took very little time; then, "Do you have a wife? A girlfriend?" when Stephanidou replied in the negative to the first. He hesitated over the second, but then nodded non-committally; it wouldn't hurt for the priest to know about Elpida, and there weren't any girls here to give her competition, he thought. Father Lambros read his thoughts; "It might be a good idea to marry her and bring her over; there are no young women here for a young man who has a mind for courting". He laughed mildly again, but then assumed a more serious tone.

"I'm afraid we must seem a sorry bunch to you; you'd be better in a city posting, or one of the larger, busier

9

islands, because there's very little here for a young man like yourself. Was that not an option?" It was, thought Stephanidou savagely, until that corrupt bastard ruined it for me; but outwardly he shrugged and controlled his inner anger, replying politely; "I was posted here and I obeyed". The priest nodded as though he understood, but continued in a negative vein, as though not wanting to give the new policeman false hope. "The island has little to recommend it to tourists, I fear; a few bad beaches, no ancient architectural sites, not even any churches or holy sites of note for devout Greeks on the religious tourist trail. The only person who's anything like close to you in age is Costas, the Australian, you'll meet him round and about and know him by his youthful appearance; Costaki, we call him, on account of his relative youth. But he's not the best company, I fear. He's unhappy, you see; he brought his wife and children back here from Australia, his parents having emigrated there when he was very young. To give the children a better life, he said, as I'm sure you know is happening all over the Greek world these days." "So there are some children?" Stephanidou interjected hopefully; he had been one of six himself, and liked to see some kids around the place. Even if they could be noisy and troublesome they were the future, and he liked to see them grow and develop. But, "No", the good Father quashed his hopes before they grew too high. "Costaki didn't check the place properly before they came, and it was just too quiet, too deserted, too old here; so his wife declared it impossible and promptly decamped to her family in Rhodes, taking the children with her. So here he is, alone and lonely and too proud to admit that she was in the right and go to join them over there. He'll crack, eventually, I think, but in the meantime he's miserable and best avoided if you're feeling a bit down yourself, which I suspect you are?"

The good priest was correct, so Stephanidou nodded and

stared gloomily into his coffee. He didn't want to hear about Costaki and his problems, because they reminded him too much of his own. Back in Athens waited Elpida, the girl he wanted to marry, but how could he, now that his career was over? She said that she loved him, that she'd be happy with him anywhere, but here? No-one of her own age to talk to, no young mothers to be her friends, with no young children to be friends to our children when they were born, should we be fortunate enough, and no young fathers to commiserate with me while they were being born. No school to educate them, so how would that work? Even if a way could be found they'd eventually have to go to the mainland, to university or for work, because there was no work for them here. And the worst would be if Elpida came here and they tried; wouldn't she, like Costaki's wife, come to hate it, grow disillusioned with both the island and her husband and decamp, returning to her mother and father in Athens and taking the children, leaving him alone and broken? Or was that the worst? What if she got tired of waiting for him to make a decision, and found someone else? In despair he turned to gesture to Giorgos to order ouzo, even though it was too early and he was on duty, but the man was already bringing it; the glass of water, the bowl of ice with tongs, and a whole karafaki of ouzo, not a just single shot. Clearly he had great experience of the depression this place engendered, and of the way to blot it all out.

It didn't take Stephanidou long to find out how matters worked locally, and to organise his new routine. Giorgos and Sofia at the kafenion would take care of housework, for both his living quarters and the office, his laundry, and would feed and water him. Sofia was concerned over food for the new Lieutenant; they were well into Lent, as he would remember (no, he didn't, but kept that to himself), so would he be wishing to fast? The other inhabitants of the village were exempt, on account of their age, and infirmity

11

in some cases, but if Stephanidou wished it she would make sure that she prepared for him only the prescribed foods, and requisite amount of meals, on the specified days, even after Lent and Easter were over. Stephanidou didn't wish it; even before he had lost his belief he hadn't been strict about fasting. It all depended on whoever was preparing his food; some observed the rules, some did not, and he usually ate whatever was put before him. Now, however, even had he wanted to observe the Great Lenten fast, he could see that it would cost Sofia a great deal of mental effort to tailor her cooking to his needs, to obtain and prepare the correct foods only. He used the excuse of personal circumstances therefore to let her off the hook; because he could sense her anxiety on this score. So "No", he told her, "that would put you to far too much trouble. I wish to fit in with my new community, and if they don't fast then neither will I, so give me whatever is the easiest food for you to prepare. I'm sure that Father Lambros will agree that this is best for all", he told her finally, and as he'd sensed her anxiety he now felt her relief; she was elderly, it wouldn't be fair to put all that on her shoulders.

He felt guilty also about Sofia cleaning and doing laundry for him, because she looked as though her housework days ought to be over. She should be sitting taking it easy with her grandchildren around her knees whilst her daughters and daughters-in-law took care of the home. But needs obviously must, and with her children and grandchildren moved to the mainland for work and schools and all the conveniences of modern life, as she told him at length, she took care of her own house and would do the same for him. And, surprisingly, when she got started, she didn't do a bad job; these old island women are a hardy breed, Stephanidou thought with grudging admiration.

He met most of the locals in the space of his first two days; they weren't many in number, and hardly anything new happened around here, so he was an item of interest and all two dozen or so members of his new community were curious to meet him. So, apart from his weekly visit to Captain Petrides, which he suspected formed a diversion for his superior also, and which took the form of driving to the main town in the antiquated police car supplied, then sitting with the good Captain over coffee and desultory conversation about criminal activities locally (of which there were none to speak), he had little to do. He tried walking around and talking to people, but that took very little time and there wasn't much to speak of, apart from the family history of each individual, and he could only take so much of that; besides, it wasn't the way it was done here, the good Father Lambros took the time to inform him. Just sit at the kafenion and talk with the old men who took up their usual seats there each morning; they would inform him of who was who and what was what within the community, as well as anything unusual which might have happened. As to anyone else, well they knew where to find him if he was needed, so Stephanidou should just sit back and take it easy and anything that needed attention would find its way to him.

A couple of days of this and Lieutenant Stephanidou was going crazy. He turned his attention back to the dog-eared files contained in the rusting filing cabinet at the station and went through them in minute detail. That also took very little time, there being only a few files outlining the details of some mundane incidents which had happened quite a few years ago. Men who had driven vans, cars or agricultural vehicles into the sides of buildings, having taken too much ouzo, mostly, or gotten into heated arguments that turned physical, whilst similarly under the influence. The only cases of note were of a girl who'd been found dead, suicide presumed, and a young man who'd gone to the Turkish mainland and never returned, the family over there having no idea as to where he'd gone either, he'd simply disappeared. But these incidents were over fifty years old, and unlikely to be resolved now.

He closed the filing cabinet and decided that physical exercise was the thing. In Athens he'd kept in good shape, which he felt to be the correct thing for a member of the Police Force, through swimming, running and regular attendance at a gym. This latter was impossible, there being no gym facilities on the island; yet we, the Greeks, invented the gymnasium, he thought with disgust, and thence the Olympics. However, he had the sea in which to swim, and ample ground over which to run; so, the relative coolness of evening coming on, he resolved to check out the layout of the area through the means of a brisk run, followed by a swim from the pebbled area nearby laughingly called a beach. A quick change into singlet, shorts and running shoes and he was off.

Stephanidou hadn't noted the topography of the island when Captain Petrides drove him to the village, he'd been too tired and full of self-pity. Now, however, he made a circuit of the local area and worked it out. The road from Ayios Andreas came from the West to the village of Palliohorio, which had a rocky shelf for a shoreline. Many years ago this had been turned into a rough harbour for half-a-dozen fishing boats by the addition of a wooden pier, rickety and unstable now, with iron hooks driven into the rocks to tie up the boats securely against wind and stormy weather. The boats, however, left unused and mouldering for many years, by the look of them, would soon fall apart of their own volition. To the left of this harbour, the land moved gradually upwards, becoming steeper on the upward incline and terminating in the cliffs which formed so much of the shoreline of the island. However, by following the flat-land path in this direction, and avoiding the uphill slope on the right-hand, coastal side, he eventually found a track to the right which lead out through another, narrower, break in the cliffs and onto a small and stony cove, edged by oleander bushes at the rear, which the locals referred to as 'the beach'. Doubling back and leaving the village on the right-hand side Stephanidou found the pattern of cliffs repeated; the village must have been founded in this natural break between them many centuries ago. However, in this direction the cliffs continued unbroken, towards the south and then curving back towards the West end of the island with no breaks for inlets apparent for as far as he could see.

This, then, formed the physical environment of Lieutenant Stephanidou's new village home, and within twenty minutes he'd taken a circuit around it easily. Not feeling as stretched as he had wished to be by his run, he decided then to challenge himself by going up the hill on the far left-hand side of the village, the furthest point from where he now was, on the right-hand side, before coming back down for his swim from the beach. It was a gradual incline over a long distance, which he judged would bring him out atop the abundant cliffs which edged the majority of the coast. The path got considerably steeper than he had expected as it neared the summit, and Stephanidou found it quite an effort, even with his excellent level of fitness. Reaching the top, he stopped to get his breath and admire the view, which even he had to admit was stunning. The blue of the Aegean stretched out to the East and South before him, with the Turkish coast to his left and the sun slowly moving towards the horizon on his right, casting a gleam upon the water and a soporific haze over the whole scene. He could make out other islands here and there, some further, some nearer, and some boats, the latter too far away for him to see distinctly whether they were large ferries or smaller fishing vessels. There were sea-birds flitting through the sky, their shrieks echoing around as they called to each other, and the scent of the scrub was in the air, this vegetation mainly dried already despite it being only spring. Magnificent in its greatness as the scene was, it had the unfortunate effect of making Lieutenant Stephanidou feel quite small and insignificant within it.

Depressed once more, he set off at a weary trot back down the way he had come.

He was more tired than he had anticipated; it wasn't quite as late as he'd thought, and the sun still had an hour, or maybe two, before it dipped below the horizon; so it was still rather too hot for comfort and Stephanidou was thirsty now, having neglected to bring a bottle of water with him. He dropped down a gear to a slower jog, and from that dropped inevitably to a walking pace. What was the hurry? No-one here would care if he wasn't at the station-house, or on the island for that matter. His mood fell still further, and he looked desperately around the landscape to try to distract himself. His eye fell on the derelict dwelling he was approaching on his right; he'd noticed it on the way up, but had given it very little attention, being focussed on getting up to the top of the hill. Now, he looked more closely.

Clearly it had once been a house, but now was in an extremely dilapidated condition, more so than any of the other buildings in the environs of the village. The doors were gone, and what was left of the wooden shutters was rotten; one touch would bring them down, he judged, seriously rather than ironically this time. The rough brick walls, bearing traces of the white paint which had once covered them, were falling down, with massive gaps surrounded by rubble in places where the falling had already been completed. The roof was gone, but a sort of plaited straw arrangement was affixed over one end, affording some kind of shelter to whoever would be desperate enough to go in there; probably the shepherd, when the weather turned bad, Stephanidou decided. The whole place was overgrown with weeds, but what must have once been the yard still boasted a rusting iron framework, bearing the dried remnants of grapevines, sitting precariously atop half-a-dozen poles fixed into the broken concrete floor upon which a few battered straw-seated old chairs with uneven legs rested at drunken angles. There was an old-fashioned iron bedstead sitting on this also, rusting as every other bit of metal on the place, wedged up against what was left of one wall and boasting an old, thin and hard-looking mattress, stained and mildewed in some places and with the stuffing bursting out in others.

It wasn't a sight to lift the mood of someone far less-depressed than the Lieutenant, but he was feeling faint, dehydrated from the heat he knew, and needed to rest. Rejecting the bed and the rickety chairs, he located a fragment of wall standing alone at the front of the place and partially shaded by some rather ragged-looking fig trees, long since denuded of their fruit. He tried to move it with his hands and, when it stayed in place, he sat down upon it to rest and hopefully regain some energy. He closed his eyes but felt dizzy so opened them again; and then, looking once again at the land around him, feeling tired and small and alone, it came to Stephanidou that the ruined house mirrored his career. Once so fine and promising, with prospects of promotion up the ladder and prosperity to follow, including marriage to the girl he'd already chosen, and hopefully children, now it lay in ruins about him, decayed and crumbling through no fault of his own, as he saw it. His whole life was out of his control and he was powerless to take it back. For the first time he thought seriously of the gun down at the station-house; had it been in his hand at this moment he would have ended it all and added his shattered shell to that upon which he sat. But it wasn't; defeated and in dark despair, he put his head down and sobbed his heart out; harsh, difficult sobs which forced their way up from his body, unwilling as it was to indulge itself in this most womanly way.

3: A MEETING

Eventually, the storm of weeping subsided and Stephanidou gulped, wiping his eyes but still resting his face in his hands. He felt ashamed for his unmanly display of emotion and was glad that he was alone, with no witness to his breakdown. Or so he thought; because, and he didn't know quite how, he gradually became aware that he wasn't alone; he lifted his head sharply and, looking around him, saw the man to his left, standing very still and quiet and just looking at him. He started at the unexpected presence, and nearly fell off of his improvised seat. He managed to rescue himself, and turned the movement into one of rising from his seat; but the other man moved then, still silent but holding out a hand, gesturing to Stephanidou to sit, and wait, which he did. The other disappeared for a few moments, during which time the Lieutenant wondered if he had imagined the apparition; but then it reappeared, and Stephanidou noticed the outstretched hand. Bizarrely, it held a tea cup, old-fashioned and fluted and edged in gold, the porcelain decorated with a pattern of tea roses and floribunda. It wouldn't have looked out of place in my grandmother's parlour, Stephanidou thought, except that it was old and cracked and chipped, like everything else here.

Then the man spoke, gesturing towards him with the cup. "Please drink, you look far too hot and it wouldn't do for you to become dehydrated." Stephanidou couldn't place the accent, but it wasn't what he was expecting; not the rough speech most usually encountered in the islands, but cultured and careful. It sounded for all the world like a foreigner who has taken great care and ended up learning to speak the language better than the natives. He took the proffered cup and gulped down the cool water gratefully, then returned the vessel with thanks. "More?" was offered, and he accepted. Once more his host departed and returned, cup brimming; and as Stephanidou drank once more, he received an apologetic explanation. "I'm sorry I don't have a glass, or a better cup to offer you, or indeed anything else by way of hospitality; I live very simply here, you see, just the well and whatever I can get to eat." Stephanidou realised that so far he hadn't said anything himself, and hastened to repair his error. "This is fine, thank you, I need nothing else."

Then, his curiosity piqued, he asked; "You say you live here? In this … place?" 'House' seemed an inappropriate description for the ruin, and 'dwelling' similarly so, but the man it seemed wasn't particular. "Yes, it belonged to my mother's family. I always meant to repair it and raise a family in it when I was young; but life got in the way, and now I have neither the desire nor the means to do so. But it provides shelter of a sort, and meets my modest needs." His manner was as modest as his needs, clearly; "May I?" he indicated another fragment of wall, asking as though he were the guest and Stephanidou the host, then without waiting for an answer he sat carefully down. "Please do give me a moment, I'm rather tired myself." He closed his eyes, and Stephanidou took the opportunity to look him over.

Tall and thin, he appeared to be, far too thin for good health. Worn black leather shoes covered the feet at the end of long legs, upon which he wore black trousers with a black shirt above; both were soiled and dusty and had clearly seen better days, as had their wearer. The shirt sleeves were rolled up to the elbow, and the forearms showed the unattractively-wrinkled and brown-spotted loose skin of the ageing. The face and head were covered in long grey hair and beard, unkempt and in need of cutting and combing. From the overall neglected appearance of the man one might have expected him to smell bad, but he did not; as he had a source of water, Stephanidou reflected, he had the means for at least basic ablutions. He couldn't put an age on his host; he must be seventy at the very least, he calculated, probably older, but it was difficult to tell, especially with the cultured voice, which sounded younger somehow.

At that moment the eyes opened; dark brown and mild, they appeared, and the mouth located below them within the beard spoke again. "I'm so sorry, I do tire easily these days. I'm afraid you'll have to forgive me, but I need to lie down now." He arose and made his way towards the rusting bedstead, and Stephanidou arose likewise, not wanting to outwear his welcome. His host sat on the edge of the bed, then swung his legs slowly sideways and up onto the mattress, stretching them out before him to assume a sitting-up posture, his back braced against the rusting frame at the head. The mild eyes were once again fixed on Stephanidou. "It's been a pleasure meeting you. Please do call again if you're passing, and feel free to drink from the well should I not be around." Then he closed his eyes, as if by way of dismissal, and lay back on the mouldy mattress, sighing with pleasure as though upon the most comfortable bed ever made. Stephanidou looked at him for a moment, then departed at a slow jog back down the hill.

At least he had an interest now, to turn his thoughts from his despair, because the old man fascinated him. Who was he, and what was he doing living in the ruins there? Many foreign nationals were living in Greece these days, he was aware, but they usually found some purpose-built holiday home or retirement property; or, if more adventurous, a traditional village house which they renovated themselves, or had done by local workmen, cursing the time these latter took whilst claiming to have come there for the slower pace of life. But to camp-out in a ruin, looking like a ruin themselves? This he had never before encountered. The question obsessed him all the way back to the station, and into the old-fashioned bathroom with the slow-running shower in which he cleansed himself before going to the kafenion to eat. There he found Father Lambros and questioned him while he ate the hot stifado provided by Sofia. She did indeed cook hot food, he had found eventually, and it was good, more than good, in fact, excellent; a small mercy which had begun to provide the interest in his days, each monotonously like the other apart from the variations in his lunch and dinner.

The priest was happy to answer the short questions which Stephanidou aimed at him whilst applying himself with gusto to his plate. "So, I see you've met our hermit on the hill, and no, he's not a foreigner, he's as Greek as you or I. Well", Father Lambros amended his answer, "he was born and raised here, but he left as a young man and spent the majority of his life in England. He only returned about seven or eight years ago, and maybe the English turned him into some kind of eccentric like themselves, because he lives in that ruin despite the habitable family home of his youth being here in the village". The Father raised one arm and indicated a street running back from the main square. "It's just down there, old and shabby like every other building here, but with running water and electricity and a degree of comfort. He did live there, when he first returned, but at some point he decided that it was too comfortable, and moved up the hill. He was coming down for the winters, and living very simply there, but this last winter he stayed up there and I fear it's done him no good. His younger brother was living in the house until he died a few months ago", the priest volunteered further, while Stephanidou finished his dinner. "He had lived in England also, and returned a few years after the older brother; but now he's in the graveyard with his parents and the elder is all alone."

"But what does he do all day? And why?" Stephanidou was still curious. The priest shrugged. "He sits, he

21

meditates, he sleeps and drinks water from the well up there. Old Sofia and the other women were taking him food, but it's difficult for them to get up there given their age and the arthritis which troubles most of them now. His brother left him some money, so he does come down and buy food from Stelios, but it's never very much." Stephanidou wondered at such a simple existence, and Father Lambros continued. "At night he's more active, or very early in the morning; he's been seen swimming off the beach at those times, not for long, just enough to cleanse himself, I suppose. He watches the stars at night, it fascinates and calms him apparently, he always enjoyed it when he was young. A couple of times he's been out with the fishermen, well, old Mandras at any rate, and they don't actually fish very much. They go out at night-time of course, it's cooler then and he's very frail now, the daytime heat tires him easily. But it reminds him of his youth, when he was a fisherman with his father and brother; he was happy then, he didn't ask much of life, I remember."

"You knew him?" Stephanidou's curiosity was increased. "Oh yes, we were boys at school together; but I stayed in Greece and he left, such is life." Stephanidou could understand the returning to one's homeland, when moving closer to the end of life, even with the eccentric lifestyle; but why leave in the first place? Especially if he was happy, as the priest had said? Father Lambros sighed. "There was some issue with a girl, the one he was to marry; she was found dead on the sea-shore, it was thought she'd killed herself." "The one in the files at the station-house? Eleni Christou?" Stephanidou was interested at the link to the old, unsolved case. The Father nodded. "They'd been engaged only a short time before it happened, and the wedding was being planned. It hit Kadi very hard when they found her, as you'd expect, because he obviously loved her very much. He wasn't getting over it very well, some people were still speaking badly of him over the matter; so his father suggested that he go and work for his uncle in England for a time, and he went but did not return until about", here the priest counted on his fingers, "seven years ago, I think". "Why were people speaking badly of him?" the Lieutenant wondered out loud. "Because she was found to have been expecting a child", the priest informed him; "but it wasn't his, he swore, and so did her father, based on what he knew about their relationship, presumably. It wouldn't have been a problem had it been Kadi's child, they'd have just bought the wedding forward; you know how it is, two young people in love". The priest sighed, as though remembering his own youthful love, then continued. "But Kadi swore he'd never taken any liberties with her, and he wouldn't have, not before marriage, despite all the usual ribbing by the other young men; he was always a very correct young man."

"Unfortunately, however", the priest continued, "another young man from the village disappeared at just the same time. Ah, yes", as Stephanidou nodded knowingly, "you'll have seen that in your files also; Nikos Osman Nikolaides. He'd gone to visit family on the Turkish mainland; his mother had been Turkish, you see, but she had died when he was young. Anyway, he didn't return when he had told his father he would and the father naturally got worried; so he contacted the family in Turkey who said that the boy had been with them but had left some time ago, to return to the island, he had told them. But he never reappeared, either over there or here; and then various people got to remembering things they'd seen or heard, and the upshot was that it looked very much as though he'd seduced the girl and run away to avoid having to face her father's anger. And that the girl, realising that her lover was gone, leaving her pregnant and unmarried, killed herself".

Stephanidou sighed in sympathy. "But in the meantime she had engaged herself to this man, Kadi, I think you called him?" "Yes, Arkadios Dukakis, Kadi for short; such a respectable family they were, but he's the only one left now and I think it won't be long before he joins those who've gone before him." The priest crossed himself here, and continued; "Unfortunately the only construction that even the most sympathetic soul could put upon the affair was that she'd had doubts about her lover, and used poor Kadi as a sort of insurance policy in case the other boy let her down. Then she would marry Kadi in that event and try to pass the child off as his, God have mercy on her soul. But when her fears seemed confirmed, she presumably found that she couldn't go through with marriage to another, so took her own life; such a terrible thing, tragic". Father Lambros sighed deeply; "But we in Greece know about tragedy, we invented it, of course, and the poor girl paid with her life and is now at peace with God's forgiveness, I pray".

"But Kadi", he continued after a pause for contemplation of the complicated nature of human affairs, "as I said he didn't get over it well. He'd been made to look foolish, at the very least, and no man likes to look foolish, least of all a proud Greek. I remember as a child, the adults tried to make us behave well by saying, If you don't do so-and-so, everyone will laugh at you. Well, it didn't bother me, I was a rascal by nature"; and here he laughed softly at the remembrance of his own boyhood, before he continued. "But it worked on most of the children, and Kadi was one of those; but it's unfair of me to say that about him, it wasn't just the threats of laughter in his case. He was just someone who naturally behaved well, if you see what I mean; deception and guile weren't in him, he expected to act honourably and would never therefore be the butt of others' humour. So he was uncomfortable now, in a position that was alien to him, and always thinking that the entire village was laughing at him behind his back, and unjustifiably so. And that, unfortunately for him, was the best outcome of the case; for, at the worst, there are always those who will not believe, and will gossip, so some persisted in saying that he was the father of the unborn child. So what with the laughter, and the gossip, and the bad memories, Kadi's life here was soured; and therefore he left."

The priest fell silent, and looked off into space thoughtfully; he appeared disinclined to say more, but Stephanidou wasn't yet ready to finish the conversation so he took the cue which the Father had given him. "I cannot believe you to be a rascal by nature, surely, a man of the Church?" Father Lambros returned from his musing. "Yes, I was the village bad boy, always in trouble, if there was mischief to be found I always found it. Whereas Kadi was the good boy, honest, well-behaved, always wanted to do the right thing and always did it. He had a temper, mind, and if he was angry, watch out! I remember once, Stelios the grocer, the father of the Stelios we have now, he took over his father's business, you know how it is. Well, old Stelios was coming back from Ayios Andreas with a van full of supplies when I was idling on the hillside, I saw him coming, and his van bounced over the road, as always, the road being in a bad state of repair even then; but this time some things, bags of flour or sugar or something, I forget exactly what, bounced right off and into the road. I was down there like a shot, finders keepers and all that. Except that Kadi had seen it also, he was going down the road, walking all the way to the next village and back to get something for his father, that was what he was like. He insisted that I take the groceries back to Stelios, but I said No, I'd found them and they were mine; but he continued to insist, and then his eyes, fixed on me so that I couldn't look away, like blood and ice they were, they always went that way when his temper flared. Well, he shouted at me that I WOULD return them and I was terrified; he hadn't even threatened to hit me, it was just his manner, you didn't argue with him when his eyes were on you like that if you knew what was good for you. So he frogmarched me off to Stelios, made me apologise and return the groceries, and

Stelios thanked him and gave me a thick ear for my trouble."

He rubbed his ear ruefully, as if remembering the blow upon it. "And then of course Kadi felt bad, because he'd made me do the right thing and I'd gotten a beating for it; and that was also what he was like, a kind and decent soul. So he took me home to his mother, who put an ice pack on my ear and gave me dinner; pourgouri with yoghourt it was, poor people's food, but then we were poor people, and it was delicious. Home cooking wasn't something I had often, my mother died giving birth to me, and my father raised me alone because he had no-one else, no sisters or other women-folk. So it was a rather rough upbringing, and maybe that was why I turned out so bad, but all credit to him, he did the best that he could whilst earning us a living and I don't blame him in the least."

"But eventually, not long after Kadi left the island in fact, and I still don't understand how, I had a revelation. God called me for his own somehow, and I knew it was the right thing for me to go into the Church. And here I am, and I thank God for calling me, because I've had a good life and I count myself truly blessed. But poor Kadi, I still don't know what is God's purpose for him. He only wanted marriage with the woman he loved, and children with her, and honest work to support them; but he's living alone as a hermit and all I can do is pray for him, pray that he may find peace in God." The priest crossed himself here, and Stephanidou almost did likewise, until he remembered that he no longer believed in a God with any purpose for him whatsoever.

Father Lambros fell silent again, as Giorgos brought ouzo, and waited while Stephanidou poured for them both. As he poured he digested all that his ready informant had told him. A sad man, but an interesting one, this Kadi, and the Lieutenant thought he might go and speak with him again; not the least because he was painfully aware that the man had probably been watching for some time while he, Stephanidou, had wept like a woman. He wanted to correct any erroneous impression this may have given whilst at the same time finding out some more about this enigmatic man. He had very little else to do, after all, but to make sure he enquired of the good Father. "Would Kadi welcome another visit from me, do you think? He said he would, but he is obviously very polite and I would not want to intrude on his privacy." "Oh yes, go and speak with him again by all means", the priest offered, "you may be able to help him, or he you, or both. I advise you to go and find him in the morning, rather than the evening, his energy hasn't been sapped by the heat of the day at that time".

"Incidentally", the priest remarked, changing the subject, "Sofia was concerned about the question of your fasting, or not, so she asked my opinion". Stephanidou remembered then his conversation with the old woman about his dietary requirements, and that he'd said he was sure that the priest would agree with the Lieutenant's reasons for not fasting; but he'd forgotten to speak to him about it. He explained this, but the Father waved aside his apologies before speaking with a solemn air. "In the village I alone fast, as befits my office, as does my wife, of course, and she prepares the correct food for us both. I do assure you that it would be no problem for her to cook for three, and you are welcome to join us and observe the correct diet in this way. It would be a shame to compromise your religious observance purely for fear of giving offence." Stephanidou felt deeply awkward; the priest was regarding him gravely, awaiting an answer to his enquiry, but the Lieutenant didn't know what to say. He stuttered a few words, stopped, started again and then gave up, defeated; he looked at the face of Father Lambros, and slowly the grave expression broke up, into a broad grin and then a laugh. "A rascal by nature, you see?" the priest intoned, through his laughter, and Stephanidou realised that his leg was being pulled; he smiled weakly himself and the Father patted him on the shoulder understandingly. "Of course it would be better to let Sofia feed you, and eat whatever she gives you; she enjoys cooking, it makes her happy, so what's the harm, eh?" He applied himself to his ouzo at this point, and Stephanidou did likewise, until the sun was well below the horizon and he retired to the station-house and a more satisfying sleep than had become usual for him.

4: A CONTRACT

On the following morning Lieutenant Stephanidou was obliged to go and see Captain Petrides in Ayios Andreas, having been summoned by e-mail for a meeting with his superior. When he arrived the Captain was absent from the police station, but was easily located at the kafenion by the harbour, taking coffee while he apparently awaited his junior officer's arrival. "I thought we could have a late breakfast here while we go over things", he told Stephanidou. What things? thought the latter; there never were any things worth discussing, he could tell by recalling those which Captain Petrides had discussed with him to date.

Litter on the streets, what could you do? The refuse collectors were sloppy and unmotivated, they were ageing, they'd been working for too long and were ready to retire, if only they didn't need the money so much. Cautioning them to take more care on their round had in the past culminated in a mysterious collection of garbage on the doorstep of the station-house, which the refuse men would swear blind had gotten there by means of the wind but professed themselves willing to remove it – for a consideration, of course.

Too many stray dogs around the place? They were culled regularly, but if people would let their collared dogs escape from the house and mate with each other, what could they expect but excess puppies? And if they didn't want to feed and raise these, which they usually didn't, they let them loose on the streets, to survive or die as fate decided. So there was an excess of mangy strays because the good people of the town couldn't be bothered to prevent there being one; and the same went for cats, for that matter. And then of course, both dogs and cats were a nuisance, hanging around begging for food and frequently being aggressively pro-active in taking what was not given freely. They also gathered into packs, and the face-offs between these, with the attendant noise and fights could be dangerous to anyone in the immediate vicinity; but the people still continued to complain whilst doing nothing to help the situation.

The woman who had reported her underclothes being stolen from her washing line had been an interesting one-off, Stephanidou thought, but as the lady in question carried a weight that had to be in excess of one hundred and fourteen kilos on a one-and-a-half metre tall frame moving well into middle-age, with presumably correspondingly-sized underclothes, she clearly watched too much television and was in the land of wishful thinking. The could do nothing to help her but stress that they would be vigilant and attempt to prevent any further acts of lingerie-larceny.

So Stephanidou sat, listened to these and other, similar, issues, ate his second breakfast of the day and thanked the self-control which made him run and swim daily now, because food and drink were becoming the main focus of his life and he'd look like the lady who lacked lingerie in no time flat without it. He also thanked his lucky stars for the existence of the intriguing Hermit on the Hill, as Father Lambros had referred to Kadi, because he at least gave the priest another topic of conversation upon which to expound, and promised something other than random rubbish, excess animals and stolen smalls to interest Stephanidou.

When he had spoken with his Captain, and eaten with him, and taken ouzo with him, the sun was almost at its zenith; so he put his foot down and drove back to Palliohorio more quickly than he ought to have, although thankfully he saw no other vehicles on either side of the road for the whole trip. He parked the car, then showered and changed into casual clothes and was intending to go up the hill to visit Kadi; however, he was unable to avoid Sofia, who was waiting for him with a lunch of octopus in red wine plus salad and fresh bread. Unable to hurt her feeling, he sat obediently and gave his two breakfasts the company of his lunch; and it was mid-afternoon therefore when he arrived at the tumbledown house on the hillside feeling uncomfortably full and the worse for wine.

There was no sign of Kadi initially, so Stephanidou took a drink of water from the well, from the rose-patterned cup which stood beside it, then around roamed the ruin in search of his erstwhile host. He wasn't on the bed outside, if the basic dwelling could be divided into outside and inside, given the absence of much that could be termed a roof, or anywhere else in view, so Stephanidou called out "Hello" a couple of times, and was rewarded with a clear if quiet response from what could have been termed the inside, in better days. Moving towards the sound, he found Kadi, lying on his back on the ground in a shaded area and moving to a sitting position at the sight of his guest. "What a pleasure to see you again; do please excuse my recumbent posture, it's rather hot in the afternoon and it does tend to drain one's energy." Stephanidou apologised in his turn; "No, please, I ought to be asking you to excuse me. I meant to come by earlier but I had to go into Ayios Andreas to see my superior officer". The hermit nodded with a knowing air. "Ah, yes, of course, I had heard that Lieutenant Polycarpou had been replaced and guessed that the new officer must be my visitor." How had he heard? Stephanidou wondered; he'd never seen the man in the village, and didn't envision the rather portly priest, or anyone else for that matter, coming up here. He didn't ask, though; he'd find out in time, of which he had plenty.

But Kadi was speaking again, as he slowly and laboriously got to his feet. "But I forget my manners; Please do sit, Officer, Lieutenant, Stephanidou, isn't it?" Again the policeman wondered how he knew, but refrained from asking and extended his right hand, which his host took. "Arkadios Dukakis, they call me Kadi, although you probably know that already, because I take it you've been speaking to Father Lambros? Of course; well, please feel free to do the same with me." Then, formal introductions being over, he returned to the matter in hand. "Seating arrangements here are very basic; I don't go in for luxury, as I once did, nothing like it, so perhaps I could suggest that you take that chair and I'll take this?" He indicated a couple of old cane-seated chairs, obviously riddled with woodworm, which he acknowledged apologetically before continuing, "You'll need to be careful, one leg is a few inches shorter than the other, and there's a hole in the weaving of the seat; but you're a young man, fit too I would have said, so I'm sure you'll manage. I can't offer you coffee, I'm afraid, but there's water in abundance in the well and if you have your own cigarettes you're welcome to smoke them. You don't? Very good, I never have myself, better to keep healthy"; which Stephanidou found somewhat bizarre, given the emaciated state of his host.

The latter continued; "Well, now we've been formally introduced; we did rather get off on an informal basis yesterday, and I hope you're feeling better today. No, no need to explain, I speak to the priest also, and he brought me up to speed, so to speak, because I did wonder out loud what a young and presumably educated man like yourself did to get himself posted to such a place; please do excuse my insensitivity in mentioning it". Stephanidou made a deprecating gesture, ready to answer, but his host continued speaking. "A good man, I'll assume you to be, trying to do a difficult job and keep the peace, then one person in a powerful position takes exception to your efforts and there goes your promising career path. There's no justice, is there? And I do know about that, no need to tell me." He stopped then, looking off into the distance, repeating, "No need to tell me", in a whisper to himself, his lips moving but the faintest of sounds emerging. Then he looked at Stephanidou again and changed tack. "There's little for you to do by way of crime here, the place is dying, what with the young people leaving for work and a more exciting life on the mainland. The old ones left behind are of the dying persuasion rather than the criminal, I fear, so your obvious talents are wasted here, as I'm sure you're aware. Warning old men not to drive with too much ouzo in them? They've been doing it all their lives and aren't about to change now."

"But maybe", the old man continued, looking at the Lieutenant speculatively, "there is a way for you to get yourself reinstated to a good city posting back on the mainland; interested?" Of course Stephanidou was interested, and said so, vehemently. His host looked him up and down again, his chin resting on his hand and his eyes filled once again with speculation, although the glint in them was not completely warm. But then he smiled, apparently with amusement. "Good. Then here's what we'll do. I shall tell you the story of my life; I take it you're interested in hearing it, about why I live the way I do, how I fit in here? Or you wouldn't be here with me, I think. The good Father Lambros will no doubt have encouraged you to get me to talk, hoping it will be good for me to do so, or for you to listen, or both; and maybe it will, who knows? It will help pass the time for you, if nothing else, but I think I can guarantee that there will be something else in it, to your advantage."

Stephanidou was intrigued, although he couldn't see how this strange hermit could help him; but his investigative instincts were stirred and he was willing to listen to what the man had to say, as the latter continued. "I hope you have plenty of time? Good; these things can't be done in a hurry, although I suspect you have more time than I do, but that's another story. Give me your time and I'll give you my tale; so long as you give me enough time to tell it, of course. No taking me in to the station-house, that's not part of the deal; until I'm ready to go, that is, which will be at Easter. Can you find enough time for me until the end of

33

Holy Week?" Stephanidou couldn't see that being a problem, he had nothing but time on his hands as far as he could see, so Yes, he'd find the time by then. "I'm going nowhere else", Kadi assured him earnestly, "there is nowhere to go and I intend to end my days on this island; unlike yourself, who have many other places to go to and wish to end your days elsewhere, I'm sure".

He thought for a moment, then, "Are you comfortable with speaking English? I thought so", as Stephanidou nodded, "you're obviously a well-educated man. I've spoken it myself for so long that I'm afraid it's rather taken over from my native tongue, and if I'm going to speak to you at length, and somewhat descriptively, then it may take over from time to time, so probably it would be better for me to use it all the time. I lived there for so long, you see, far longer than I lived here in my youth; but I've returned to my roots and here you are to help me round things off. Perhaps in future you could come here in casual attire, as you have today? If and when you turn up in uniform I'll know you're here in your official capacity, rather than in friendship. Do we have an agreement? A contract between us? Good".

Stephanidou, although having given his assent, was rather puzzled nevertheless by his host's references to taking him to the station-house, as though he was to be arrested, and his assurances that he was going nowhere which sounded as though Stephanidou expected him to abscond. Was he going to confess to some unknown crime? Intrigued despite himself, the Lieutenant decided that the only way to find out was to listen to the man, although he still didn't see how anything he learned here could help him get his career and his life back on track; but he was willing to wait and see. Did he have a choice, in fact? How else was he to spend his days? His formal duties took so little of his time, and he could only run and swim so far. Nor was he sure that he liked being so obviously transparent that Kyrie

Dukakis – for Stephanidou had decided to keep things formal for the present, until he knew more about the man - assumed in him a desire to hear the hermit's life-story; which he was obviously going to tell whatever the case might be.

First, however, there was another proviso; "I'd like you to record what I'm going to tell you", as Kadi moved to the rusting bedstead and rummaged under the old blankets sitting in a heap at one end of it. He brought out a portable recording machine, not the latest technology but not the oldest, Stephanidou judged. "It has a battery", Kadi continued, "but it does need re-charging at regular intervals. Would you mind doing so each day, at your station-house? The electricity is turned off in my old house in town, you see, and this" – he gestured at the ruin behind him and shrugged his shoulders. Stephanidou assented, Of course he would do so, it would be no problem. His host smiled; "Thank you. So if you would be so kind tonight, we can begin tomorrow? It's getting late now, and I'm rather tired. If you could come earlier in the day that would be helpful, your official duties allowing, of course; I'm fresher in the morning. You can? That will be good. So I'll see you then". He closed his eyes, which Stephanidou took for his dismissal, and headed off back down the hill to the village, his dinner and his bed.

5: IN MEDIAS RES

The next morning Stephanidou returned to the ruin, with the battery of the recording machine fully-charged as promised. He'd mused during the evening on the things he'd found out about the old man and, in a spirit of detective work which made him feel as though he was actually working rather than sitting around waiting to die, he'd opened a file on Kadi. 'Has a temper, Father Lambros says' he typed, and 'Seems to expect me to arrest him' on the next line. As case notes went it was hardly Eliot Ness on Al Capone, he'd reflected ironically, but who knew? He'd closed the file and slept rather better than he had recently, and now here he was hoping to hear something else to add to it, as well as to give some interest to his day.

His host was waiting for him, perched on his old bed, and welcomed his guest in his impeccable English, then waved him to a seat. Stephanidou settled down on the rickety chair previously designated as his to listen as the man commenced. "As you've spoken to Father Lambros I'm sure that you're aware of the important parts of my early life? Of course; then you will appreciate that it was an unhappy time for me and I'm not comfortable with talking about it, at least not yet. I'll get to it, when the time is right, but for the moment we can skip it and go straight to when I left the island and went to England. Do feel free to go and help yourself to water when you need it and, should you need them, the latrine facilities are over there." He waved an arm and pointed towards a crumbling outhouse at some distance from the main building. "Very basic, I'm afraid, but they provide what's necessary. Comfortable?" Not as much as I could be, Stephanidou thought, but he nodded anyway and Kadi continued. "Then I'll begin, or ought I to say, end?"

"I hated England at first; so huge, so noisy, so crowded, and loud, and bad-smelling to a nose accustomed to simplicity. The salt smell of the sea and the dry smell of the scrub on the breeze, the animals, the flowers in spring and my mother's cooking; these natural aromas were replaced by petrol fumes and the mingling odours of food from many nations in the take-away food shops that abounded in the East-End street to which I was taken by the driver who collected me from the airport at my uncle's orders. I'd learned English at school and been good at it, applying myself to it with the determination I had given to all my studies; but I hadn't used it much since and it came to my mouth with difficulty now. It was hard therefore to have any meaningful kind of conversation with the man, so I contented myself with looking out of the car window, and wasn't impressed by what I saw. Dull, overcast weather, clouds, periodic rain, and far too many cars; if every car on the island were to drive past our terrace back home, continually, it would take years for me to count this many, I thought."

"The place to which the man delivered me was equally unimpressive; a doorway on the street, sandwiched by two shops, which was opened eventually in response to his hard knock by a thick-set middle-aged man; a Greek, thankfully." "You'll be staying here, sharing with me", I was told by Alkis, for that was his name. "We'll eat, and then you'd better get some rest. Your uncle wants to see you tomorrow." "I unpacked my bag in the small bedroom to which he showed me, designated as mine; it was shabby, it could have been much cleaner and my mother would have had apoplexy if she'd seen it, but it was my home for the foreseeable future and I had to make the best of it. Then Alkis took me down the street to one of the take-aways, a

Greek kebab shop, where we got food which was nothing like that I'd had at home but at least bore a passing resemblance to it. Having eaten, I lay down on the cramped, narrow bed and tried to order my thoughts on the disastrous turn my life had taken until I finally slept the sleep of the exhausted."

"On the following day Alkis took me to the promised meeting with Uncle Michalis, at his office building in an area better than that in which I was now living, but not by much. I'd never met my uncle before, he'd left the island when I was too young to remember him, but I could see the resemblance he bore to his younger brother, my father. He was taller yet more thickly-set, greyer of hair and beard and clad in a smart suit, rather than the shabby shirt and trousers of the fisherman; yet the shrewd eyes and curve of the lips with which he greeted me were unmistakably those of my father."

"He shook my hand, then looked me over and pronounced me the image of my father as a young man. His manner was affable, if somewhat offhand, but then he'd have refused to take me on if he was still harbouring hostile feelings towards his brother, I thought. He spoke, and came straight to the point". "So the father wants more for his son than he wanted for himself? Understandable, I suppose I'd have done the same had I been blessed with a son. So, you'll stay with Alkis, he'll show you how things work around here and keep an eye on you. I'll see where I can fit you in; is there anything you have a particular interest in, business-wise?" I had to reply that there wasn't; I'd been a fisherman and would be one still if it weren't for circumstances. He cut me off there; "No need to go into those yet", and he fixed me with a direct and cold stare. "Don't think you're going to get an easy ride just because you're my nephew; you'll earn your keep, like everyone else here, and you'll have to start at the bottom, as I did. It's the best way to learn, and if you do well you'll move up quickly. Maybe you could start at the docks? At least you'll be near water, maybe you'll catch a fish; we'll see".

He laughed at his own humour, then. "OK, Alkis will get you started; he'll pay you each week too. I've found a teacher for you, we need to get your English fluent, if you're going to be staying here; Alkis will show you where and when, oh, and a driving instructor, he'll show you. So, unless you need to see me sooner, and you can ask Alkis to fix it if you do, I'll see you in a few months and see what progress you've made all around, OK?" I nodded, because there wasn't anything else to say; my uncle clearly had everything under control and I was to fall in with whatever he had arranged for me. He shook my hand once more; our interview was obviously over. He ushered me out, into the care of the waiting Alkis and into my new life."

"In point of fact, I started this new life as an unskilled labourer on a small development not far from where I was living; I hoped it was just a filler while my uncle found something better, because it wasn't what I'd pictured myself doing for the rest of my life. But Uncle Michalis had taken me on and I had a duty, a contract with him, I felt, to work hard and show my gratitude. So I fetched and carried, loaded and unloaded, dug holes and helped clear away what I'd dug; I worked with a will and did my best for the time that I was there. When work was over, I returned to the flat over the shop and the care of Alkis; sometimes I was given a lift, and sometimes I walked. I preferred this latter, in terms of getting to know the society in which I found myself; it was one of immigrants from many nations, both on and off the building site, including myself. Alien to each other and the place, we were nevertheless living alongside each other and doing the best we could; I just hoped my situation would improve, and soon."

"I didn't have too much time to dwell on my circumstances though, because the driving lessons and English lessons kept me busy in my so-called free time. The driving wasn't a problem, I'd learned when I was a conscript and, although I hadn't used it much back home, it came back to me very quickly. All I had to adapt to was driving on the other side of the road, plus the busy London traffic; all? It wasn't easy, the culture-shock of so many vehicles compared to the minimal traffic of my quiet island, but my instructor, John, took me first to a large disused lot awaiting development into a housing estate to practise before letting me loose into the traffic. It helped me work-wise, because when Alkis reported my rapid progress to my uncle, he moved me to work as an assistant driver, with a man named Nick. Sometimes we were couriers, delivering packages that had to be somewhere fast, sometimes goods from Uncle's import operations. The most important part for me, however, was that Nick would let me drive when we were out of town, on quieter roads; which gradually grew to include inner London and led to a driving test, which I passed with ease, hence the cessation of the driving lessons."

"I was glad of this for another reason, namely that I'd had to pay for the lessons myself, something which Uncle Michalis had neglected to mention. The cost would be deducted before Alkis paid me each week and, although I suspected that my uncle was getting a special rate, it didn't leave me with much after paying my share of the rent and household costs, electricity, food and the like, plus a woman to clean the place once a week. It was the same with the English lessons; the teacher provided for me, Tim Mountain, was very helpful and, apparently being very well-spoken himself, at pains to get me speaking English as well as possible and as fast as possible, but I knew it would take much longer to master this than the driving had. I didn't mind too much; I'd sit at home and work hard on the tasks he set me, as I had when at school, and during the day at work I'd be using what I'd learned, so I progressed fast. The homework kept me busy and didn't cost anything extra, so I never got bored."

"For the little leisure time I had left I read; it was an extension of my English lessons, really, but the sooner I got my language skills up to speed the better, I thought. There were a few old books lying around the flat, and these I worked on, slowly and laboriously at first but improving as time went by. When I'd got through those I found the local library, with some better reading matter available for free, and began to work my way through that as well. I watched TV too, which similarly helped with both the language and the culture of the country. I liked to keep in shape though, and these were largely sedentary occupations which didn't help maintain my usual level of fitness. While I was on the building site it hadn't been a problem, because the work was manual; once I was driving, however, I needed something else to counterbalance all that sitting. I found a swimming pool not too far away; it didn't cost too much and although the indoor nature of it, complete with the strong smell of chlorine, was a poor substitute for the Aegean, it did the job. So I was up at the crack of dawn several days each week, at the sessions for lane swimmers, before I went to work. In this way I passed my days and night, with little time left over for anything else, most notably women. I was glad of it; I was not ready yet to venture my affections again."

"When six months had passed I was interviewed again by Uncle Michalis. He deliberately asked me questions which required long answers, and listened attentively to my much-improved English. He smiled initially, but gradually a frown appeared on his face." "The vocabulary and grammar are good, but the accent is not", was his comment; "I suppose I ought to have expected it from putting you to live and work where I did". "He spoke to me in English now, I noted, albeit with a strong Greek accent, and he clearly wanted me to do better than he had done in this. He had a point, though; he'd given me a good teacher in Tim, who worked hard on my pronunciation during our lessons, but for the rest of the time I was interacting with the multi-cultural East End community of which I was a part, and the way they spoke English was certainly not with what was known as Received Pronunciation. So a move was deemed desirable for me, and soon thereafter I found myself sharing a flat in Knightsbridge with Tim, who was under instructions to get me speaking the Queen's English as quickly as possible. I rather fancy he succeeded, although of course if I myself hadn't worked hard it would never have happened. It's an odd thing, language"; and here Kadi paused to think and then proceeded to pursue a red herring for a few minutes.

"Each language has its own pitfalls", he mused. "English I found difficult because there are no accents of any type written down to tell one where to put the stress. They're present in Greek, in a simplified form nowadays of course, and we native speakers tend to leave them out when writing because we know how to pronounce the words. But English; nothing, you just have to buckle down and learn how to stress words, and if you get this wrong, which of course happens, the natives laugh at you for doing so. I wouldn't have minded, but most of them don't speak it well themselves, by any means. Learning a foreign language, you may or may not have noticed, often means that the person learning knows the target language better than the native speakers. The English, for example, seem to have a problem with the use of apostrophes, if you're familiar with those? Yes, and you're entitled to get your usage of them wrong because it's not your native tongue; but I've seen shop signs, TV credits, newspapers even, where someone has got it wrong. I remember it being discussed once at a drinks party which I attended, and a woman, a teacher, declaring that they should just stop using them because they confused the children. Well, I had to stop myself from saying, 'Why? Because you can't be bothered to teach them? You're a teacher, it's up to you to clear up any confusion that the children may experience.' I didn't say this, of course, but what to do when those who ought to be responsible for education don't want to educate? I mean, really; self-control is what's needed, in both teacher and student."

He stopped then. "I do appear to have gone off at a tangent, which of course is not what you need. But you'll have to indulge me at times; we'll get you sorted out, never fear." He smiled wearily, seeming tired and disinclined to return to the main thrust of his tale. He appeared thirsty, yet when Stephanidou offered him the rose-patterned cup, which was half-full and which he had been holding, Kadi refused, albeit politely. "No, I thank you, I'll be fine without; but I admit that I could do with a rest. It's good to talk to you, to get it all out there and in there" – he indicated the recording machine – "but I'm unused to talking at length, you see. So perhaps you could excuse me now and we could continue tomorrow? Thank you; I hope it's been of interest to you." He held out his hand, which Stephanidou took briefly, then lay back on his rusting bed and closed his eyes.

The Lieutenant took himself back down the hill, slowly on account of the growing heat and not forgetting to take the machine to recharge the battery. He hadn't been there for too long, but it added another dimension to his day and he was grateful for that, although unsure of how the reminiscences of this old man would be of benefit to him. Whatever, he thought, I've agreed to listen and who knows where it will go? So nursing his mild curiosity he returned to his lonely station-house with no telephone messages, no e-mails and no reports of any local criminal activity – not that he'd been expecting there to be any – so he showered and went to the kafenion to find out what Sofia had for his dinner.

6: WARMTH TO THE COLD CASE

He awoke late the following morning, having drunk too much red wine with the hearty giouvetsi of lamb with which Sofia had greeted him on the previous evening. Of course, it was his day to drive to Ayios Andreas and meet with Captain Petrides, and he was going to be late. There wasn't really any hurry, neither of them had anything much else to do, and the Captain would happily sit and drink coffee for that much longer if Stephanidou phoned and told him that there was a delay. But he didn't want to do that; he liked to do things by the book and if he'd said he would be there at eleven in the morning then he ought to be there at that time. It would look bad otherwise, late for a meeting with his superior officer, unthinkable; such things counted against you when promotions were being considered. Then he he switched into reality mode; promotion? What promotion? I'm finished, so why should I care? But nevertheless he did care, and was glad that he wasn't letting his standards drop, not all at once, anyway.

He took a fast shower and dressed in a clean uniform, had a speedy coffee and gulped-down breakfast at the kafenion, then was in the car with the key in the ignition. Of course, it wouldn't start; he'd known it was going to happen sometime, but it had to be today, of all days. Jumping up and down with frustration he went round to the garage and summoned Costaki, the unhappy Australian, who opened the bonnet and performed various mechanical checks in an irritatingly slow manner, then pronounced that it wouldn't be going anywhere today, or for a couple of weeks maybe. It needed parts, and they would have to be ordered and sent from the mainland, and who knew how long that could take? He shrugged his shoulders dismissively when Stephanidou pressed him for a more exact estimate. His whole attitude was curmudgeonly, the Lieutenant decided; life had treated him badly, he apparently felt, and he wasn't inclined to treat anyone else in a better way. You've picked the wrong man here, my friend, he addressed Costaki silently, I'm in the same boat as you. He had to prevent himself from putting the man out of his misery there and then, so he thanked him as civilly as he was able, before taking his life in his hands and cadging a lift with old Stelios in the latter's antiquated van.

The grocer had long since given up running a large operation; he still kept his old shop on the square, but in a far more limited way to match the equally limited population of the village. He went regularly into Ayios Andreas to pick up supplies which, he said, kept him active whilst giving him an interest and an income of sorts. This information had been known already to Stephanidou via the offices of the good Father Lambros, but Stelios imparted it himself anyway, whilst crunching gears and proceeding slowly up hilly stretches of the road which they were always in danger of rolling back down again. Stephanidou reckoned that the old van must still be the one from which the grocer's father had dropped supplies which had been appropriated from the road by the young Lambros, before Kadi had forced him to return them; and he voiced this thought with as much humour as he could muster. "Oh no", Stelios replied, he'd only had this one for about thirty years, and it wasn't up to much. "That old van, that could *go;* we had a really good mechanic at the time my father was running it, and he kept it in top notch condition; not like now, with only Costaki, who's competent at best. A pity he disappeared so suddenly, that man; I always wondered what had become of him." And Stephanidou discovered the disappeared mechanic to have been Nikos Osman Nikolaides, the assumed lover of Eleni Christou, who'd gone missing at around the same time that she'd been found dead.

"I remember well the time when they found the girl dead, and that Osman was missing not long afterwards", continued Stelios. "I'd returned from my National Service the night before they found her body; awful to think that, while we were all in the kafenion celebrating my homecoming, she was out there dying, killing herself." "Or being killed?" asked Stephanidou; "was there any chance of that, do you think?" "Oh no, all the men were at the kafenion, and those who left early were the fishermen, and all seen by the others to go out as usual. The women were at home, of course, but why would any of them want to kill her? I suppose there were the usual jealousies, you know, she was extremely beautiful and all the young men wanted her, and the other girls were aware of this. But to drag her to the top of the cliffs and throw her off? Too extreme, and it would take more than one woman, I think; a conspiracy of women? No, my friend, this is a simple island in Greece, not Hollywood."

Stephanidou agreed that it was rather far-fetched, but he persisted. Was there any possibility, did Stelios think, that Osman had returned and killed her? "There's always a chance", Stelios supposed, "but surely someone would have seen him, and no-one did. But why return to kill her, and risk getting caught? Easier to just slip away scot-free and leave her to take the consequences; it wouldn't be the first time, in the history of the human race". Here Stelios stopped talking, to apply all his skills to nursing the antiquated van up a rather steep incline, and Stephanidou had to be content with that. He was thoughtful for the rest of the trip, making perfunctory answers to the old grocer, who didn't notice because he was happy to have a new audience for his stream of chatter.

The trip into town passed without incident, and Captain Petrides gave his junior officer a ride back to the village afterwards, making sympathetic noises over the broken-down car. It was mid-afternoon by this time and Stephanidou, who had eaten lunch in Ayios Andreas, found himself faced with the prospect of a second, because he'd neglected to inform Sofia that he'd be eating away today and she had prepared for him a light lunch – light by her standards – of keftedes made with tomato plus a salad with feta and fresh bread on the side. He was still feeling full, but he couldn't bear to disappoint old Sofia, who he was increasingly regarding in the light of a new mother, or grandmother, and the meal was one of his favourites, after all. So he managed to eat it all, Sofia being inclined to grumble if he ever left anything on the plate, and then felt too full to do anything but retire to the shade of the station-house for a light doze after a couple of anti-indigestion tablets.

He awoke several hours later, when the sun descending towards the horizon and the correspondingly falling temperature made it clear to him that evening was coming on. The relative coolness reminded him for some reason of Kadi, and that he hadn't been to see the old man today; so putting on his running kit he hastened towards the hill to repair his error. He found the hermit sitting on the ground before his dwelling, resting his back against a section of crumbling wall, facing West and watching the sun going down. He raised his hand in welcome as Stephanidou appeared at a light jog, and waved aside the latter's apologies for the lateness of his visit and the reasons for this. "No problem, my friend, you have your work to do and I'm just an old man with nothing but my memories to occupy me"; which reminded Stephanidou to switch on the recording machine, at which Kadi smiled and continued. "Mind you, I worked hard in my time; to call me a workaholic would have been an under-estimation of the dedication I gave to business affairs. But it took some time for me to get to that stage; I had to learn my uncle's business, and so much else, before I arrived at that state of affairs." He paused for a moment, then continued, as Stephanidou sat himself on the ground like his host and leaned against a section of wall.

"As I was telling you, I moved in with Tim the language teacher and began mixing with his upper-class group of friends, the better for me to learn not just the English tongue but Englishness of the upper-class variety. Not before Tim had put me through a rigorous course in Received Pronunciation, of course; what would be the point of exposing me to these people while I still spoke with the multicultural inflexions to be found in the East End? Because, having decided that I had what it took, my uncle was grooming me for success, and I felt rather like Pip, being socially-educated by Herbert Pocket, if you know *Great Expectations*? Charles Dickens? No? Not to worry, I haven't read it either; I tried Dickens but he does go on so" (As do you, Stephanidou resisted the urge to say, then rebuked himself mentally for his impoliteness, albeit of thought rather than speech) "and I'm afraid that I gave up, eventually. But I did see a film based on the story; I used to watch all sorts of films when I wasn't working, or learning English, but of course I watched the films to help me to learn English. Whatever was on the television I watched, some good, some awful, and frequently I didn't understand a word of what was being said".

"Incidentally", and here Kadi pursued another language-related red herring, "if you ever want to improve your English don't, ever, do not, watch *EastEnders;* it's another foreign language all over again. It hadn't been made, fortunately for me, when I was first over there, but much later, in the 1980s when it had, I remember having a French student working for me temporarily. She was the daughter of a business contact out there, and he wanted her to improve her English, so I agreed to have her at my place for a month or so to keep him sweet. Well, she got on well with one of the secretaries, who took her home for dinner one night, and she came in looking really distressed the following morning. It turned out they'd watched *EastEnders* and she hadn't understood a word, which had totally undermined her confidence in the English she knew already. I had to send her off with the Chelsea crowd, my brother's friends (I'll tell you about him, in the fullness of time), the well-spoken lot that she understood totally and who praised her English to the skies. I had to sweeten them, of course, pay for the drinks and dinner and so forth, but it could have totally scuppered my business relationship with her father, which was worth far more. Such a mess; I never did a favour like that again, I can tell, you, far more trouble than it was worth".

He stopped again and laughed, at himself as much as anything. "I've done it again, haven't I? Gone rambling off on a tangent, losing control of the plot; but then I've always had to fight to keep control, you see. It all adds to the bigger picture, though." Stephanidou nodded; 'Has to fight to keep control' was mentally noted to be added to his file on Kadi, who continued then. "Well, anyway, there I was, improving my English and, when that sounded correct, my manners with Tim's group, and not doing badly at it either. They were such a confident bunch of young men and women, and why wouldn't they be? Some of them were well-educated, some not; some were holding down posts in the professions, the city, politics, while others were just socialites with time on their hands and money to spend. All of them were well-connected, though, and therefore the heirs to the pinnacle of their society, those who would rule it, run it, the politicians and law-makers and captains of industry; one of the latter being what my uncle had decided I should become."

"It was time, he felt, to bring me in closer to him, so work-wise I was moved into an office, in his main place of business, and set to learn the organisation and paper-work side of things, rather than the manual labour part. Now my

English was up to speed, more than, I'd have said, I could cope with this. What was I doing, exactly? A bit of this and a bit of that; I started writing up bills of lading, for both importing and exporting goods, and then there was the bidding for contracts, shipping and building and service providing, railways, both nationally and internationally. I was rather more than good at it, if you'll excuse my saying so, but what's the point of false modesty? I was good at it because I was so organised; I committed things to heart with ease, so I always knew which business was up for grabs, as they say in England, who else was up for it and how we could outbid them. I kept my ear to the ground and my uncle in the loop and we continued to prosper."

"After another few months my uncle summoned me to dinner with him again, and this time he announced himself satisfied with my newly-acquired pronunciation, as well as the grip I'd gained on the business. Then he considered me and spoke solemnly and to the point." "You will be my heir, Kadi; Rinoulla and I were never blessed with children, and you have become like my son. You are good with the business, more than good, and I bless the day my brother sent you to me." "His heir; I'd never expected anything like that. My uncle's mention of my father brought it home to me vividly that I'd always expected to return home at some point; but this was not the time to mention it. I thanked him sincerely for the honour he did me, and from there on in I was with him each day, accompanying him through his working day and learning the business from his personal perspective. But when he retired at night I continued, going back to the offices and looking through the work that I used to do, and which was now being done by others; I wanted a hands-on approach to all aspects of the business and to be as much in control as I possibly could be. I was aware of other people, business associates of Uncle Michalis, who had encountered problems, failed altogether in one extreme case, because they'd trusted certain things, important things, to others who'd failed to do what was necessary and let their employers down. This was not my way; my uncle had given me a chance when I needed it, and I was not going to fail him."

Kadi paused here and looked up at the sky. It had been getting dark whilst he had been speaking, and now the stars were beginning to appear here and there in the soon-to-be-night sky. "I think that will have to suffice for today", he recommenced, and Stephanidou acquiesced; he'd been late in arriving and couldn't reasonably expect the man to go on into the night just to suit him. Besides, Sofia would have his dinner waiting and would be upset if he let it spoil; never mind exactly how he'd manage to eat it, given that his double-lunch was still making itself felt in his abdomen. So he took his leave, along with the machine for recharging, and made his way back down to the village at a slow jogging pace. Upon arrival, he opened his file on Kadi and added 'Has to fight to keep control' at the end.

7: THE LIST GROWS

The next morning saw Stephanidou up very early and swimming; he hadn't managed to fit this in on the previous day, which surprised him given how little he had to do in the way of official duties. Yet he seemed to have found enough to fill his time with the local community, chatting at the kafenion with the other men and getting to know about their lives. Old Themis, for example, had been a shepherd, Tryfon a carpenter, and they were related by virtue of having married identical twin sisters. Unhappily, their wives were now departed, and their children working in Canada, leaving the men little to do but sit and reminisce over coffee in the morning and ouzo later in the day. His visits to Kadi, however, were becoming the chief interest of the Lieutenant's day; the old man's story perhaps wasn't the most riveting in the world, but Stephanidou was finding it interesting nevertheless and each evening found him looking forward to the next edition and trying to work out for himself what was going to happen. Perhaps it would be boring; Kadi married, had children, supported them and grew old doing so. But in that case, why the retirement to live as an itinerant hermit in his old home? Why the austerity of his existence? And why had he assured Stephanidou that he could help him get his life and career back on track? The Lieutenant felt sure that an ordinary life couldn't lead to such an outcome, and the only way to find out was to go and listen to some more. He towelled himself off and walked back to the station-house to shower and dress, then a leisurely breakfast preceded a walk up the hill to the story which awaited him.

Kadi appeared pleased to see him so early. "I have far more energy at this time of day, and it hardly seems any time at all since you were here last, so I do remember where I left off last evening." And, as Stephanidou switched on the recording device, he continued. "I do believe that I mentioned my brother yesterday? Yes, that's right, his crowd of friends who helped the little French girl. Well, it was one of the better times of my new life when my brother Iannis came to join me, and it was so good to see him again. Uncle Michalis let me go to meet him at the airport, to give him a more promising start over here than I'd had myself. I felt more at home at last in London by now, and was driving confidently in the busy traffic in one of Uncle's cars, so I didn't need a minder to watch over me anymore, and our emotional reunion and greeting was followed by exuberant conversation in our native Greek. Iannis had become disillusioned with life on the island after our troubles; he never referred to what had happened, but we both knew it was there and I was grateful for his wholehearted support, for which I never felt able to repay him adequately."

"Things had improved after I'd left, he told me, but there were still a few who looked askance at my family. My parents were coping, although clearly missing their eldest son, which broke my heart; although when Iannis had broached the idea of following me they had put aside their own needs in order to make him happy. The island was dying, he told me; not experiencing the steady growth in tourism to be found in those islands better equipped for the purpose, the place was stagnating and the younger people leaving. They were going to the tourist islands, to work the summer season or to set up their own businesses; or to Athens, to study and find a profession which they could follow over there. Or they were going further afield, to Canada, Australia, Britain, where they had relatives who had left years ago and could help them to a start in life there; as my uncle had done for me, and was now to do for

Iannis."

"So Iannis, having had an interview with Uncle Michalis similar to that which I'd experienced, was set on a path as I had been, with the difference that he had me there, a loving brother to help and guide him and smooth the parts of the course which had been rough for me. His career path was different, however; he'd always shown a flair for mathematics when at school, and now the world of finance attracted him greatly. He naturally gravitated towards the financial department of Uncle's offices, and that was where he was placed, happily soaking up knowledge from the staff like the sponges which the Ancient Greeks used and which, as I'm sure you know, are still harvested near the island of Kalymnos. So Uncle pulled a few strings, which obviated the need for Iannis to have a degree, and got him some industry-specific training plus a post in a brokerage firm in which he himself had an interest. The salary was low, but Iannis could learn from the bottom upwards and in time hopefully rise from the lowly task of buying and selling into an advisory and then a discretionary role. He took to it like a duck to water and his future looked fixed."

"As for myself, I was becoming successful in the business and, strangely, it was my honesty that played a large part in making me so. I say strangely, because I had become gradually aware that my uncle's methods weren't always above board. This wasn't my way and I wasn't too happy with it, but it was his business to run as he saw fit. I told myself that I could change things when the time came for me to inherit, and I hoped that would be a long time in coming, for to hope otherwise would be extremely disrespectful to Uncle Michalis. But in the meantime I always tried to proceed as honestly as his system would allow me to, and it came to be known that if I said I'd do a thing, it was as good as done. My word was my bond, and that counted for a lot; a verbal contract, if you like, and although some Hollywood mogul once said that a verbal contract wasn't worth the paper it was written on – he was joking, it was assumed, or not reasoning correctly – my verbal contracts were worth everything, as time proved."

"Some people were sceptical, though, naturally suspicious, it's the way of the world and I accept that. Most people took me on trust and found out that their trust wasn't misplaced, but there were those few who were essentially unable to do so. I remember one, a man who wasn't happy and was convinced that I'd cheated him. He barged his way into my office with a grievance which, if he'd thought about it, was a result of his own incompetence and nothing to do with me. I was opening the post at the time, paper-knife in hand; some people have secretarial staff carry out such mundane tasks, but I like to see what's coming in as soon as possible, it's the side of me that likes to be in control, you see. I wonder what became of that paper knife? It was a pretty thing, if potentially fatal, like some women I have known" (Eleni Christou? Stephanidou wondered) "... Well, as I was saying, he was aggrieved, but that was no excuse for his rudeness; he was shouting, he made some adverse remark about my mother, and before the words were fully out of his mouth he was staggering back against the wall with his hand to his cheek. It was covered in blood, the same blood which now covered my paper knife; he had sustained a three-inch gash on his cheek. I saw the bruises and scar later when it had been fixed up; it's lucky he wasn't standing closer or holding his head higher or I'd have cut his throat and then the outcome would have been significantly worse for both of us. I was unaware that I'd lashed out, but that was my temper for you, the red mist would descend and wham ... But the word went around after that, and people were careful of what they said to me; it was said that if my eyes flashed, beware, because my knife would flash an instant later. Complete nonsense of course, because I never went armed."

As Kadi was considering his next words, they were both

startled by Stephanidou's mobile phone, which suddenly rang, loudly and unexpectedly; the Lieutenant would have sworn it was the first time in weeks that anybody had called him on it. The call proved to be a summons to Captain Petrides, who had driven over to Palliohorio for want of anything else to do, and was waiting at the kafenion hoping to pass some time with his junior officer. So Stephanidou could do nothing else but apologise to Kadi and leave, cutting short the man's story, to his own disappointment but he received a deprecating gesture from the old man; "There's enough time, we'll get through it, don't worry".

Stephanidou was thoughtful on his way down the hill, but forgot his thoughts until later, after Captain Petrides had partaken of lunch with him, to the delight of Sofia who responded to the occasion of two men to feed with a classic kotopitta preceded by bread, olives, salad and skordalia. Far too much wine was taken with the food, so the Captain was taken back to Ayios Andreas by Stelios, who would collect Petrides on his grocery run tomorrow and bring him back to collect his car. As they disappeared down the road, Stephanidou made his way to the station-house and his bed, where he passed the afternoon heat in satisfied slumber. Awaking in the relative cool of the evening, he remembered his thoughts and added 'Pretty but potentially-fatal women, Eleni Christou possibly?' and 'Red mist of anger, scarred man with paper-knife' to his file. Then he went to find Father Lambros in his usual place at the kafenion. With as much tact as possible, and with today's story in mind, of the man at whom Kadi had lashed out and consequentially scarred, he reminded the priest of what the latter had told him about Kadi's temper.

Was it possible, he wanted to know, that perhaps Kadi had had something to do with the death of Eleni Christou? That he'd somehow found out about her deception and taken his revenge, throwing her over the cliff? The priest, aghast, dismissed the suggestion as totally impossible, but the Lieutenant persisted. "Where was he, when she died?" "Oh, out fishing with his father and brother, as usual", the priest responded. "They all used to fish at night, our few boats; you've seen them, still sitting down there, rotting?" Stephanidou nodded. "Except for Mandras, he still goes out occasionally, and Kadi goes with him when the mood takes him; I expect it reminds him of his youth, before all this happened. But I think I've told you that, already?" The Father recalled himself to his original purpose. "Anyway, Kadi was out that night, I walked down to the harbour with him myself. I'd gone to their house to try to cadge something to eat from his mother and Kadi was finishing his dinner; he gave some to me, that was what he was like. Then we walked down and off he went in the boat, the same as always."

"I was there when they came back the following morning, the whole village was. Word went round that the first boat coming back saw something on the shore and went to investigate; and it was her, lying dead at the far end of the beach. She'd gone off the cliffs, the post-mortem said later, injuries consistent with impact following a fall from a great height. Well, they put one man ashore to run and alert the police, and the doctor, and they put her in the boat and took her to the harbour wall. The village had started to gather when they arrived, as they brought her ashore, covered with an old tarpaulin. Kadi's family were in the last boat to come in; he collapsed when he saw her and, before God, I never want to see such a sight again. Such grief! I don't who know was the worst, Kadi or her parents."

Father Lambros shivered at the recollection, and Stephanidou had to put aside his idea of Kadi as a murderer; which it pleased him to do, albeit somewhat reluctantly, having developed as he had a certain regard for the old hermit which didn't really encompass him being a vicious killer. The idea was ridiculous, he decided, you've been out here in the sticks for too long, your brain is going soft. And with the idea of preventing his brain from softening any further, he politely declined the priest's offer of more ouzo and pleaded an invented headache to give himself an excuse for an early night.

8: GABRIELLE

Stephanidou couldn't get to Kadi as early as he would have liked the next day, as there was an incident in the village to which he had to attend. An incident; some excitement! The widow Chrisafy, old Georgina, had a cat, her beloved companion since her husband had passed away some years ago, which had apparently disappeared and which she was accusing her neighbour, Panayiotis, of killing. Stephanidou knew the cat, a mangy, ugly and bad tempered creature; it had hissed at him and bitten him when he had tried to stroke it the first time they'd met. He'd thanked his lucky stars that his Tetanus vaccination was up to date, or he wouldn't have given much for his chances. So privately he wouldn't have blamed Panayiotis for killing the thing, because he'd have killed it himself, given half a chance. However, as the neighbour flatly denied the accusation, and as there was no body to be found, Stephanidou had to explain to the widow that he couldn't charge the man on the basis of her unjustified claims, but that he would keep an eye out for the creature and ask everyone else in the village to do likewise. No more could he do, so he took a coffee to refresh himself and then set out up the hill to hear more of Kadi's story, with his own words 'No body' and 'Unjustified claims' going through his head. You want to solve the cold case for something to do, he told himself, but you can't make Kadi guilty just because you want him to be. He put the thoughts out of his mind and resolved to be extra-polite to his hermit host.

"I told you about my brother's arrival, did I not", Kadi began when Stephanidou had settled himself and switched on to record the old man's words. "Well, not so long after he was established here my uncle decided that both he and I should change our names to something more English. Uncle Michalis you see had changed his own name, and wished me to do the same, when he saw that I was doing very well indeed in the business, and made me his heir. He'd decided early on in his life here that he himself needed a better pedigree; I mean, a poor immigrant who'd got started in the East End just wouldn't cut it with the upper-class toffs, as he put it, who were running the show. The name change alone wasn't enough for my uncle, though; he had invented himself a whole different past, which he explained to me obscurely by saying, 'I never know when I might need to disappear'. He fitted me into his fictional life, so I became known as Edward as my brother became James, keeping Kadi and Ianni for those close to us to use, which was pretty much each other and our uncle."

"Whatever name I was known by was immaterial to me, however; and although Arkadios Dukakis went into hibernation, he still came out occasionally, most notably when I returned to the island to visit my parents. It was one of only three trips I made back here, until I returned this time, almost seven years ago, and I did manage to enjoy the experience to some extent, despite the bad memories threatening to overshadow the good. My brother had stated the obvious, not long after his arrival in the UK, in telling me that I ought to visit our parents; they missed me and weren't getting any younger. I wanted to see them, obviously, but not to go back to the island. So I put it off for as long as I could, but eventually knew that if I didn't go soon it would be too late, they both being in poor health by now. So I made the journey, and arrived during the afternoon; it felt strange being there again, and I wasn't sure what exactly I was feeling."

Here he lapsed seamlessly into Greek; he did this, as Stephanidou came to realise, whenever he spoke of the island and his life there in both the past and the present.

English for England, Greek for Greece he used; it was as if his memories were enshrined in his mind in the languages in which he'd lived them. So he continued now in his native Greek as he spoke of the island. "The place was changing, in line with what my brother had told me; it was quieter, there were less people, many of the younger generation having left to find work elsewhere. Those who had stayed behind were ageing, including some of my own generation and some of our parents, including mine. It was an emotional reunion with them; they didn't know at what time I'd be arriving, the ferry times being erratic, and I got the driver who took me from Ayios Andreas to drop me outside the village so that I could walk in."

"The place looked the same, but older, dingier, the roads more in need of repair than ever and the buildings requiring several coats of paint by now. There was no-one around the square as I walked in and, on an impulse, I walked down to the harbour rather than to our house. The fishing boats were still there, much as they'd been when I left, except that most of them looked unused, derelict, if that word can be applied to boats. One was clearly in use however, and an old man sat on the quay beside it, mending nets; my father! Not that old, but he looked it, so lined of face, so grey of hair; I stood still, not too close to him but not too far away either, and just gazed at him. Gradually he became aware of my presence; he looked up and started when he realised that he wasn't alone, then he recognised me and struggled to his feet, tears filling his eyes. I went up to him and we embraced each other, my eyes wet also; it was an emotional reunion."

"As we approached the house my mother came running; still strong, still agile, although she too had become grey of hair. Life had not been kind to either of them, but my mother had not let it affect her as as much as it had my father, it seemed. Had she been looking through the window, or had she somehow sensed my presence, in the way that mothers do? She never told me. My father was calling out as she came towards us, 'Our boy is back, Androulla, God be thanked', and she repeated this as she hugged me to her in a fierce embrace. Too thin, she pronounced me, and ushered me into the house where my welcome was that of a hero. Odysseus himself had not a better, once he'd sorted out the suitors, obviously. I was glad to have returned now, despite the fact that my parents were looking so much more worn of face and thinner of body, although I felt guilty at the extra weight which I had put upon their shoulders before I left." (Stephanidou wondered at this, but let it go as a reference to the false engagement). "I spent most of my time with them, only being there for one week as the business could not spare me for longer, and they were happy to have me around the house, sitting with them and talking, as well as eating and drinking. My mother seemed to want to feed me all the meals she hadn't made me while I had been away." He laughed softly and Stephanidou, thinking of his own feeding-up at the hands of Sofia, sympathised silently.

"As to the rest of the place", Kadi continued, "I saw those of the community who were still there, the older and ageing, and they appeared glad to see me; time appeared to have healed whatever ill-feeling might have existed towards me. Apparently Kyrie Nikolaides, Osman's father, had left the island; I wasn't the only one with bad memories to try to put behind me. Eleni's parents I did not see, to my regret; Chrystis, the father, had always been fair to me. They were visiting family on the mainland, I was told, with the young son who miraculously had been born to them a year or so after Eleni's death, and I was glad for them to have some consolation in the face of their loss. I heard about how Lambros, that bad boy, had been called by God, but didn't see him then as he was serving elsewhere at the time. I did wonder, though, at our respective fates, so different from what we might have expected. I made myself walk around the place, the beach, the cliffs, it didn't take long, as you know by now, and it hadn't changed much, if at all; small out-of-the-way places rarely do, and this village was no exception. So there were no new buildings, or people, or anything else to cover over the memories of my youth there; and those which had been the most recent when I'd left, those which were the reason for my leaving, still managed to overshadow all else and I was glad on that score when it was time to leave."

"So there was a reluctant leave-taking with my parents; a final farewell, as it happened, as they both were dead within a year of my visit; it was as if they were hanging on to see me again before they allowed the cancer, which it transpired was eating at them, to win the battle they'd been fighting with it daily. I went for their respective funerals, my father first, my mother following within months, and Iannis and I said our last goodbyes at their gravesides."

"When we returned to England" (and here Kadi moved seamlessly back into English), "I buried myself in work; this was to be my life from here on in, I reasoned, there being nothing and no-one for me to return to in Greece, so I might as well do it correctly, as well as I possibly could. For leisure, I worked out at the gym and swam; I'd stopped living with Tim by now, my English being rather good if I do say so myself, and moved into a much better apartment, in a block with a residents' private gym and pool in the basement. I shared it with James, so that he had support whilst he settled into his new life and acclimatised himself to his new country. We were all the family we each had now, and it felt good to be close for that time; we both understood that it probably wasn't going to be a permanent arrangement, and indeed James moved out after about a year. My little brother had settled into life in England with amazing speed, and was becoming quite a ladies' man, resulting in interesting encounters for myself with scantily-clad young women during the night or early morning, in the kitchen or bathroom or hallway. Quite apart from the fact that I was developing into a loner, and disliked strangers in my personal space, I found the proximity of all this nearly-nude female flesh unsettling; because my own love life was a wasteland."

"The unfortunate experience of my youth, you see; well, it would be too little to say that it still bothered me, too much to say that it haunted me, but it had certainly had a profound effect upon me and I was unwilling to look for love again. You will say, no doubt, that it didn't have to be love, and I'd agree with you; it was the 1980's by now, attitudes to sex were much more open and free, certainly in England, and I could have enjoyed many affairs with no strings had I so desired. However, my old need to do things correctly still had me in its grip; I might not want commitment, but the majority of the young women whom I encountered via my brother and my other male contacts were certainly looking for a more permanent arrangement. Other men might take advantage of them, but that was not my way, not then."

"So I buried myself in sport, and books, and education; I'd discovered the Open University and other forms of distance learning, and was quite happy to bury myself in literature and art as a form of relaxation in the evening. I did well at these pursuits because, as when I was at school, I saw the thing as a contract; If I applied myself I would get good results, and this is what happened. I discovered the works of Shakespeare in this manner and, although it took much work to get to grips with the archaic language and to understand it, when I did so it felt very rewarding indeed. I particularly identified with Othello, if you know that particular story? Yes? Good, then you'll appreciate my also having felt like an outsider trying to get onto the inside, and of course my sad experience with Eleni felt somewhat akin to Othello's marital issues. Of course, I had in no way been suspicious of Eleni, who was unfaithful, whilst Othello had been manipulated into suspicion of the innocent Desdemona. Still, it does rather highlight the complicated nature of human relationships, does it not?"

"So I studied, and exercised, and encased my heart in ice; and it might have stayed that way for the rest of my life, had it not been for Uncle Michalis, who noticed everything including my lack of a love life. 'You work too hard, Kadi', he scolded me, 'and that's good for business and for me; but for you, you need to take some time out, relax, enjoy life. I have never seen you with a woman, you know'; and he smiled with understanding at the look I turned upon him. 'Yes, I know about the past, about her'; he paused as I flinched at the unwelcome memory. 'But you need to put that behind you, leave it in the past, where it belongs, and move forward. Women, the right women that is, are a delight, a treasure, a pleasure to be enjoyed; but they can also be useful to us, necessary to help with business which we men cannot transact for ourselves'. I was uncertain of his meaning, and it must have been obvious to him, because he laughed again; 'You must meet with Gabrielle, I insist upon it. If you are to learn about the value of women, she is the one to teach it'. So I bowed to his greater experience, and his veiled command, and duly if reluctantly met with Gabrielle."

"Later you will hear me speak of Aphrodite, but for now it's her Aunt Gabrielle of whom I speak. Her mother was Italian, her father a Greek who travelled in foreign parts and brought her home with him when he came back to settle, eventually to have two daughters with her, Athene and Gabrielle. Aphrodite's father was an Italian sailor who jumped ship in Piraeus and into the arms of the dark-eyed girl, Gabrielle's older sister Athene, who bewitched him when she served him in their father's bar by the port. She wasn't interested in being one of many women in many ports which he visited, so she played her hand well; he converted and they married. It was the same God, so why not worship him in the Orthodox as well as the Catholic church? But serving drinks in her parents' establishment wasn't his idea of a profitable way to spend the rest of his life, and his native Naples was a poor place, so they found their way to the East End of London, where by chance he met my uncle and fell in with the latter's business schemes. He did rather well for himself in this way, and became my uncle's closest friend and right-hand man. So his wife Athene sent for her younger sister, Gabrielle, to come and make a better life for herself in London. My uncle met her, and the rest as they say is history."

"He couldn't marry her, having a wife already, but Gabrielle was a philosophical soul and being his mistress was better than her prospects in Piraeus had been. Anyway, as his wife she couldn't have helped him via the methods which she was later to employ. The story I heard was that my uncle couldn't get what he wanted from a difficult business associate by any means, and was fuming about it. But Gabrielle, who'd seen something in the man's eyes which she had seen many times before, asked him privately to meet her for a drink one evening. He did so, and returned with her to her apartment, where he stayed until the following morning; at which time he contacted my uncle and made a deal which gave the latter almost everything he wanted from the deal with no loss of face. He didn't even have to make use of the tape-recording which Gabrielle had made of the encounter, unknown to her partner of the night. What a woman! as my uncle said frequently afterwards; being a pragmatist he realised that she could be a valuable asset to him when sharing her bed with others as well as himself, and as she had no issues with doing so he accepted the situation gladly. Their union was sealed for life thereafter."

"Gabrielle, Queen of Courtesans; a dark beauty, black-eyed and raven-haired, classical, mysterious. Past her prime now, in her late forties at best and maybe twenty years older than me, I judged her to be; I would never ask, God forbid, but she would have told me honestly had I done so. She had been mistress to a number of men, always at the behest of my uncle, whose interests were uppermost in her scheme of things. Important men they were, within the circles in which I was now moving, but discreet Gabrielle had never told anything to anyone of her relationships with them; which was a cause of great respect from her ex-lovers, and a major attraction to any considering becoming her current lover. Which included myself; for I found her fascinating, attractive in her assured and lazy sensuality, which encroaching age and clothing could not hide."

"At our first meeting, decreed by Uncle Michalis, she looked me up and down with amusement and laughed; 'Well, Kadi mou, your uncle tells me you have need of my experience?' I must have blushed, like the virgin I was, and she patted my cheek reassuringly; 'You're embarrassed that he knows what he does about you?' I assented, quietly; I was concerned over confidentiality in any relationship which might ensue between us, and she had sensed this. 'You wouldn't want him to know any more?' She laughed again and didn't wait for an answer; 'You think I'll kiss and tell?' I was over-sensitive to being made a fool of after my early experience with Eleni, so, 'Yes, anyone who kissed and told on me wouldn't do it again', I assured her; 'It's hard to kiss when your lips have been slashed, to tell when your tongue has been cut out and thrown to the dogs'. I was ridiculous, overly-dramatic and threatening, but she just looked at me and laughed her lazy, sensual laugh. She was totally without fear, and I came to respect that in her. 'Kadi mou', she told me, 'if I were to write my memoirs I could make a fortune, but I wouldn't live long enough to enjoy it. I was told, when I was younger, not to fuck with the big boys; but I fuck with them because that's what they want from me. But I keep my mouth shut, unless they want me to do otherwise'. She paused and stroked my cheek again; 'So, what do you want me to teach you?' I took her hand from my cheek and kissed her palm, then looked her directly in the eye; 'Everything'."

"And I'm rather afraid that has to be everything for today"; Kadi broke off with a yawn, which he stifled with one hand. "I'm feeling rather tired, my energy is low, you will have to excuse me." No, Stephanidou insisted untruthfully, not at all, of course, he'd been rather late anyway; and so on and so forth, until he found himself on his way back down the hill feeling rather warm and uncomfortable and miffed at Kadi's breaking off of the story just as it was getting interesting. Women had come into it, along with the prospect of sexual encounters being retold, about which Stephanidou was not averse to hearing but was also disturbed by. Kadi had touched on the subject of sex, and simultaneously touched a nerve in his one-man audience.

Stephanidou was uncomfortably aware that his own sex life, like Kadi's for some years when he had first gone to England, was non-existent. Further, the parallels between himself and the old man were closer than the latter knew because, despite it being the twenty-first century now, and sexual relationships being much freer in Greece as well as in many other parts of the Western world, Stephanidou had refrained from entering into such a relationship with Elpida, his intended bride. Like the young Kadi, he had wanted to do things correctly, but now he was unsure as to whether he had done the right thing. On the one hand, it was good that he hadn't entered into an intimate relationship with Elpida, because now he was stuck on this dying island and didn't know whether they had a future. On the other, however, he had no tender memories to fall back on, and no prospects of anything else to take their place.

To be perfectly crude about it, as Stephanidou put it to himself, he wasn't getting any, so he was frustrated and food was rapidly taking the place of sex in his life. I may not be fasting in terms of food, he thought, but I'm making up for it in terms of fasting from sex. Ruefully he felt his waistline, which was becoming noticeably softer, he thought, despite all the swimming and running, due to the ministrations of Sofia, the new domestic goddess in his life. Sofia, it seemed, lived for cooking. It had been fine when she had had an active, healthy husband and three growing sons to provide for, she'd been in her element. Now, however, the sons were all living on the mainland or the islands which benefited from tourism, that being where the work was, and she only got to cook for them when they visited each year in August. Additionally, Giorgos these days was suffering from gastric issues, which he treated via self-medication with ouzo and only certain simple foods which he'd found via trial and error to keep things in order digestive-tract wise.

So Sofia's need to feed others was frustrated within her own hearth and home, and she looked elsewhere to satisfy it. The now-deceased Lieutenant Polycarpou had eaten little, preferring to drink; but now, sensing in his replacement an appreciation, via his compliments and the empty plates which he returned to her, she pulled out all the stops. She found in Stephanidou a surrogate son, and her culinary skills experienced a renaissance. Stifado, moussaka, pasticio, kotopitta, spanakopitta, yemista, if he named it she would cook it as well as other, complementary, dishes besides. Even the simplest dishes, such as plain green beans in oil and lemon, drew sighs of pleasure from her new-found disciple, and she stepped up to the plate, the hot-plate as Stephanidou liked to joke, in order to please his palate. You're too thin, she told him when he remonstrated at the gastronomic portions she served up to him, You need feeding up and you've no wife yet to do it for you. Tell me about it, thought Stephanidou; but in the absence of the sexual pleasures of wedded bliss, his only other recourse was to those of the table. Sofia knew he'd eat it, once the food was set before him, and she'd got his measure in this; he knew when he was beaten, and had stepped up his daily running and swimming routine in order to body-combat his expanding waistline and forget his lack of love.

9: AN EDUCATION

When Stephanidou went up the hill the next morning he wasn't in the best of moods. He'd slept fitfully, after dinner at the kafenion and several cold showers, and gotten very little sleep for his pains. He'd then drunk too much coffee to try to wake himself up and eaten too much breakfast by way of comfort. Sofia had been delighted and, he reflected gloomily and with justification as it turned out, he could expect even larger breakfasts in the future as a result. So he was feeling tired on the one hand and lifted by a caffeine high on the other, and bloated on both from his over-indulgence at the table.

Climbing the hill in the increasing heat wasn't the best activity therefore, and he actually stopped halfway up and considered walking back down again. What am I doing, he asked himself, coming up here every day to listen to the life story of a crazy old man? Why do I need this? Because he said that he could help you, although you seriously doubt that to be the case, but you have a niggling idea that there's something more going on there. The man's fiancée died in suspicious circumstances, her lover disappeared off the face of the Earth, and Kadi himself had a violent temper, by his own admission and the testament of the priest. He seems to have had a watertight alibi though, also through the offices of the priest; but I still feel there's something I can't put my finger on.

There's his life in England as well; he appears to have been very successful, although I haven't yet heard the whole story, and I can understand the return to Greece later in his life. But the hermit lifestyle? He could live much better if he still had money, so maybe he lost it all? Well, you don't have anything else to do, his pragmatic persona added, so you might as well hear the whole story and see what you can get out of it. At least when you're listening to him you're not thinking about your own situation and depressing yourself any further. Can I get any more depressed, though? Stephanidou had thought seriously again, in the wakeful small hours, of the loaded gun in his desk; but he put the thought from him swiftly now, squared his shoulders and continued up the hill. Might as well go with the flow and see what, if anything, came out of it.

The old man must have seen Stephanidou's stop for consideration on the hillside, because he referred to it obliquely, the latter thought, when he arrived at the ruin. Propped up on his bedstead, Kadi waved an arm in the direction of Stephanidou's route up the hill, which the latter took as a reference to his having stopped and stood still for a while; then his host spoke. "I suspect that you're beginning to wonder what you're doing, listening to the no-doubt boring reminiscences of an old man like me? Well, if you keep listening you'll have an answer by the time I'm done, I'm sure of that."

"In the meantime, does is occur to you that you and I are similar in some ways? We both had a particular future in mind for ourselves, but things didn't work out as we had envisioned. I always expected to live my life on this island, but I had to leave and was able to return only a few years ago; while you expected a bright career in the thick of things, the city lights and so forth, and here you are on an island which you would cheerfully never have heard of, if you'd had your way. My lot is rather ironic, you know; I always expected to live in this house, and here I am. It was my mother's family home, but my father had his own house, and never had enough money for them to do anything with this one. I wanted to renovate it myself, and live here with a wife and raise a family, but it was not to be. I could do it now if I wanted to, of course, having worked on a building site when I first went to England. I have many of the skills, but what would be the point? I have no plans to marry." And he laughed softly and jeeringly at himself, the laugh with a bitter note which sent a chill through Stephanidou.

"It's not just you and I, either", Kadi continued; "the others in the village, old Sofia and Giorgos, Stelios and Mandras, all of them, they all expected to have raised their children to follow them. Fishing for Mandras's sons, the grocery shop for those of Stelios and the kafenion for young Giorgos; as to Sofia and the other women, to pass on their household skills to their daughters and have their grandchildren around them by now. It didn't happen though; the children are gone, to the mainland, or Australia or Canada, wherever there was work for them and a life in the larger world. Which of course is what you had, but here you are, listening to me because there's precious little else for you to do. Someone who's in control of how human affairs progress is having a very good laugh on our account, you may be sure."

Stephanidou was touched on the raw by this reference to his own situation, and suddenly realised that Yes, he could indeed feel more depressed than he had on the way here. It must have shown on his face, because Kadi addressed him then with almost savage passion; "Feeling sorry for yourself? Get out of it, then, your current career. There's still time, put the corruption and the rottenness behind you and start afresh, you're young enough." It was almost a plea, but Stephanidou shook his head; No, he couldn't do that, this was what he wanted to do with his life and to leave would mean that the other guy, the bad guy, had won. "Then you have to find a solution, a way for you to take control, to rise again"; Kadi had calmed again now, and was speaking reasonably. "So while you try to find a way you might as well listen to someone's else's story of a rise, and a fall, and a rise again. A spectacular rise and an equally spectacular fall; mine, and you have me here to tell you of it. Shall I continue?" Stephanidou nodded bleakly and the old man spoke again. "It's difficult for me to talk about the past, I sit and think of it and of whether I could have done anything differently? Telling you will help me to rationalise it all, I can go through it chronologically, in an orderly fashion, and try to make sense of it all. You can judge for yourself, and possibly help me just by listening, as I can possibly help you just by telling."

"So, we were speaking of Gabrielle, who was important to me; she wasn't a trophy escort, which wasn't what I was looking for at that time, but she was a prize in her own way. I wasn't in love with her, nor she with me; we had both been allotted a task by my uncle, and were obedient to his wishes. It sounds somewhat ridiculous to say that I entered into the arena of sexual pleasure at the orders of my uncle, however that is what I did. It has to be said, though, that I was more than happy to do so. I had wanted to wait, correct young man that I had been, for my wedding night with my bride; but that had been denied me, and I had kept clear of women thereafter through fear of something similar happening again. But it had been some years now, and I was ready, in fact I was yearning, for the close physical contact and intimacy that was a sexual relationship with a woman. Once I had embarked upon my relationship with Gabrielle I remembered my fellow conscripts from my National Service days, those who had made night-time trips to certain houses in the back streets of the town near the camp, and was glad that I had not followed their example. Doubtless the authorities had vetted those places and the women who inhabited them, and found them to be clean; they did not want the young men to return home riddled with God-knows what to pass on to their future brides and father a race weakened thereby. Yet to me it seemed a soulless transaction; pay your money, take a number and get in line, for what? An impersonal coupling with an unfortunate woman made desperate by circumstances. Not for me, and I was relieved that I had waited, even if as it turned out I had waited for Gabrielle rather than Eleni."

"Much later, when my Magdalena told me stories from *The Epic of Gilgamesh* about the wild man Enkidu and the priestess from the Temple of Love who initiated him into the arts of love-making, I remembered Gabrielle. She was exactly what I needed at that time, and she taught me well; I even found an added *frisson* later, when I was lucky enough to find my Magdalena a virgin still, in passing on what Gabrielle had taught me, and taking pleasure simultaneously in remembering when I had been the virgin to be taught. Later, when she'd taught me all she had to teach, when we both knew that our time was passing, she passed me also; on to the next, to whom she introduced me. Wise Gabrielle; and she found me a treasure, a pleasure, but pain also, pain and pleasure, together. But that came much later."

"Gabrielle didn't just teach me about physical, sexual pleasure, but undertook my cultural education also; probably at my Uncle's behest, but I never asked her. She finished me, polished me, took what knowledge I had gleaned about social life in Britain and expanded it, explained what I didn't completely understand and corrected those things which I thought I had mastered but had in fact got wrong. A great percentage of this teaching, it has to be said, took place in her bed, between bouts of intense sexual activity which I have to confess I enjoyed immensely and of which I couldn't get enough. It wasn't the correct, formalised relationship which I had wanted when young, but by now I was compromising my need for correctness in many ways; real life just wasn't like that, I'd learned, so I'd learned to compromise, when I couldn't do otherwise."

"Compromise, of course, has no place in tragedy, which was a part of the education to which Gabrielle exposed me outside of her bed. The arts, theatre, opera, music and painting were made available to me, and I have to say that I lapped them up. I'd discovered distance learning, as I've told you already, and was enrolled on one course after another, to study in depth. But it was Gabrielle's duty to take me to see paintings I'd only seen in books, hear the music played live which I'd only heard recorded, and watch plays which I'd only seen on television or video acted in live performances, on stage. We were constrained, of course, to those plays which were in performance somewhere; otherwise we'd content ourselves with videos which we'd watch in Gabrielle's apartment, comfortably curled up on her sofa with a bottle of wine before we moved to her bed for the night."

"Ancient Greek drama was an important part of this education for me, being in my blood, of course, as it's in yours. Both both tragedy and comedy, of course, but the former tends to be seen as more important than the latter, and far more examples of it have survived, incidentally. I'm sure you know that the original drama festivals were dedicated to Dionysus, that god of chaos who sits in opposition to the law and order of Apollo, whom I'd followed exclusively. Now I realised that equal respect must be paid to both. One of the plays to which Gabrielle took me was *The Bacchae* of Euripides, in which the king, Pentheus, who opposes Dionysus and tries to deny his godhead, comes to a sticky end. You know it? Good. I also read Thomas Mann's *Death in Venice*, in which Gustave von Aschenbach also dies for living too orderly a life and denying the need for a little Dionysian chaos. So, with these examples before me, I realised the need for a little disorderly behaviour in my own life; and sexual experience outside of marriage filled this need."

"In opera also I found that I leaned more towards the tragic, rather than the comic, stories. The first performance to which Gabrielle took me, Puccini's *Tosca,* brought out an empathy in me with the doomed heroine, Floria Tosca.

She'd tried to live well, for her art, for her love, so what had she done to deserve the truly terrible situation in which she found herself, she asked in her aria 'Vissi d'arte'. Of course I identified with her; all I'd ever wanted was a simple life, home and honest work, wife and children, but I'd been exiled for an honestly-made mistake and was living in a way I could never have imagined. Gabrielle found me too thoughtful after that particular performance, and I didn't stay with her that night, making my excuses by way of an impending heavy schedule the next morning. She didn't say anything, wise woman that she was, but the next few operas to which she took me were *Buffa,* rather than *Seria*. It was no good, though; I was hooked on the tragic."

Stephanidou didn't hear this last part, being focussed on Kadi's reference to 'an honestly-made mistake'. How had he made a mistake, other than getting engaged to a woman who was trying to make a fool of him? He could mean that, but to the Lieutenant's ears it didn't sound like it. He applied himself to listening even more closely, to see what if anything else of interest was disclosed, but Kadi had closed his eyes in the manner which Stephanidou had come to recognise as the signal for the end of that day's chapter. He took his leave, and the recording machine for its daily recharge, and made his way thoughtfully back down to the village.

He had an unexpected treat that night. The weather being favourable, old Mandras had decided to take his boat out, and invited Stephanidou to come along. Not for the whole night, he informed his guest reassuringly, he was too old now for the dusk-till-dawn fishing expeditions of his youth, but a couple of hours, maybe three if all went well, and would the Lieutenant like to get a feel of what life here had been like? The Lieutenant would, very much, he was told; for, although Stephanidou was finding his days rather well-filled somehow, he welcomed any novelty that presented itself and a spot of boating by night appeared to him in that light. Having accepted however, and eaten more dinner than usual (because he'd need fuel against the night air, he told himself and Sofia, who wasn't arguing with him), he had misgivings as he dressed for his nautical novelty. He recollected the tired appearance of the boats by the harbour wall, old and rusting and decidedly unseaworthy; was he setting himself up for a watery death? But apparently old Mandras did go out sometimes, he remembered distinctly Father Lambros telling him so, and that Kadi had gone with him on occasions; and both were still alive. So Stephanidou waved aside his negative thoughts and went to the harbour for the trip which awaited him.

In the event Mandras proved a more than capable sailor, experienced in and sensitive to the caprices of the ocean; it had been his life, after all, and Stephanidou soon found himself forgetting his misgivings over the seaworthiness of the vessel and enjoying the smell of the salt and the feel of the night breeze on his face. Mandras had sensed his nerves when they first set out, and laughed to himself; when his guest visibly relaxed, however, he allowed himself to give a reproof to the latter. We build them strong out here, our boats; no chance of any problems on a night like this. Stephanidou had to agree; it was spring, and the water still rather cold, but the breeze had a gentle warmth in its undercurrent. There was a little cloud, but not enough to obscure the half-moon which cast its rays over the water and the stars which gleamed around it. He thought of Kadi observing these at night, to relax himself, and possibly for more. Stephanidou remembered feeling small, up on the cliffs in daylight, on the day when he first met the old hermit, and now he felt small again; however, in a positive manner this time. Yes, he was small, but still a part of it all, this earth, this ocean, this sky and the heavenly bodies shining down on him; he felt at peace.

Then he saw the cliffs, pale surfaces moving from the sky to the sea in the light of the moon; he could make out the beach nearby, and was involuntarily reminded of Eleni Christou falling from the former and being washed up on the latter. Then he thought, What if she wasn't alone? What if Nikos Osman had been with her, what if it was a lovers' leap together? All bodies didn't necessarily wash ashore, perhaps the young man had been carried out to sea, rather than in to the shore, by currents which Eleni's body had eluded? Why should I think that? he wondered; Nikos Osman had left the island and not returned, the records of the investigation at the time were clear, plus Stephanidou remembered his conversation with Stelios on the way to Ayios Andreas. Nevertheless, a good investigator never discounts anything which could be possible, the Lieutenant told himself, and filed the thought for later.

10: APHRODITE

He slept well that night and awoke early, just as the sun was emerging over the horizon in a deep red glow. He felt refreshed in both body and spirit, and gave the credit to the sea air and the change of scene. He decided to ask Mandras to take him again, if he should go out; Why live on an island if you never partake of the sea on your doorstep? he asked himself. His upbeat mood continuing, he decided to go for an early swim before his shower and, after throwing on a singlet and shorts, set off at a light jog to the beach. The sound of birds was in the air, including the crowing of a cockerel which appeared to be standard issue in small villages, Stephanidou thought with amusement, but no people except perhaps Stelios busy in his store and Sofia thinking about preparations for breakfast; but those were indoor activities, and no-one except himself was venturing forth at present.

Or so he thought, until he arrived at the beach and was greeted with the sight of someone swimming; maybe not swimming exactly, but far enough from the shore to be totally immersed up to and over his shoulders, moving back and forth slowly before turning towards the shore and moving in that direction. Stephanidou realised with fascination that the man was Kadi and, for some reason decided that he didn't want to be seen by the hermit. It was too late to retreat the way he had come without being detected, so he moved quickly down and behind the thick bushes which lined the beach to the rear. Making sure he was well-hidden, he watched as the man emerged from the water, his total nakedness showing clearly the extreme emaciation of his body as he moved towards the right-hand edge of the shore, fortunately the furthest away from Stephanidou in his hiding-place. The old man proceeded to dress himself in his usual black clothes, which were spread out on the rocks bordering the shore here and which Stephanidou presumed Kadi had washed in the water before immersing himself. Neither man nor garments could be totally dry, he thought, but at least they were clean; and he watched as, dressed eventually, the old hermit moved slowly to the back of the beach and up the track towards the village.

Stephanidou was glad that he had hidden; he had given the old man his dignity in so doing, he felt, and was also glad that he had remained undetected. He took a good, long swim himself then, shivering at the coldness of the water at first entry but plunging in without hesitation. In the water rather than on it this morning, he thought, I enjoy the benefits of the sea from all perspectives. His good mood continued as he jogged back to shower off the salt before partaking of breakfast with a good appetite, which earned him the approval of Sofia and of Giorgos also; for it was not lost on Stephanidou that if Sofia was in a good mood her husband appeared to benefit, and gave the credit to the Lieutenant when the latter's appreciation of her cooking was the reason. So with the sun of their joint good feelings shining on him, he set out to visit Kadi.

He found the old hermit sitting on one of his rickety chairs, which he had moved out into the early morning sun, with his head back and his eyes closed as if sleeping. He sensed the presence of his guest, however, opening his eyes and smiling lazily as he waved Stephanidou to another chair, presumably placed in the sun for the visitor's benefit. "It makes one feel so good, a morning swim, does it not?", the host enquired of the guest, making it clear to Stephanidou that he had in fact not gone undetected at the beach. His confusion was obvious to Kadi, who laughed lightly and self-deprecatingly. "Do please excuse me for mentioning it, but I couldn't resist it; I thank you for respecting my privacy and dignity, so please don't feel embarrassed. I too have hidden in those bushes and seen naked bathers come ashore, in the distant past. I remember one couple in particular …". He paused and sighed and Stephanidou couldn't quite identify the emotion displayed as either positive or negative. Which couple? he thought; Eleni and Osman were in his mind after his thoughts near the cliffs last night. Surely they hadn't swum together, they'd have been seen; possibly they had, and by Kadi? But his musings were interrupted by his host; "Fortunately it's not illegal now, as it was then, to swim nude, so you won't have to arrest me; it still can be offensive, though, which is why I go very early or very late to perform my ablutions, so you may have to caution me." He laughed gently, and Stephanidou dismissed the idea with a wave of his hand; his host now seeming disinclined to continue with that topic, he indicated that Stephanidou should commence recording and started upon a new one.

"It is now time to speak of Aphrodite. I saw her first at one of Gabrielle's parties, across the floor talking to some other man, some nonentity who didn't register with me. Her gaze met mine and I was smitten; as clichéd as it gets, but that's how it was. I couldn't tear my eyes away, and neither could she; her mouth was moving in the direction of her companion, but her eyes were looking directly over his shoulder into mine. Gabrielle, ever-intuitive and attentive to the needs of her guests, realised what was going on and intervened for the comfort of all. Taking my arm, she swept me over to the pair; 'Henry darling', to the man, 'I have someone who's desperate to meet you, and I absolutely insist that you meet her'. Then, relinquishing my arm, and taking his, which he willingly gave through the obedience which we all gave to Gabrielle, she paused only to introduce the eye-entwined couple; 'Edward (using my English name, of course), this is Aphrodite, my niece; Aphrodite, this is Edward, Michalis's nephew; look after him for me, would you, darling?' And she was gone, towing Henry in her wake, which I sensed rather than saw, because I remained gaze-locked with my new companion."

"She was well-named; Aphrodite, Queen of Beauty and Love. Part Italian, part Greek, a younger version of her aunt, as dark as Eleni had been blonde, as experienced when I met her as Magdalena had been innocent when she came to me later. Suffice to say, Aphrodite left with me that night and we were inseparable for the next week. I was in love, or lust, or both, and totally in the grip of my passion. I didn't care about Aphrodite's past or present or anything else, I knew that I was going to marry her and be happy at last. My uncle had to understand my absence from work for that period of time; after all, he had pushed me back into the arms of a woman, and his ploy had succeeded rather better than he had expected. So he gave me the week, but made it clear in messages that he expected me by his side as usual on the following Monday. This wasn't a problem, as it happened, because the curse which regularly visits all young women visited Aphrodite on the following Saturday night, so she encouraged me to return to work on Monday."

"My uncle laughed indulgently when he saw me, but restricted himself to a comment which was not totally insensitive; 'You're looking well, better than I can remember; the change in your lifestyle suits you'. That was all, and I busied myself with catching up on what I'd missed while Uncle Michalis brought me up to date verbally. One item puzzled me though, as I went through paperwork new to my eyes; 'I thought this contract was going to Davidson, but it's been drafted as if for Marston, a mistake?' My uncle didn't even need to look at the document, he knew very well to what I was referring and laughed with some regret in his tone. 'Well, yes, but Marston wasn't very happy after what you did to him, and I'll need him in the future so I have to keep him sweet; this seemed the best way, we can give something else to Davidson'. 'After what I did to him? I don't think I've even met him'. I looked quizzically at my uncle and he looked embarrassed, a new mood for him, in my experience, as he answered. 'Henry Marston; he was at Gabrielle's party'. But I shrugged in continued ignorance, and he looked away from me; 'Gabrielle told me; you took his fiancée from him'."

"My jaw dropped in shock; 'Aphrodite?' I could say no more than that. Uncle Michalis nodded and shrugged himself. 'He was with her when you met, they were engaged; but he should know that women can be fickle. Make the most of them when they're with you, and then … well, there are always more'. My head was reeling with the shock, but habit took over and I controlled myself, forcing myself to smile and nod, with a rueful air, then I moved rapidly on to business. 'I see you have a meeting with Crawford at eleven; we'll need to get going soon'. Subject closed, by mutual consent, and the day progressed according to plan; I drove, parked, fetched, carried, took notes and whatever else was required of me, outwardly. Inwardly, however, I kept coming back to Aphrodite. Her fiancé; she was committed to one man, yet she just upped and left him in the space of an evening for another? I was dismayed, I'd already experienced one disastrous relationship with a fickle fiancée, I didn't need another. I realised that I owed it to her to hear her side of things, but I wasn't hopeful."

"When I returned home that evening she was waiting, open-armed and with kisses ready on her lips, but she backed off when she saw my face and I didn't waste any time. 'Aphrodite, what of Henry Marston?' She looked at me for a long moment, then shrugged; 'What of him? My uncle says you were engaged to him, last Saturday, when we met'. She smiled in her lazy, sensual manner then; 'I met you and fell in love; in love with you, out of love with him'.

I couldn't believe her casual manner; Did you even tell him? 'Of course I did, he called me the next morning and left a message; I sent him a text while you were in the shower'. I could barely speak at her attitude; A text? I thought, and, 'Behind my back?' I managed out loud. She frowned then, with something like irritation; 'No, to spare your feelings. He's nothing to you, or to me now, why are you making such a big deal of it?' She turned to go to the kitchen; 'My stomach hurts, I need a hot pack, we both need a drink, then I'll fix us something to eat'. Subject closed, apparently, her dismissive manner said so as clearly as her departure from the room; and I remained, exasperated but still too infatuated to pursue the matter."

"We made up, if what had occurred could be called a row; more a difference of opinion, with the subsequent ignoring of the matter a tacit agreement between us to differ. It changed me, though; a reality check had occurred. Although I still adored being with Aphrodite, in bed with her mostly, enjoying her lazy sensuality and pleasure in the act of love, my thoughts had turned away from marriage. I thanked God that I hadn't proposed to her already; if she could turn her affections from one man, no less than her fiancé, to another, so easily, what was to prevent her from doing it again? I couldn't take the chance, given my history; instead I took my uncle's advice and made the most of what I had with Aphrodite while I had her."

"She noticed the change, though; she didn't mention it, but something in her manner told me that she realised she had lost a part of me and was trying to get it back. She did her utmost, in ways both large and small, to please me; not through subservience, that was never her way, but somehow what I wanted was always supplied without my having to ask for it. She had an apparently natural way of pleasing a man without seeming to make any effort; indefinable, but it was there. She was her aunt's niece, after all, and I'd called Gabrielle Queen of Courtesans, so I suppose Aphrodite had learned it from her, or it was in their blood, who knew? Wonderful mistresses, but doubtful wives; it sounds so old-fashioned nowadays, but that's the way it was. And if Aphrodite realised that I had contemplated marriage and was now doing so no longer, she managed to bind me to her in another way which I hadn't considered. A few months after our meeting she informed me that she was pregnant."

11: BIBI

At this point Kadi temporarily ceased his narrative, in order to move onto his bed in the shade; the sun was well-risen into the sky by now, and the warmth was building. Stephanidou moved also, into the shade and balanced on the best of the broken-down chairs, after having fetched some water in the rose-patterned cup, which he offered to Kadi, who took a small sip before continuing his tale.

"Another almost-marriage, and another baby on the way; at least I knew that this one was mine. If Aphrodite was a natural courtesan, she played by the rules of being a kept woman; one man at a time. She ditched Marston when she met me because that was how it worked; I was yours but now I'm his. End of. And now her impending motherhood showed yet another side of her; excitement at what was coming, wonder at the life that was growing inside her, and an enthusiasm for me to share it. Which unfortunately I couldn't."

"I was not pleased with the turn events had taken. Retaining as I did some of my old need to do things correctly, I didn't want a child of mine born out of wedlock; but neither was I going to be railroaded into marriage with a woman I had my doubts about just to make the birth regular, as it were. So I compromised, and accepted that the child would have unmarried parents, as the lesser of two evils. I also had to accept the change in Aphrodite, irksome though I found it could be. I was still sexually-infatuated with her, and couldn't get enough of her; and although she was still the sensual, earthy creature she had been at first, her desire for sex decreased in ratio with her increasing pregnancy. When she was willing, moreover, I had to take her with care, for fear of doing some damage to the precious cargo she carried in her womb, and I had need of much self-control during this period."

"When Aphrodite eventually had her baby, in the middle of the night after a wild drive to the hospital, things changed yet again. But I had expected this, because babies inevitably change things. It had been that way when my mother had Iannis and I was no longer the only one, the only child, focus of both parents, doting mother and proud father. Child no longer, although only five years old; You have to help us to look after him, Kadi-mou, from both, and I didn't mind the idea, small though I was. Here was someone I could protect and control, as my parents protected and controlled me. So when Aphrodite gave birth, things were different because they couldn't be otherwise. She doted on the little girl, carried her constantly, gave her the breast on demand, kept her in a cot beside our bed, from where she could reach out and bring her to the bed if necessary. I tolerated it all, most of the time; I quite liked to see her, the earth-mother, baring her breast and suckling her young. I became a part of the process, sitting up next to her, arm around her, naked as we were in bed when the little one cried to be fed."

"At other times, though, I had to be firm; she would put the sleeping child in the cot, then lean on one elbow and look down at her adoringly, unable to tear herself away. I had to remind her that she was my lover as well as the child's mother, desirable to my eyes as she reclined there, naked and warm and kindling my mounting passion. I would take her in my arms and kiss her, firmly letting her know that the infant had to take second place now, while her lover needed her. She would submit to me, torn I could tell as she moved her body but found it difficult to tear her eyes away from the cot. I would touch her cheek, firmly again, and turn her face to me and look into her eyes as I caressed her. Slowly she would move from submission to active passion as I teased her body, awakening her own need so that, even if the child whimpered lightly, she would have no focus but our mutual desire as I brought her to a climax, slowly and methodically. She was still my woman, earthy in her sensuality, and it drove me mad with desire just to see her, naked or clothed. I wanted to take her, over and over again; there was no end to my wanting her."

"Until the child grew older, that is. Initially I'd had little interest in her, although she was mine. Newly-born, she looked much as other babies, apart from the sprinkling of downy dark hair on her head, and I found her much as I had found them in the past. I'd indulge Aphrodite's obsession with her, a new mother wrapped-up in the wonder of her creation, but gave the child little attention beside that. Aphrodite obviously noticed that I was taking little part in the Adoration of the Wunderkind. All-too-frequently I'd hear, Kadi, do come and look, or, Kadi, do listen to her, or, Kadi, see, she's smiling at you; the latter being just wind, of course. Sometimes I'd come in from the office and find Aphrodite sitting on a sofa with the child in her arms, playing a game of nonsense-speak and tickling with the little one, who was gurgling softly back at her mother. A pretty sight, but one which I wasn't a part of, and Aphrodite would not stop the game or look up even to acknowledge my presence."

"There was one evening when I decided that I *would* join in the game, with resentment, I regret to say, and because I wanted to make my presence felt; this was my home and I wouldn't be ignored. So I went over and held out my arms authoritatively; 'Let me hold her'. It was an order, not a request, but obediently the mother passed the precious bundle to the father, glad that for once he was taking notice of his offspring. I took the child with curiosity, but I still couldn't feel anything, try as I might, and I did try, to my credit. I looked at my daughter blankly, willing some paternal pride to rise within me, but nothing came; she looked right back at me in the same way, indifference for indifference, I felt. I gave her back to her mother and went to have a shower."

"But things changed when the little girl was about two or three months old. I'd come home, more tired than usual from being stuck for over an hour in a traffic jam caused by an accident. The child was crying and wouldn't stop, despite all the efforts of Aphrodite, who looked exhausted, with large dark circles under her eyes as she paced the room with the brat in her arms. I was grumpy with it all, the backed-up traffic followed by the crying child, hence my calling her a brat, for the first and last time, in my defence. Was this tiny tyrant going to spoil what was left of the evening when I so needed to rest, as did her mother? I went over and gestured to Aphrodite, who willingly passed her to me, glad for once of the respite, before she collapsed onto the sofa."

"I was firm with the child, overly-so to the point of harshness, I'm afraid, in both tone of voice and in the way I held her; 'Come here, cry-baby Baby'. She stopped mid-scream and looked into my face curiously, and I looked back, returning stare for stare as I assessed her. The dark down had turned into a bundle of brown curls, thick and unruly and so much like my own had been, as a child. The little hands, warm and pink and pudgy with rolls of baby fat, extending from the arms of the little lemon-coloured woollen matinee jacket which she wore. Old-fashioned it was, but Aphrodite had insisted on knitting it and other items while she had waited for the one who was to wear them upon her entry into the world. There were little matching mittens for when the weather was colder, and matching bootees which adorned the little feet, as pink and pudgy within them as the hands were above. The eyes, as dark as the hair, observed me solemnly from above the chubby little cheeks, one of which I stroked now in wonder. Maybe it tickled her, for the eyes lit up as they fixed on my face, the little nose wrinkled and the rosebud mouth curved wide open in a smile of delight as the little hands and feet waved and kicked her pleasure for me to see. One of the hands, in the general area of my face as I bent closer to observe her, caught my face and stroked it with the fat of five little fingers, such dainty digits that I couldn't help but grasp them gently. I felt myself go pink with pleasure, and as I did so this little one burst into giggles, a baby's crowing with delight, and she coo-ed and chuckled and touched my face again. I moved my hand and caressed the chubby, baby-fat encased little wrist; then she burst into yet louder chuckles, bouncing in my remaining arm and waving both little fists, little feet encased in their knitted bootees kicking for all they were worth. On that instant I fell in love with her, my little Bibi."

"She had been officially named Michaela Gabrielle, for my uncle and Aphrodite's aunt, but from that moment she became Bibi. Cry-baby Baby, I had called her, but I dropped the 'cry' and she became Baby-Baby, then B-B, turning naturally into Bibi. Aphrodite's baby but mine too, this fruit of my loins, my offspring. I thought about those words, later, words which we all so carelessly use without thinking about their genesis. I remembered nights filled with desire spent with Aphrodite, looking down at her pleasure as I took her with my own, man and woman, one flesh, as I enjoyed her and she me, her climax coming just before my own. And when we lay in the aftermath of love-making, a third was conceived within the mother, with the seed of the father, and this child was the result. Flesh of my flesh, and of hers, our child, the result and living proof of our union. For the first time in my life I thought I understood why parenthood was so important to so many, even if they never thought of it in those exact terms."

"Aphrodite understood that something important had occurred. She sat and watched us, as I observed the child intensely and the baby gurgled back at me, not demanding her child back, as the protective mother in her usually did.

She let the wave of love that broke over me and consumed me take its course, as I stood and cuddled the little bundle of love that was my daughter. I was not just a proud father, though, caught up in the moment. I knew that, although now she was so small, she was growing and would continue, and one day she would be grown enough to go out into the world. God help anyone who tries to hurt her, I vowed; I'll protect her, now and then, savagely if necessary. Any man, when she comes of age, or even before that, who tries anything, anything at all, will have me to deal with. But then the wave broke, and I felt calm and contentment; everything as it comes, I thought, plenty of time before she's grown. I took the infant over to the sofa, where I sat down with the mother and together we coo-ed over and admired this physical manifestation of our love. If only I could have stopped the clock at that time."

"I need to stop here, though"; the old man broke off from the tale, clearly emotionally-affected by it. "I'm not used to talking so much and I'm very tired now. If you would excuse me, we can continue next time?" Of course, Stephanidou agreed; he was getting tired himself now, with having risen so early, and hungry, although he was enchanted by the entry of little Bibi into the narrative and hoped that things would take an upturn from here on. He'd heard about Gabrielle, and Aphrodite, he mused, and a Magdalena had also been mentioned but not enlarged upon; he'd make a note of her for future reference. He fetched some water from the well for Kadi, who'd taken to his bed and seemed disinclined to leave it, although he must be in need of water. However, he only drank a sip of it, albeit gratefully, before falling into a light doze. Stephanidou left him and went down to the village to find Sofia fretting in case he was late for the lunch of yemista which she had cooked for him, and to which he did full justice before taking to his own bed for a siesta before an evening jog and dinner, ouzo and conversation at the kafenion before a restful night's sleep.

12: A VOICE FROM THE PAST

If it had happened to anyone else they would probably have put it down to divine intervention; but as Lieutenant Stephanidou had become an atheist by that particular point in time, he didn't. He had to admit, though, that you couldn't have written it. Although yes, he contradicted himself, that was probably the only way it could have happened. Writers, the best ones, could do anything, that was the beauty of writing. Who though? One of the ancient greats, as they were in Greece, after all. He wasn't keen on Aristophanes or Aeschylus; Euripides was his favourite, but for this particular task he'd most likely have chosen Sophocles, because, well, look at his Oedipus. A man, sent away at birth because it was prophesied that he'd kill his father and marry his mother, grows up not knowing who he is, then meets and kills his father and marries the widow, to have four children by her and then discover that she is his mother. Such coincidences; but then of course it was his fate, and you couldn't avoid your fate, was the message sent by this story. The hands of the gods were in the matter and what the gods say goes; which brought Stephanidou neatly back to divine intervention. Whatever.

The fact remained, though, that coincidences did occur, and in this instance he benefited from them. Coincidence Number One; An unexpected phone call from Captain Petrides one morning, when Stephanidou had only been on the island for about a month. A brief conversation to the effect that the Captain had to go to Athens in a hurry because his father was ill, most likely dying. The correct sympathetic noises made by Stephanidou met with thanks, but the father had been ill for some time and it was not unexpected. But Petrides had to go now, this minute, because there was a boat he could take leaving in the next half-hour, for another island from whence he could make his way to the capital, and if he didn't catch that he'd have to wait until tomorrow afternoon. So you're in charge for the foreseeable future, he told Stephanidou; I've left an explanatory note on the door here and your mobile number for anyone that needs you, and the keys will be at the kafenion for you to collect. You'd better come over here once a day to keep an eye on things. I've also set up an auto-response on my e-mail so that any messages that come there will be informed that I'm away and pass on your contact details. Good luck and see you whenever.

So Lieutenant Stephanidou had a temporary local promotion and was Number One in the Force on the island; it sounded impressive, until he stopped kidding himself; he was usually number two of two here, so it wasn't actually that great. It did give him the opportunity to leave the village daily though, instead of once each week, which meant he got to drive to Ayios Andreas and look at the four walls of the station-house there instead of his own. He only did that for ten minutes though, before he decamped to the kafenion by the harbour and drank their coffee and ouzo with a different sea view before driving back to Palliohorio. But it was a change of routine, which ought to have been a good thing except that it interfered with his visits to Kadi, who was very understanding. "Do come whenever you are able, don't stand on ceremony; you have extra responsibilities now, the security of the entire island rests upon your capable shoulders, I do comprehend your changed circumstances." And he lapsed into that mildly sardonic laugh which Stephanidou understood by now to be directed at the world in general and not at him personally.

Ultimately, though, the temporary change to his professional status benefited Stephanidou in terms of Coincidence Number Two which, had it not been for

Coincidence Number One, would have happened to Captain Petrides rather than himself. It arrived in the form of a phone call even more unexpected than that which took the Captain away; from Athens Police Headquarters and one Captain Pavlakis. They'd received information from the Turkish Police which pertained to the island, a case gone cold from about fifty years ago. There was probably nothing to be done about it now, it having been such a long time ago, but Captain Pavlakis was sending over the Turkish Police report by e-mail, along with a witness statement. "Not a formal statement as we know it", the Captain apologised, "more a personal account, a bit rambling, you know? But the old man was dying and in no state to write the thing out on the form, so they sat at his bedside and recorded him as he spoke. They transcribed it in Turkish, and it's been translated into Greek now also, so have a read and see if there's anything to be done with it".

Activity, gold dust even! Lieutenant Stephanidou thanked Coincidence Number One, which had taken Captain Petrides away at this time, and savoured the reading of the statement. It was by one Kamal Mustafa, eighty-two years old at the time of making it and now deceased. In his youth he had been a fisherman, but he would gladly ferry people up and down the Turkish coast in his boat for payment and, as his statement read;

One night in 1972 I took a young man over to the island of K .... I didn't usually go out at night, except when I was fishing, but he paid me well because he couldn't find anyone else to do what he needed, which was a bit out-of-the-way, he said. When I agreed without knowing exactly what he wanted, because the money he offered was so good, you see, he gave me the details. He wanted me to take him over to the island after dark and drop him off at a small cove between the cliffs to which he'd direct me; quietly, cutting the engine and going in on the oars for the last part because he didn't want to be heard or seen. Then I was to row out again and wait for one hour, within which time he would return, bringing someone else, and I would take them back to Turkey. Who else? I wanted to know; I didn't want to be ferrying criminals around, I didn't need trouble with the police any more than anyone else. He hesitated, but then he owned up; A girl, he said, they won't let us marry so we're going to go someplace where we can be married. Well, it sounded a bit underhand, but it wasn't that long since I'd been in love myself, I still was, she was my wife by now and we had children, and he looked so sorrowful. Plus, I couldn't refuse that kind of money so I put aside my misgivings and agreed.

It wasn't a long trip, it's only four miles out there, and the weather was good; a partial moon and clouds, with only a small breeze, so we made good progress. He sat there and I could tell he was impatient; he was humming a tune, a little love song it was, so I said something like, Dreaming of your dark-eyed beauty? No, he said, her eyes are blue, and her hair is blonde. That's unusual for these parts, I thought, and I said so. Yes, he told me, she's different and that's part of her charm; I'm different myself, so I suppose it formed part of the attraction between us. Well, I said nothing more but I recognised him then; I'd known when he came to me that he looked familiar, but I hadn't placed him. The Greek, they called him over here, Nikos the Greek, and Osman the Turk they called him on the island. His father was Greek, you see, and his mother Turkish; he lived over there but visited family here quite often, but the poor lad didn't really fit in either place. So maybe the best thing he and his girl could have done was to go elsewhere, somewhere big where they'd be immigrants, true, but they'd blend into a crowd of others like them rather than stick out like sore thumbs here.

Anyway, I put him ashore and he told me to give him one hour; if they didn't come by then I should go and he'd arrange something else. The girl didn't know when to expect him, he told me, mobile phones not having been invented then and even landline telephones being few and far between in these parts, but she would have been looking out for him each night and hopefully they'd meet up quickly. I wished him luck and rowed offshore, not too far but enough to be out of view of the coast. He couldn't find her quickly enough for me, because if we got away in the time he'd allowed we'd be gone before the fishing boats of the village went out. I could just make them out in harbour down the coast to my left, so I hoped he'd take as little time as possible because I was feeling a bit spooked now, left on my own and involved in something not quite above board. I'd felt alright about it when he was around, with love and hope in his eyes, but left to my own devices I started to feel in the wrong.

Well, the time began to pass and it was very quiet, apart from the breeze on the sea; and then I heard a noise from the shore. Like a shout it was, short and strangled was how I'd describe it; it startled me, nervous and jumpy as I was, and I looked over to the land and I just saw a white flash of something, because the moon was out from behind the clouds just then, it was falling towards the base of the cliffs and then there was a noise, not too loud but I heard it clearly in the silence, a thump or a splash, or both, as it hit the water. I didn't know what it was, a sheep or a goat which had wandered over the cliff edge maybe? Unlikely, but it had been known to happen. I couldn't help myself, I rowed over, I could see it floating, and when I got there, I felt sick to my stomach. It was a girl, may Allah have mercy on her; clearly dead, she had a hole in her forehead where she must have hit a rock, I suppose, and her hair! Even wet and with blood from her head streaked through it I could see that it was blonde, a very light blonde, and it shone eerily in the moonlight.

It would be too much of a coincidence for one girl to fall from the cliffs on the same night that another girl was eloping, I thought, and besides, with that hair she had to be *the* girl, I knew, his girl, and something must have gone badly wrong. I didn't know what to do; I wanted to go and tell someone, but if the planned elopement had been discovered then there was every chance that it was her family who'd thrown her over the cliffs, and who knew what they'd done to the boy? And if I raised the alarm it would be guessed that I had been involved in this, this abduction of a Greek girl by a Turk, because abduction would be how they'd see it, and his being only a half-Turk wouldn't matter to them; and I, another Turk involved? My blood ran cold and I panicked, I didn't want to be a part of this, I just wanted to get away. The boy had paid me in advance, it was well over the hour which I was supposed to give him by now, and I could hear the voices and the noises of the men in the fishing boats preparing to go out for the night. I left the girl floating and rowed hard till I was well out, I've never rowed so hard in my life, then I put the engine on and got away from there as fast as I could.

Well, I tried to put it out of my mind and carried on with my life, but the story of the dead girl reached me over here. You know what it's like, people talk, boats go from place to place and the stories go with them. And then the police came around the coastal area, looking for the boy and trying to find out if anyone had seen him around that time; and I should have told them but I kept my head down and kept quiet in fear of my life. Because I'd heard by then that she'd been pregnant, and that the boy had disappeared, and that it was thought she'd killed herself because he'd deserted her; but I knew better. I knew that he'd returned to the island, but someone else must know also, and that someone was keeping quiet too; why? Because that person or persons had done for the boy as well as the girl, it had to be that; and if I got involved they might decide to get me too, and I was frightened. I was young myself then, I had a wife and children to support, what would they do if anything happened to me? And if the family (it had to be they) didn't get me, the police here might take a dim view of my having kept quiet in the first place, not to mention my involvement in the abduction of a girl. So I just kept quiet, and it has haunted me at times; but now I'm dying and it's on my conscience and I would like to make a clean breast before I go.

The statement finished then, and had been signed by the Turkish policemen who had been present and recorded it to the effect that they certified it to be a correct and true transcription, and so on and so forth. Stephanidou became thoughtful; a forward-looking man, he had just been spoken to by a voice from the past which might change the future, and to his advantage. So the boy had returned, and no-one appeared to have known anything about it, until now. The girl had gone over the cliff within an hour of his return, and the boy had then disappeared and was still missing; but was somewhere on the island, apparently, unless someone else who wasn't talking had taken him away. If he'd left of his own free will, Stephanidou reasoned, he'd had a boat paid for and waiting to take him; so why find someone else to do the job? Unless he'd stayed on the island longer, and left at a later date; but no-one had seen him, apparently, and it would be difficult to remain undetected in such a small place. It followed therefore that whatever had happened to him would seem to be against his will.

Who stood to gain from Osman's disappearance? The girl's father? No, he'd been at the kafenion with the other men of the village all evening and late into the night, the enquiry notes from the time clearly said so. Her mother? She'd had an alibi which placed her at the house of a neighbour who'd recently had a baby and was feeling unwell; and in any case they were both dead now. Had Osman killed the girl, and then taken his own life, his body undiscovered? Perhaps they had jumped over the cliff together, Osman sinking or floating away, to sink later, and only the body of the girl seen by the Turkish boatman? Why would either of those things happen? The boy could have just run away, as had been assumed, if he wanted no more to do with the girl, so why return and kill her? Similarly, why take a lovers' leap to death together, when they could leave and marry and be together elsewhere? Improbable, Stephanidou decided; leaving Kadi as the only obvious candidate. He'd been taken for a fool, tricked and trapped by the girl, and who knew whether Osman was in on that also? Kadi had a sense of honour which would have been outraged, and a hot temper, that had been established, which would certainly have been roused if he'd found out about the deception practised upon him. But, and it was a big But, he had a watertight alibi. He'd been seen at his house by Lambros, who had accompanied him to the harbour after he'd had his dinner and seen him go out in the boat with his father and brother; and the entire village had been on the harbour-side with the body of Eleni when they had returned.

Nevertheless, the question still exercised the mind of the Lieutenant. Did Kadi do it somehow? He may have gone out that night, but the Turk waiting offshore heard the boats preparing to go out at around the same time that he saw the girl go over the cliff. Did Kadi somehow kill her, and potentially Osman also, before he went out fishing? But Father Lambros, just bad-boy Lambros back then, saw him at home, eating his dinner immediately before he went to the boat, and saw him sail out of the harbour, which would have considerably lessened the margin of time he had to commit even one, let alone two, murders.

Stephanidou tried to work it out, over the next few days. Had Kadi gone out with the boat and somehow got back to shore, with the assistance of his father and brother, to commit murder? No, that didn't fit with the girl floating in the sea before the fishing fleet went out. But the Lieutenant worked on the theory anyway; he thought that he might

101

work out the time it took to run from the beach – as the only place where Kadi's father could have put him ashore – to where exactly? He didn't know. He asked Father Lambros if Kadi had been a fit young man; the Father was puzzled, but answered him. As fit as any on the island; we were poor, there was not too much food so we didn't overeat, and our labour was manual, fishing, farming, no sitting in front of a computer screen as they do nowadays.

So back to square one and a rethink. Had the girl been alive when she went over the cliff, or killed elsewhere and her body thrown over in the hope that damage sustained from the fall and landing would cover the fact that she had been dead already? No; the Turkish boatman claimed to have heard a sound like a shout as she fell, but that could have come from whoever threw her over, Stephanidou reasoned. But why make a noise which could give you away? It didn't make sense, and he came back to her family; the parents were dead now, but had there been any siblings? Any brothers, keen to avenge their family honour? He'd asked the priest, who had told him that Eleni had been an only child, although her parents it seemed had been granted a miracle a year or so after her death. A son, a change-of-life baby had been born; but he obviously hadn't been around when Eleni had died. He'd left the island, like so many others of the younger generation, and was living somewhere on the mainland.

Stephanidou felt exasperated with himself; he was becoming obsessed with this old case, this cold case, and why? Most of the people involved were dead, and those who were still living had alibis, so why was he so concerned? Because new information has come to light, he told himself, and it was his duty as an officer of police to investigate, even if ultimately he turned up nothing new. He recalled that Kadi had promised to have told his entire tale by the week after Easter, which wasn't that far away now; so Stephanidou could only hope for fresh disclosures to help him fit the pieces of the puzzle together. But nevertheless he continued to mull things over in the hope of a breakthrough.

13: HOLY WEEK

With his new obsession fresh in his mind, and given that he wasn't fasting, Stephanidou had completely forgotten the advent of Holy Week, which would not have bothered him, given his current feelings towards religion. He'd been reminded, however, when Sofia had brought his breakfast to him this morning and remarked that tomorrow afternoon she'd be baking Lazarakia, so he'd have those to look forward to in the evening. So it would be Lazarus Saturday tomorrow; Stephanidou remembered then the sweet, spiced breads which his mother had made when he was a child, and which he hadn't eaten that often since. Sofia's version of them would, he was sure, be excellent, like all her cooking; just thinking about them was a poignant reminder of his happy childhood, upon which he reflected as he returned to the station-house. Why are we all in such a hurry to grow up? he asked himself. I suppose many of us would go back, if we could; but I, right now, need to move forward.

He controlled the sentimental feelings of nostalgia, firmly filing them in the folder marked 'Past' in his memory and focussing his thoughts on the present. He prepared himself to return to Kadi to see if he could glean any more clues from the old man's story, and was in two minds about whether to tell the hermit of the Turkish boatman's death-bed confession or not. He decided on the latter; to tell might shock something out of Kadi, but equally it could put him on his guard and prevent any further information slipping out. Best for the Lieutenant to keep it to himself, therefore, until such a time as he judged it useful to disclose the information; if such a time ever came, that was. More immediately, he was hoping for a more uplifting story-line, now that baby Bibi had entered into it, but Kadi picked up the thread of his tale with a sombre air.

"In the week after little Bibi stole my heart, I asked Aphrodite to marry me. My child deserved all the protection I could give her, including the legal rights that went with being my acknowledged offspring; and I was willing to put aside my lingering doubts about her mother in order to achieve this. I've never understood those people who live together and have children, but claim that they aren't ready to make a big commitment like marriage; aren't children the biggest commitment to each other which any couple can make? Marriage is easy by comparison, in my opinion, so it wasn't difficult for me now to consider marriage to Aphrodite."

"My proposal wasn't received with the rapturous acceptance that I might have expected, however; I could see the thought flash through Aphrodite's eyes that I only considered her good enough for a wife now for the sake of our child. So there was resentment, but also good sense in her; she knew that it was to her benefit as well as that of little Bibi for us to be married, and she didn't need me to point out the enormous financial benefits to her, my being my uncle's heir, both if I lived and if by any unfortunate chance I should die. I didn't mention immediately the possibility of divorce, which I had considered an option, should she find me as easy to leave as she had Henry Marston; but privately I determined to have a pre-nuptial contract drafted which would make it extremely difficult for her to do so. Because if I was prepared for her to leave, I was not letting our little daughter go; if it came to it Aphrodite could stay and have the baby and the money, or leave and have the money but not the baby. But I let it go for the present, as we discussed our marriage plans."

"While this was going on, I was making the most of little Bibi; I wanted to be a part of everything that concerned her, even down to changing nappies and bathing her, which

tasks Aphrodite jealousy guarded as part of her parental
province. But she took pity on my constant requests and
allowed me to watch, then perform these rituals under her
close scrutiny. Bibi was allowed to wear modern all-in-one
suits now because one day, in my besotted condition, I'd
gone into a baby store and bought up half the shop on the
grounds that she would look so sweet in all the little clothes.
This particular action had melted Aphrodite's heart and was
mostly responsible for my being allowed to be a part of the
bathing and changing routine. I went toy shopping also,
although that seriously backfired when the four-foot teddy-
bear in which I indulged actually frightened little Bibi into
loud cries of distress. Shamefacedly and with deep remorse
I had to return it and get a more realistic small one, furry
and cuddly with a sweet expression on its little face to
match hers. Thereafter I let Aphrodite buy the toys, and was
rewarded by being allowed to go shopping for them with
her and our baby, just like any normal family; but the sight
of my little one in the grimy city streets set me thinking.

I'd wanted to move to the country before, because I liked
to watch the stars in the clear night sky. I used to watch
them when I was very young; they fascinated me. I used to
help Themis the shepherd sometimes at night, when the
fishing was poor, just because I liked the peace and the
night sky. I was supposed to be watching the sheep, but they
were happy enough grazing so I just lay back and looked at
the sky. There was little if any light pollution there, back
then; unlike London, where it's usually difficult to get a
good view, even on a clear night. If business commitments
hadn't required me to be there constantly I'd have moved
out before, right into the country, got an estate with no
neighbours and big, clear skies both day and night, weather
allowing. Now this became a necessity; little Bibi must
have the best I could get for her, and that included clean air,
not the pollution of London choking her little lungs.

My uncle was willing to give me an advance on my

inheritance, when I explained what it was for, so I put my people to work, and soon found somewhere suitable in Kent, to the south and east of London. It meant a huge commute for me, not being rich enough yet to afford a helicopter on a regular basis, so I'd have to stay in town in the apartment sometimes in the week, but I'd make sure that I had all weekend whenever possible to be there with them, my darling little one and her mother. Peace, quiet, with acres of land and a good distance from the nearest neighbours and any major roads; and the skies were huge and unpolluted by city lights, so I could indulge my star-gazing to my heart's content. Maybe when she was older I could start little Bibi watching them, too; but it wasn't to be."

The old man paused at this point and sat, staring blankly before him, and Stephanidou knew that he was back there, in the time of whatever had happened. Then Kadi took a breath, as though to continue, but did not, and repeated this action several times. It was as though he was reluctant to continue, but then he took a huge breath and forced himself to speak, almost spitting the words out of his mouth against his will.

"It was about one week before we were due to move to the country house when I was awakened by the screams. Aphrodite's screams, beside the bed, beside the cot, chilling and heart-broken and calling out little Bibi's name, over and over, and mine too. I was awake instantly, 'Aphrodite, what is it, calm down, what's happened?', looking at the little cot as I did so, knowing without being told, grabbing the phone and calling 999 followed by the private clinic where Bibi had been born. I don't know which paramedics arrived first, but the explanation was the same from both, when she'd been taken and examined and the formalities gone though. Cot Death; Sudden infant death syndrome; words no parent wants to hear, one of their worst nightmares, but we were hearing them now. All the precautions we had taken were as nothing; that plump little form, smiling and chuckling and waving little fists and feet with chubby, dimpled baby fat around them, now stiff and cold and unmoving."

He did stop then, and Stephanidou looked over and saw the tears running down the old man's cheeks; his own cheeks felt wet, and he realised that he was crying too. They sat, companions in misery, until Kadi composed himself enough to say something; "I'm afraid I can't say any more now, you understand; I'll see you tomorrow?" Stephanidou nodded slowly and rose to leave; but first he went over and put his hand, both gently and firmly, on the man's shoulder. And Kadi responded, putting his own hand over the Lieutenant's, as if to draw strength from it; a bond was established between them then.

Stephanidou walked slowly down the hill; he was more upset than he would have liked to be by the story of the child, thrust upon an unwilling father who then fell in love with her only to have her cruelly taken away. How much worse could it be for someone who'd wanted the child, spent all their time before the impending birth in preparing for it and all their time afterwards in loving the baby, only to have it all come to naught? He tried to lift his mood; after all, it was only a small percentage of families who were affected in this way. He remembered his many siblings; his parents had never lost a child, so it was likely that he'd inherited that ability. But would he ever get the chance to father children? His mood dipped again as he remembered the stalemate of his current situation and his relationship with Elpida which hung in the balance. She'd said that she'd wait for him, and emphasised this in the phone calls which he made to her; with unfortunate frequency, he feared, because what did he have to offer her? He could see no change in his circumstances occurring any time soon, and preferred not to hear the despair which he found it hard to keep out of his own voice gradually spreading into hers.

He spent a depressed evening, eating little and incurring

the concern of Sofia, who could see that something was wrong and didn't therefore scold him for his lack of appetite; instead, she told him he was a good boy and patted his head affectionately. Touched, he squeezed her hand before making his way to his bed and an early night. Fortunately, however, he fell into a deep and lasting sleep as soon as his head hit the pillow, and awoke refreshed to make his way up the hill for the next episode.

14: LAZARUS SATURDAY

Kadi wasted little time on formalities when Stephanidou arrived; it was as though the next chapter had to be gotten through as quickly as possible, which suited both host and guest as neither wished to dwell on the death of little Bibi. Kadi spoke quietly, without preamble; "Somehow we got through the appalling necessities, the things that had to be done and which I won't go into here; I still feel the pain, I have no need to intensify it. And then, what? Life had ceased to have any meaning. There was no point in getting married now, no point in moving to the country; we sat in the apartment like zombies and I just went over and over it all in my mind. We'd been aware of the risks to babies, so had read all the pamphlets and websites, followed all the advice and it still hadn't been enough. I hadn't been able to control circumstances, I hadn't been able to protect her and save her and I felt like the worst father ever. I beat myself up mentally until my head was spinning and I badly needed sleep, but sleep wouldn't come."

"Aphrodite I'm sure was in just as bad a case as I, but I was unable to be there for her as she needed me to be; I failed her in that, and I paid the price later. We were both sunk in our respective griefs, and put on black mourning; we ought to have comforted each other, and Aphrodite did try, eventually, but I shut her out; with hindsight, maybe I ought to have married her then, shown her that I needed her for herself, not just as a means to formalize the birth of our child, the little girl we'd now lost. But I couldn't think straight; I was in a permanent daze, shattered, like a massive tree felled, paralysed and petrified. My uncle had been very understanding; I was to take all the time I needed, the business had functioned before I came along and would do so now. Somewhat tactless, but that was his way and I understood what he meant, if I understood anything at that terrible time. All I knew was that I'd lost my little girl and I might as well be in the grave with her."

"Aphrodite, once the initial shock and grief had passed, was stronger than I was in this; she came to me one day and put her arms around me. I dissolved in tears and she just held me as I sobbed my heart out, adding her tears to my own. Eventually she tried hard to help us both begin again, get past this and move on; 'Kadi, it's bad, but it's life, it happens, but it's not the end. We can have other children'. I cut her off with a fierce look and she shut up and left the room. Other children? Did she really think I'd go there again? It wouldn't be my Bibi, it would be another child completely, it might even be a boy, and there would be no guarantees of love or life for that one any more than there had been for my little girl."

"I lost trust in Aphrodite then; I remembered how she'd almost casually dropped her fiancé Henry Marston when she met me, and how she'd become pregnant without consulting me. I was sure that she'd stopped taking her contraceptive pills then, although she claimed to have only forgotten a few, and I was worried that she'd do the same again now, to replace little Bibi with another baby, much as she'd replaced Marston with me. And although I had lived with the latter, the former was totally unacceptable to me."

"I wouldn't have left her, I couldn't have been that cruel, because she was hurting almost as much as I was; but I withdrew from her sexually. I didn't want to take the chance of her getting pregnant and blaming faulty contraception, so I adopted what I knew to be the last word in this. No sex meant no pregnancy, and if she decided to find someone else to oblige her (although in fairness I'm sure she wouldn't have done so) then it would clearly not be mine any more than Eleni's child had been, and I was no more

minded now than back then to father another man's child."
(Had that been an option? thought Stephanidou at this;
wasn't Eleni dead before he knew of her pregnancy? He
filed the thought for later reference and dragged his
attention back to Kadi as the hermit continued).

"So I stopped making love to her, and of course she
noticed, me having been so keen before. I had headaches,
stomach aches, I was too tired from work, I didn't feel like
it now, and so on and so forth; all the excuses which other
men I knew complained of in their wives. She tried to get
me in the mood, of course, and I frequently had need of far
more self-control than I'd ever needed in the past. But I
kept my resolve, painfully on occasions, and finally told her
that the loss of our child had affected me in this way also;
which she had to accept."

"So she stopped trying and, in her turn, withdrew into
herself. I gradually came to realise that she had taken to
drink, to get her through, and I remonstrated with her about
the amount she was consuming. But she flew at me
verbally, screaming at me; 'Leave me alone, stop trying to
control me, you're not my father, I can drink as much as I
like and when I like. I need it, I don't need you so shut up
and leave me alone'. I saw no sense in prolonging the
argument so I did as she demanded, but I wasn't happy. I
could only hope that in time she'd find the effects of the
drink worse than the feeling she was trying to blot out with
it."

"Personally I couldn't afford the luxury of alcohol to
dampen my grief because I needed to be operating at
maximum efficiency to do business effectively. Work
became my saviour, the more so because, in the months
after we'd lost little Bibi, my uncle had suffered a heart
attack; not a major one, but serious enough to let him know
that he needed to slow down and take things more easily. I
felt guilty, because I had been taking on more of his
business duties before our loss, but afterwards he'd told me

to take as long as I needed and assumed the whole workload himself again. So now I threw myself into the business, out of respect and care for him and also to keep myself from thinking about little Bibi."

"Poor Aphrodite had no such support to fall back on, though; men and motherhood had been the focus of her life, and now she was deprived of both. I feel guilty, looking back, at doubting her commitment to me, because it wouldn't have been difficult for her to take a lover at this time, given that I wasn't there for her. But she stuck with me and didn't so much as look at another man; I know, because I had her watched, discreetly of course, and I felt bad about having done that as well, afterwards. But there it is, it was what it was, and instead of another man Aphrodite took to pills along with alcohol to get her through. She concealed this from me, mainly because I was working all the hours I could, and she was usually asleep by the time I got home, pills taken and the containers presumably hidden where I couldn't see them and give her another lecture like that I'd given her over the drink. I returned home late one night to find a bottle of pills and an empty glass beside her on the bedside table. At first I thought she'd fallen asleep and tried to waken her; but she was cold to my touch, and then I realised the meaning of the pill bottle next to the whisky bottle. Pills and alcohol; a lethal combination, and Aphrodite pale and cold and dead in our bed."

"It was never ascertained whether she took her own life, or whether it was an accidental overdose; another woman in my life to suffer an ambiguous death." Kadi stopped speaking at this point and Stephanidou, looking up as though from a trance, saw the traces of tears on his cheeks; but his voice was steady as he spoke again. "You'll have to excuse me now, I'm feeling rather overcome with it all; I'll see you again tomorrow, I hope?" The Lieutenant nodded, and turned to go as the man lay down painfully and turned away.

Stephanidou was glad to go, if he was truthful. He was still more upset than he would have liked to admit over the death of little Bibi; he'd been entranced at the story of Kadi finding love for her and was heart-broken over her end. He loved children, as he'd told Father Lambros; they were the future, and Stephanidou was very much a man of the future. But now, to have the death of her mother also, it was unbearable. He wanted to offer some comfort to the doubly-bereaved old man, for it clearly still affected Kadi very much, no matter how long ago it had been; but he'd been dismissed, and the hermit appeared to be sleeping now. Stephanidou walked slowly down the hill and took too much ouzo from Giorgos before once again eating too little of the dinner which Sofia had made for him and incurring looks of concern from her. Sorry for her sake, Stephanidou rallied all his resources and managed some of the Lazarakia which she had made for him, complimenting her on the lightness of her baking. Reassured, she nevertheless hoped that his appetite would return soon; maybe, as he had not fasted during Great Lent, an involuntary fast was being imposed on him from above? Perhaps; he smiled at her and went back to the station-house to shower and sleep, after noting on his file that Kadi 'Suggested that he had known about Eleni Christou's pregnancy before her death',.

15: PALM SUNDAY

The next day he arrived at his usual time, to find Kadi sitting up and pleased to see him; but Stephanidou felt that he must acknowledge the strain felt by this strange storyteller on the previous day. "Look here, I'm interested in hearing what you have to tell, but it clearly affects you and I don't want you to put yourself through any pain by bringing up all these old memories; so if you want to stop I fully understand." But Kadi waved a hand dismissively; "Thank you, but it's quite alright; if I don't tell it all I'm thinking it anyway, so I feel pain whatever the case. Better to pass it on to someone who takes an interest and who might benefit". So Stephanidou nodded, and seated himself, and Kadi continued:

"I got rid of the London apartment and took a new one, without all the memories, both good and bad; because even if I thought of the former they inevitably led me to the latter, and that was unbearable. I felt a deep sense of guilt because I hadn't been able to protect and save either my daughter or her mother; I hadn't been able to control the situation. I'd taken every measure known to mankind to protect little Bibi, but Death had laughed at me and taken her; then I'd tried to control the situation with Aphrodite by withdrawing from her to prevent another baby coming, only to be lost like Bibi, but I'd lost Aphrodite instead. I still couldn't let go, however, I couldn't hand control of my life over to whatever deity rules us; I didn't like the way He controlled things so I fought Him, or Her, and tried even harder to take control of my life, of everything and everyone around me."

"I buried myself in work even more than I had before; my uncle had been resting at home as his doctor ordered, but had been advising me, summoning me to his presence at times or making a multitude of telephone calls. I felt that he was still doing too much; there was an urgent need for me to get up to speed on everything pertaining to the business, and gradually I took the reins from him. I did well, but not well enough it seems; Uncle Michalis suffered another attack, a massive one this time, which proved to be fatal. I didn't even have time to see him and say goodbye and thank you for all he had done for me; he just collapsed one day, on his way to have dinner, and was dead within minutes."

"I mourned my uncle, but I knew he wouldn't approve of my sitting around grieving forever; as his heir I took sole charge of things then, and I know he would have approved if he had been looking down on me. Work became my life; I lived and breathed it, ate and drank it, until events forced me to slow down. My brother, James as he was now called, was instrumental in making me take some time out from work. He had done well since he came to England, a fully-fledged city trader now, very good indeed at what he did and extremely useful to the business. He wasn't as immersed in work as I was, though, but then he wasn't running the entire show as I was, and he hadn't suffered the personal losses which had been my lot. He had a social life; he followed Formula One and horse racing, played rugby and squash and had a group of friends with whom he shared these interests, young men for the sport and young women with whom he became amorously involved periodically, but nothing serious, nothing lasting. 'I'll know when I meet the right one, he used to say, but there's no hurry'."

"He tried to get me to share in his social activities, but sensitively, with none of the nagging, such as, You need to get out and get a life again, you've had a rough time but no sense in brooding over it. None of that kind of thing, that wasn't my brother's way. Instead, he'd invite me to go to this or that occasion with him, and I'd usually refuse; so then he'd turn up at my apartment with a couple of friends, both male and female, claiming just to have been passing. And he succeeded, to some extent, in getting me to socialise again; my sense of good manners couldn't help itself when James and friends turned up on the doorstep, I had to give them drinks and make conversation, and when they decided to go on from my place and have dinner, naturally they invited me and out of politeness I went, of course. I knew, of course, that it would be at my brother's instigation that a beautiful young woman would be sitting beside me, apparently eager for my company; yet when I spent the night in the beds of those young women it was fully my own choice."

"At all accounts, I owed my partial re-emergence into life to my brother, to whose support I already owed much after my unfortunate and disastrous early engagement, and did my best over the coming years to repay him. After he'd shown me that there was still a life outside of the office I began to do a few things on my own again. I rediscovered the gym; I moved into a new, much plusher apartment than that in which I'd been living, a soul-less transitional place where I'd showered and slept post-Aphrodite. My uncle had been involved in the building of a smart new apartment block, overlooking the river, and this had just been completed, under my auspices. I bought the penthouse; eventually I bought the entire block. It had private parking in the basement and a private gym for residents on the ground floor. I'd never had any issues of weight or fitness, but now I rediscovered the pleasures of working-out every morning before I started work. It became the basis for a daily routine, so essential to someone with my love of order and control, and even if I'd spent the night elsewhere I would take myself to the gym before returning to my apartment, from whence I could keep in touch with my various business interests via phone or the internet whilst showering and preparing for the day ahead."

"Night-time would find me trying to watch the stars

from my penthouse terrace when there was enough clear sky. I thought again about taking a house in the country, away from the urban light pollution, so that I could just sit outside at night and look up, up at the universe and the myriad stars in the heavens, and pretend maybe that I was still on the island, still a poor but happy fisherman with a penchant for star-gazing. But what would be the point? It was impractical for a start, I needed to be in the city, where the action was, able to attend meetings and catch a flight fast if necessary. Plus, even if I could attend to do business from there, and I could afford to commute by helicopter now, what would I do for the rest of the time? In town I had theatres, galleries, opera houses, restaurants, a whole host of places to go and people to be with to blot out the fact of my total loneliness. I'd never been bothered by being alone when I was young, up on the hillside with the stars, or on the seas waiting for the fish to come, when I sometimes went out without my father and Iannis. But now being alone was the illustration of an absence; no Bibi, no Aphrodite, no family, no-one. There was James, true, but he too needed to be in the city, as a working trader, he couldn't run his business from out of town so would only be able to visit occasionally, at weekends. At least in town I was able to see him often, have dinner with him, play squash with him when he suggested it."

"There were of course women in town too; no-one who became close but easy pick-ups, one-nighters, because I had needs like anyone else. I don't think I treated them badly, they were always willing and I was generous to them, they didn't lose by what happened between us. It wasn't ideal; I dislike using condoms and would have liked a real relationship, even given my unfortunate track record in that department, but none of us falls in love to order so I made the best I could of my situation. I never had women in my home, for such I felt my apartment to be by now, but always went to theirs, or took them to a hotel; I didn't need the complication of trying to get rid of them in the morning if the night hadn't turned into anything more lasting. If it had, they were brief affairs, of maybe two or three months, and never became serious. I didn't feel good about using these women in this way, but they didn't have to sleep with me, it was their choice to do so."

"Nor was I totally callous; I might meet someone and think there was something more to them, and give them the opportunity to capture my interest for a longer time. But after a while, usually a short while, I'd find that I was bored with them; whatever it was that had shown me the potential for something more had not lasted, not developed, so I'd drop them. Gently, of course; I was always generous to them, however short or long the encounter, and they didn't drive away after the last goodbye empty-handed. Eventually I found myself with a chauffeur who was not only a suitable driver but also a good-looking young man with a way to him, which I was to regret bitterly in time. But before that he'd drive the women back to wherever they came from and, if he fancied his chances, he'd try his luck and frequently ended up consoling them, meaning that I was not subjected to tearful and embarrassing phone calls from those who took their dismissal badly. Good luck to him, and to them, I thought."

"So I worked during the days, and played with a variety of casual amours during the nights, and prospered, financially if not emotionally. I looked in the mirror one morning and saw, what? A sophisticated businessman, surrounded by the trappings of success. Groomed to within an inch of my life, hair and beard immaculately trimmed, expensive cologne, Italian tailoring, hand-made leather shoes; standing in a penthouse apartment in one of the more fashionable areas of the city, surrounded by designer furniture and with costly works of art on the walls. I was able to walk out of there and have the most glamorous women without even asking; they would approach me and, even if I knew they weren't doing it for my personal charm, I didn't flatter myself when I considered that they were getting the charm as a bonus. No overweight fat-cat here, depending on his money to get women; a fit man, a daily user of the gym, fastidious and clean and able to give them as much sexual pleasure as they gave me; more so, in some forgettable cases. So yes, all the external trappings of success; but inside, emotionally, dead. I put that part aside and concentrated on business."

He stopped speaking and took a small sip of water from the rose-patterned teacup which Stephanidou had thoughtfully left by his side, then, "I think that's all I can manage for today. I do hope it's enough for you, there's so much to get through but still enough time for it all, I think?" Stephanidou agreed; it hadn't been that long a session, but Kadi seemed to have tired more quickly than had been his wont. However, having not eaten much breakfast due to the previous evening's ouzo, Stephanidou was feeling hungry; Kadi must be also, for that matter, he thought, and asked if he needed anything brought from the village? Sofia he was sure would be only too glad to prepare something for the old hermit. Kadi shook his head though, and replied politely; "That's most kind of you, but I have everything I need. I don't eat much, you see, although I'm sure Sofia would be only too glad to provide me with much more. Please do give her my regards, and Giorgos, of course." He closed his eyes then, and taking this for his dismissal, Stephanidou took himself back to the village, his dinner and to think on his continuing fixation with the case of Eleni Christou and Nikos Osman Nikolaides.

16: HOLY MONDAY, HOLY TUESDAY

His fixation was arrested the next morning by a phone call; "I'm back", the tones of Captain Petrides told him brightly, "and I have a surprise for you". Before enquiring as to the nature of the latter, Stephanidou began to offer condolences for the Captain's father, but Petrides brushed these aside. "Thank you, but they're not needed, not yet, anyway. He wasn't looking so good, they'd put him on a new drug and I suppose his system hadn't reacted well to the change. By the time I got there, though, he was responding to it and things are looking more hopeful." So Stephanidou offered his best wishes, and only then asked about the surprise which his Captain had mentioned. "Old Manolis is bringing it now; I'd come myself, but I'm rather tired from the journey. So enjoy your surprise and take the rest of the week off, you've earned it."

"I suppose of course there are no urgent matters on which you need to bring me up to speed?" Petrides continued, as an afterthought. Stephanidou told him about the Turkish boatman's deathbed confession, the text of which was on the desk of his superior; but he played down the importance of the thing, concerning events of over fifty years ago as it did. Petrides agreed with him; "Nothing much to do about it now, but it will make interesting reading". Apart from that, Stephanidou assured him, the island had not experienced a crime wave in the Captain's absence and everything else was as quiet as the grave, as it usually was. "Good, then enjoy your leave, and celebrate Easter", the Captain told him; "it's Holy Week, I'd quite forgotten it myself, what with the unexpected visit to my parents". Stephanidou hastened to assure his superior that

121

he too had forgotten it, until reminded by Sofia, not adding that in his case it was his discontent with religion which had caused his memory loss. And so they each rang off, with an agreement to meet up when the religious festival was over.

Phone call over, Stephanidou took himself over to the kafenion for coffee while he awaited the arrival of Manolis and his surprise, which duly turned up and Stephanidou was indeed surprised. No inanimate package this, but a person; a real, living breathing body in the shape of his old friend from the academy, Artemidou, called Socrates by everyone for reasons which Stephanidou couldn't recall right now. It was quite a reunion, and the whole village turned out to see, excitement in their midst being an extremely rare thing. Ouzo was ordered, and lunch, and Sofia busied herself to prepare something extra special while the guest, having assured her that he was exempt from fasting on account of a medical condition (a polite lie, in fact), deposited his things at the station-house and freshened up before the meal. Another mouth to feed! Sofia couldn't believe her luck, especially as Manolis had had the foresight to bring with him the groceries which she'd ordered from town and which Stelios had been going to get for her this afternoon. Her kitchen thereafter resonated with the sound of pots and pans and her elderly but firm voice singing, folk songs which were not heard here so much any more.

What was Socrates doing here, of all places, his old friend wanted to know? It turned out that he'd met Petrides, who he also knew and who had gone into HQ in Athens on his return from his visit to his father. As they caught up over a drink, Petrides had informed him of Stephanidou's posting to the island and, as Socrates was just off on leave himself, and going to visit family in Rhodes for Easter, he had decided to make a side journey in the company of the Captain and see his old friend. So here he was, only until tomorrow, when he'd have to catch the evening ferry, but he was happy to camp out in the station-house for tonight. So they talked, and drank, and ate, and drank some more and talked some more, and Stephanidou thought he'd died and gone to heaven, forgetting his new status as a born-again atheist.

He didn't feel that way in the morning, though; it was fair to say that if a crime wave had broken out in the village overnight neither man would have been in any fit state to fight it. Stephanidou's consumption of ouzo and wine was reminding him of its continuing presence in his body via a throbbing pain in his temples. Socrates was in like state, albeit not with the additional back-ache suffered by his host, who had sacrificed his own bed to his guest and slept on the rickety fold-up camp bed supplied with the accommodation. Showers were taken, and tablets for the headaches, with plenty of water followed by coffee and breakfast which the thoughtful Sofia supplied to them at the house, having noted their presence long into the night outside the kafenion. Only then did they feel well enough to actually talk about more serious matters, like Stephanidou's dead-man posting to this remote island; for it had become clear that Petrides had also disclosed the reasons for the posting to Socrates, who raised the subject in a no-nonsense manner.

"I'm going to speak to you straight, Stephano, and I mean it for your good, so please don't take offence at me, OK?" Stephanidou tensed, but nodded anyway. Socrates was known for his blunt speaking, but he was popular, well-liked by almost everyone who met him, and they knew that whatever he said was intended for their best; so they tended not to take offence. He continued; "The boss, the old man, he wasn't so bad, you know, look up his record and see; he did good things in the past and got recognition for those, commendations even, and he was well-respected. His methods weren't always orthodox, not what would be considered correct, these days, but maybe he learned that sometimes you have to bend the rules a little to get the correct results".

Stephanidou made as if to interject here, but Socrates held up a hand to stop him and continued. "He'd built up a complicated network of contacts, informers and so forth, I don't know the details but it's what everyone says, and you, with your bull-in-a-china-shop honest approach, were in danger of damaging it. Well, you wouldn't be told, wouldn't wind your neck in, were so sure that your way was the right way. He thought you needed to be taken down a peg or two, and he certainly did that, because here you are"; and he waved an arm around the old, shabby station-house with the squeaky ceiling fan.

"The trouble with you, Stephano, is that you don't consider what's gone before, he continued, you don't have enough respect for the past. You think of the future, and that's good, but too much, and that's not. I know it sounds clichéd, but you have to know where you've come from to know where you're going; the past informs the future." "And what about the present?" Stephanidou wanted to know. Socrates didn't hesitate. "It's where the past and the future meet, or collide, depending on how you apply them to each other. The now is where we negotiate between them", he told Stephanidou, who recalled now that his friend had been nicknamed Socrates at college because he was so philosophical.

Stephanidou didn't know what to say now. In the past he'd have protested and blustered and insisted that his way was correct; which was exactly what Socrates was telling him about himself. Now, however, he was willing to consider what his friend had said; he needed to think about it at length, and that would take time. So he thanked Socrates gruffly and muttered something to the effect of, maybe there was something in what he was saying, and Stephanidou would think about it. And Socrates knew that his message had hit home, and might do his friend some good; so he changed the subject, suggesting that a hair of the dog, or several, could be in order before he had to get his things together and head back to Ayios Andreas to get the ferry. Stelios would take him, going into town as he was on a supply run for his store, so the two men spent a final friendly couple of hours at the kafenion, with lunch provided by Sofia, of course, before Stelios was ready and Socrates and his suitcase were stowed in his car and on their way.

It was only when his old friend had departed, waved off not just by Stephanidou but by Father Lambros, Sofia and Giorgos and anyone else who happened to be around, that the Lieutenant realised that his brief excitement was over and it was back to business as usual. Alone again, naturally, he thought, using a line from an English song, or film or whatever, that he'd heard somewhere. No, he corrected himself, not alone; he had his little community here, Father Lambros, Sofia and Giorgos, Mandras, Stelios, even the surly Costaki, to name but a few. Then he remembered that in the excitement of the unexpected visit he'd neglected to go and see Kadi yesterday. It was mid-afternoon by now, but they'd have time to get through some portion of Kadi's tale, if the old man was willing; and maybe to make amends for yesterday's absence Stephanidou would disclose the new information regarding Eleni Christou and Nikos Osman Nikolaides and see what he might find out from the old man regarding this. He hastened up the hill to repair his error.

He found the hermit lying down within the crumbling walls of the house, in a shady spot to counter the afternoon heat. He apologised profusely, but Kadi cut him short; "No need to apologise, I'm delighted to hear that you had a visitor, a breath of fresh air from the world outside. We have enough time left to us, however" – here he paused - "I do need you to get here every day for the rest of the week; will that be possible? Wednesday, Thursday, Friday and Saturday; we'll be finished on Saturday, and I guarantee that it will be to your advantage". Stephanidou assured him that he would be there each day as specified, all day if

125

necessary, assuming that Kadi had the strength to go on at some length; he had the time, Captain Petrides having given him leave.

He then imparted his news regarding the confession of the Turkish boatman, but to his disappointment Kadi didn't react in a shocked or otherwise surprised manner. He merely put this head on one side and pursed his lips slightly, considering the information. "So, it seems that all secrets come out eventually", was his only comment before checking that his audience was comfortable and switched-on in terms of his recording device and then taking up the thread where he'd left it two days ago, having first checked Stephanidou's remembrance of where they'd got to.

"So my life went on; work, more work and social occasions which were really business opportunities. It was an exciting time, business-wise, and I was in the thick of it. The London Docklands development was happening, and I was heavily involved in that. I redeveloped the slum area where I'd lived when I first arrived in the country, think of that. I built a football stadium not far from there, and bought the Premier-League team who became resident within it. I invested in racehorses, I watched them and enjoyed the experience, I gambled on them and I won; I had a knack for it. I rubbed shoulders with sheiks, and other royalty, and did very well indeed out of such connections. Development in Dubai was underway, and I was very much a part of that; it was opening up and being built up, and I was right in there gathering up contracts for so much of this money-generating regeneration. So it went on, and on; and ten years later I looked in the mirror again and saw the same man looking back at me. So many years older but so much richer, still successful in business, and fit and presentable; and still dead inside."

"Another ten years passed; I looked in the mirror one morning as I dressed and thought, Kadi, what have you become? A fifty-five year-old man looked back at me, going grey in both hair and beard, outwardly a suave, suited man of business, speaking impeccable English and head of my uncle's empire which had prospered under me since his death. But inwardly? Empty and cavernous, like the house of my mother's family back at home; decayed, derelict, full of weeds and rubble and memories of betrayal, sitting alongside those more recent ones of lost love, of my daughter and her mother." This house? wondered Stephanidou; and memories of betrayal associated with it? He stored the thought for later and continued to listen.

"I needed to stop this; so many people would sell their soul for what I'd got. I'd worked hard for it, certainly, but at least I didn't have the financial worries that beset so many others, far from it. So no more self-pity, time to get on and work, the panacea for all my ills. I remembered that I had the annual charity dinner that night; James had reminded me, though I hadn't been going to bother, but I supposed I might just as well. My PA Imelda would have booked me a room in the venue hotel, as she always did, and I might find one of the hostesses attractive enough to interest me for the night; I usually did, and on that night I didn't want to be alone. I needed to hold someone, just for the feel of their flesh to make me feel in that I was connected to the rest of humanity."

"Speaking of which, I recalled that I'd seen Gabrielle again recently; we'd lost touch to some extent, my being so busy and involved in business, she being much older and retired to a great extent from the social gatherings of the past. She'd been greatly saddened by the death of my little Bibi, but that of her niece Aphrodite had affected her very badly; and my uncle's demise following not long afterwards, she had given up on the world and retired from social life to a major extent, going out only occasionally. My uncle had left her very well-set up for the rest of her life, and she'd never want for anything financially. She must have been nearly seventy by now, I recollected, or already

127

there, but was still looking good for her age. She'd always been voluptuous, and was so now, in the extreme; but she was still immaculately turned-out, hair dye and cosmetics and Botox having been employed to supply what Nature had ceased supplying, even though she rarely saw anyone on whom to make an impression. Once a courtesan always a courtesan, artificial but warm, in Gabrielle's case, I thought; and thinking of her I naturally thought of Aphrodite, so like her in so many ways but so genuine in others, as in when she had discovered motherhood. I thought with distress then of the child she'd given me, little Bibi, and how I'd lost them both; I was remembering when I was able to *feel* … I put the thought sharply from me and called Shine, my chauffeur to take me to the charity event."

"When I'd checked into the hotel I took myself to the room where the dinner was being hosted, on the first floor. A dark-haired hostess met me at the door and gave me a broad smile of recognition, which I returned in a more muted form before she preceded me along the corridor, the better to display her now rather tawdry charms. I'd sampled them a couple of years ago, after this same function, and frankly they hadn't been worth the cost of the condoms I'd used with her. But I'd been generous the following morning; the money wasn't much to me, but a great deal to her, and she'd done her best even if she hadn't been bright enough to get paid up front, and other men would certainly have taken advantage of that. Now I appraised her, finding her backside grown rather larger than it had been and just about getting away with the tight skirt she'd squeezed it into. Her legs had thickened also, they'd be better in flatter shoes rather than the regulation stilettos, the Fuck-Me Pumps, as some feminist-type had called them. All told, I doubted she'd be working here again next year."

"She made sure I was seated and went to get me a drink; I thanked her when she returned with it, albeit distantly, hoping that my reserved manner would dispel any illusions she might have about us renewing our acquaintance. What is wrong with you, Kadi? I asked myself as I took a good mouthful of the whisky. You're a multi-millionaire, possibly a billionaire, but here you are picking up two-a-penny tarts at a glorified stag do; Panagia mou! I used an expression Greeks would use where the British would say My God!, or Christ!, calling rather on the Queen of Heaven, the Virgin, My Virgin, literally-translated. And then she heard me, and answered my prayer, because I saw her; My virgin; *My* virgin."

"I didn't know that Magdalena was a virgin, of course, when I saw her first, seating another man at the other side of the table. I couldn't move; I would have said I was turned to stone, but it was the opposite. The cold man of marble became flesh again, the hot blood coursed through my veins, as it had what seemed like so long ago. Eleni! Eleni? Of course it wasn't, it couldn't be, all these years later, even had she lived she'd have been in her fifties, like me, not a seventeen-year-old girl as she had been when she died. But before me was the doppelgänger of what she had been, back then, the white-blonde hair, the eyes; but there was more, I thought, as I watched her carefully."

"I'd recovered myself by now, it wouldn't do to let this lot see me with my heart on my sleeve. I just wanted to gaze at her, all night long if necessary, but obviously I couldn't do that, how would it look? The jokes and the sniggers behind hands, I knew the kind of thing, Du Cain's fallen in love, how about that, Old Eddie's losing it, must be going senile a bit early, time to re-think our dealings with him, see what territory we can wrest from him? (Du Cain, Eddie; Stephanidou filed these gleanings for reference later). Old? Fifty-five wasn't exactly ancient, but it wasn't the first flush of youth either, and everything was relative in this game. So, Control, control, keep your thoughts to yourself and act as usual, just look at her occasionally, as you do at all the rest of them. So I guarded myself carefully, drank in

129

moderation and ate, when the food came, made desultory conversation with my neighbours. Fortunately I had Caldwell to my right, as talkative a man as any born, so all I had to do was feed him the occasional question, prompt him, and he'd be off, his flow of words requiring only a nod and a look now and then; leaving me free to observe her, surreptitiously."

"I couldn't tell much about her from her clothes as she was wearing the cheap-looking uniform they were all obliged to wear. They did have some choice, I noticed, wearing either fishnet stockings and suspenders or less-provocative lace-topped hold-up stockings; my girl was wearing the latter, which said something in her favour, I hoped. She was doing her job, initially getting guests to their correct tables and seats, escorting them to the men's room when required, fetching drinks, making conversation and being pleasant in general. She didn't seem quite right here though, it seemed to me, she didn't fit. I could tell whenever one of these charmers made a suggestive comment to her because she blushed, innocently and becomingly, which had the unfortunate effect of them making more comments, to instigate more blushing."

"I couldn't work her out; innocent? If so, what was she doing here? This annual event was notorious for the sexual offers made by the guests to the hostesses, which had had the effect, over the years, of attracting a certain type of girl; those hoping to profit from their bodies over and above what they earned as hostesses at the tables. At best, a rich man amused enough to keep them around for a while and supply whatever they were skilled enough to wring out of him by way of cash and gifts. At worst, the night after the dinner in his bed, making sure they got cash up front; and I'd experienced them at best and worst. Maybe my girl played on her innocent looks, I decided; I remembered seeing *Miss Saigon,* the virgin in the whorehouse-bar, but how often did that kind of thing happen in reality?"

"Whatever the case, though, I was intrigued enough to find out, and I had to have her. I was owed this Eleni look-alike and the gods had given me justice, seemingly, however long it had taken them. James had seen her too, and wanted her; I could see him looking, from his table just over from mine. He could whistle for her; to hell with brotherly love, this was every man for himself, I decided. I observed her leave, escorting someone from the other side of the table, presumably to the men's room and, as I discerned a need to go there myself I followed, hoping maybe for some interaction in the corridor. I was out of luck in this however, but I did find James waiting for me when I emerged. 'I know what you're thinking, Kadi, but she isn't Eleni, we both know that, she just looks like her, uncannily so, but she's just some girl we know nothing about with a striking resemblance. Be careful.' 'Of what?' I asked him, but he just shrugged. He was correct, obviously, she wasn't Eleni, but that didn't stop him from wanting her too; and I couldn't have that, I was the eldest and Eleni had been for me, not him, however much he may have wanted it the other way around. She had to be mine and I was going to make sure that she was."

"Returning to the table I found her there, passing drinks and fending off advances to the best of her ability, which didn't appear to be that good, for the rest of the interminable dinner and speeches. When the latter were over at last, I saw her once again, moving towards the corridor, and decided that it had to be now, or never. James had seen her go also, and I detected a determination identical to mine in his eyes; he was off to get her too, and I had to be ahead of him. I moved as fast as it was possible to move without giving the impression of speed, encountered Philip Corven in my path, and acted swiftly. 'You want that contract, don't you? The shipping lines?' His eyes lightened, of course he did. 'Then get to my brother now, immediately, keep him talking, ten minutes, don't let him brush you off, ten minutes and we have a deal.' He raised his eyebrows briefly, but I didn't care any more what any of them thought, I had to claim what was mine. But Corven knew when he was well-off and asked no questions; 'Right-oh', and he sidelined James with skill. Clearly his rugby days had left him with all the right moves; I heard him begin, 'James, old chap ...' , but no more as I was in the passage and searching for her."

"I found her backed up against the corridor wall by that drunken shit Inglis, who'd made too many indecent comments to her at table in far too loud a voice. He was attempting to assault her, and I saw red rage like blood in my eyes. It was the Turk with Eleni again, and I would have killed him where he stood, had there been an iron bar to hand. But there wasn't, fortunately for both of us, and, Control, control, Kadi mou, as my father used to say, Words will wound as surely as weapons and hurt you less also."

Stephanidou, whose head had shot up sharply at the reference to the Turk, Eleni and an iron bar, was currently having to exert all his control; he managed to remain outwardly impassive, as the old man continued, seemingly unaware of what he'd said and of Stephanidou's sudden movement. "I used my own iron bar of control and fought him with words, some sarcastic comment about his wife, plus a look that would have frozen the alcohol in his veins. Bastard; he slunk away, he knew what I was capable of, when roused, he'd heard the story of the paper-knife and he wasn't going to risk it. Good to remind them occasionally that they'd be better off keeping me on-side. But here I was at last, myself and the girl sizing each other up, and I hadn't got a clue what to say to her; I was like a tongue-tied teenager."

"Which is rather how I feel now", Kadi trailed off, "the tongue-tied part, not the teenager; it's been a long session this afternoon, and I need to rest. We've much to get through, and we will; tomorrow I'll tell you of Magdalena, for it was she that I met at the dinner, and the day after that, well, we'll be done by the end of the week", he concluded, "so have patience, my friend, and your reward will not be long in coming".

"One thing more though"; he waved Stephanidou back to his seat and held him there with a penetrating look. "It's obvious to me that you haven't worked out who I am yet; who else I am, that is, because clearly you are by now well-acquainted with Arkadios Dukakis. If you had found out, I'm sure that you would have been here in uniform early one morning to apprehend me officially. So I suppose I shall have to give you a clue, but do remember please when you find the answer that it was I who made it possible; I controlled the process."

"Well, you can be sure that my name is not Rumplestiltskin, if you've heard of that particular fairy-tale character? No? It was one of Magdalena's, on one of her university modules, and worth looking up as it pertains to knowing someone's name being the key to knowing them completely. Although in my case, as in many others, it was an assumed name, so does it count? So many people invent new names for themselves, and new selves with the names; an interesting digression for which you'll have to forgive me, but there's so much to learn in this world. Maybe back in ancient times I was a philosopher? An interesting speculation, for which unfortunately we have no time now."

"So, to my assumed name. My uncle had changed his own name because, as he so enigmatically put it, he might need to disappear at some time, although that never came to pass. He chose Edward as his given name, for reasons best known to himself, and Ducan, as a nod to our patronymic, Dukakis. So he became Eddie Ducan, and he must have been a prophet, and a poet, because it rhymes with Lucan, if you're familiar with that particular refugee from justice? Yes? Of course, he's attained international notoriety, I believe. Well, he didn't commit his particular crime until 1974, well after my uncle had chosen the pseudonym which he passed on to me, as his supposed nephew, and the refugee from justice parallel works very well with me also. My uncle was Old Eddie and I was Young Eddie, to distinguish us from each other, you see. Well, when he saw that I was doing very well indeed in the business, and made me his heir, he decided that I needed a better pedigree; I mean, an immigrant coming in via the East End just wouldn't cut it with the upper-class toffs who were running the show, as he put it. So he came up with as good a history for me as he could, and Young Eddie Ducan I became; and that's enough. I'm not going to do all the work for you, and I can see that you're itching to get back to the station-house and find me on the Internet, so please do be my guest. Search for Eddie Ducan to start with, on the correct site, of course, and I think we both know which that is; be a bit creative and you ought to be able to come back here tomorrow morning and tell me who I was."

He arrested Stephanidou's departure once more as the Lieutenant got up, trying not to appear too keen and failing miserably, and extended his right hand; "I'd be obliged if I could shake hands with you now, as in friendship, because I feel that when you come tomorrow it will be in your official capacity. I'll know by how you're dressed, of course. But please do remember to honour our agreement; I shall have more to tell you tomorrow, and on the next day, and on Friday the final part, or the first, it may be, which will be of use to you as an officer of police. But I shan't be going anywhere with you tomorrow, or the two days afterwards, for that matter; be so good as to leave me here until the next day, that is, Saturday, when I will be at your disposal. But until then my time belongs to her; it's in the contract, you see. Now you ought to go and spin your straw into gold, and then perhaps we can make magic for you."

Stephanidou was curious as to the meaning of Kadi's reference to his time belonging to a woman, by contract; however, he was far more interested in checking the more concrete information which the old man had given him. So, having taken his leave for the day, he hurried back to the station-house and consulted the list he had been making on his i-Pad, adding those items which he had gleaned today, so that the final product read as follows:

'Has a temper, Father Lambros says'.
'Seems to expect me to arrest him' (for what?)
'Has to fight to keep control'
'Pretty but potentially-fatal women, Eleni Christou, possibly?'
'Red mist of anger, scarred man with paper-knife'
'Suggested that he had known about Eleni Christou's pregnancy before her death'.
'An honestly-made mistake' (other than getting engaged to the wrong woman?)
'Memories of betrayal associated with ruined house (his mother's)'.
'A lovers' leap together? Double suicide?'
'Eleni and Osman, nude bathing together?'
'Du Cain's fallen in love …. Old Eddie's losing it' (= Eddie Du Cain/Ducan?)
Turkish boatman's confession; Nikos Osman Nikolaides had returned to the island;
had Kadi known?
Did Osman kill Eleni?
Was Osman killed? By whom? Kadi/Eleni's parents?
'The Turk with Eleni again, and I would have killed him where he stood, had there been an iron bar to hand'.

A bit of digging around on the Interpol site with the names Eddie, Ducan and Du Cain and Stephanidou found what he sought. There it was; he found himself looking at a photograph from which Kadi looked right back at him. It was a prison mug shot, but unmistakeably Kadi, maybe ten years younger, neater, with shorter hair and beard, but the eyes glaring at the camera, with chips of ice and fire in them, were unmistakeable. The Lieutenant checked out the accompanying profile; Edward du Cain, served four years in Great Britain for various white-collar offences, insider trading, money laundering, bribery, false accounting and so forth. Released early on parole but broke this and disappeared, to date not traced and still at large. Not the worst criminal in the world, not a murderer, but no police force likes to be made a fool of and the British police would be glad to have this man apprehended.

It won't do me any harm to have found him either, Stephanidou reflected as he showered and changed, but I felt that there was more to it, there has to be more to it. What about the bad memories at the ruined house, Eleni and the Turk and the iron bar? But Kadi had promised more and he would just have to wait for it. In the meantime, he silently addressed the man, you can be sure that I'll make the most of what I have, and then you, O Kyrios Dukakis, will be well and truly nicked, as they say in English! Mulling things over, he realised that he was very hungry indeed; he took his evening meal from Sofia at the kafenion, earning her praise for eating two very large portions of her moussaka. Then he returned to his bed and slept like the dead, yet was still up early to go and get the next chapter of the story.

17: HOLY WEDNESDAY: REVELATION

Dressed in his uniform, as Kadi had predicted, Stephanidou arrived at the derelict house on the hill. He was greeted by Kadi, lying in the shade upon his bed and remarking, "I'm glad to say that I appear to be on schedule, today being Holy Wednesday and focussed around repentance and confession; because you will find that I am now, and have been for some time, engaged in the former; for the latter, that is coming, have no fear. You will have to bear with me, I'm afraid, but it will be worth your while".

He smiled from the bed where he lay and heaved himself into a horizontal position, indicating Stephanidou's uniform as he did so. "It seems to me, from the look on your face and your attire that you have worked it out, Lieutenant; so do tell me who I am; or who I was, in England, at any rate." Stephanidou tried to speak solemnly, but felt rather ridiculous in so doing in the face of Kadi's by-now familiar sardonic grin; and instead his words came out weakly and rather wearily. "You are known in Great Britain as Edward du Cain, who served four years in prison there on charges relating to insider trading, money laundering, bribery, false accounting. You are currently wanted there for breach of parole upon your early release from prison."

Kadi laughed, clearly amused. "Very well done, good work, that's exactly it. You need a new name, Kadi, my uncle told me, when he realised my potential and took me to work at his side. Your real name? Arkadios Dukakis sounds too different, too foreign, to mix easily with these old-school-tie types, and you need to mix easily to do business with them. I consented, out of respect for him, and because he was right. Interestingly, it wasn't difficult to fit his own assumed name, Eddie Ducan, to my real one. My given name of Arkadios, hence Kadi, was derived from Arktos, Greek for bear, so Edward, from which Teddy is derived as a diminutive, worked well. Ducan, which he'd derived from our mutual patronymic of Dukakis, as I told you earlier, he now changed into du Cain. I protested that this still sounded foreign, but Uncle Michalis was adamant. A Greek name is far-foreign, a French one near-foreign, my boy; the history of England is intertwined more recently with that of France and besides, you know that I do much business with the French, so the name will open doors for us there."

"He had a good imagination, Uncle Michalis, and explained the name thus. According to his version, we both came from a poor and remote area of the Peloponnese, which he had left as a young man to seek his fortune in England. I on the other hand was the offspring of his flighty sister Despina and one Peter du Cain, an Anglo-French hippy wanderer with whom she had become infatuated when his peripatetic pathway brought him to her village. She had thrown up family life to join him on his travels, and died giving birth to me in a far-flung region of the Atlas mountains. My father, perceiving a baby as a hindrance to his lifestyle, took a diversion to deliver me back to my mother's village and, having discharged his duty as a father, as he saw it, departed for lands unknown and was never seen again. I was found one morning on my maternal family's doorstep, with a note like that carried by the bear on Paddington Station asking them to Please look after this child, the son of their deceased daughter. So I was raised there, learned some English at school and, when old enough, despatched to Uncle Michalis in England for him to find something for me to do with my life."

"Uncle was pleased with his invention; it was a romantic story, and I came close to believing it myself, although I queried why I needed it. 'Just in case anyone asks, Kadi'; omitting to use the new name himself. No-one ever did, except one man, far too inquisitive, with whom I was

138

performing some task one day; 'What part of the Peloponnese do you come from anyway?' I gave him a cold stare; 'What's it to you?' He hedged, uncomfortable; 'Nothing, just making conversation, you know'. 'Well, it's the same part my uncle comes from, why don't you ask him?' He backed off, and the word went around that the Boss's nephew didn't welcome questions about his private life any more than the Boss himself did, so whatever people may have thought they kept it to themselves."

"The story of my imaginary previous life wasn't totally foolproof, however, as I pointed out when my brother Iannis, now to be James, came to England a few years later. 'If my mother was dead and my father disappeared, how could I have a younger brother?' I asked my uncle. He didn't hesitate; 'He's your cousin by my brother, you were raised together like brothers (that part was true, at least) so he's taken your surname to make the link clear, OK?' Whatever made Uncle Michalis happy was fine by me, and his wisdom became apparent later; because any of my early East-End acquaintances who recognised Eddie Ducan in Edward du Cain would just think that Young Eddie had gone posh to try to fit in with the big boys, the public-school types, and good luck to him."

"So the formal but correct name for the circles to which Uncle Michalis aspired for me was chosen, and there was the new me; Edward du Cain, businessman, with a new passport to prove it, courtesy of my Uncle. He sorted out all the other matters for me too, permanent residence status when I'd been in the country for five years, citizenship application thereafter, and of course I passed the language test with flying colours. Uncle Michalis oiled the wheels, through unorthodox methods, I'm afraid, but all was done in the new name which was on the new passport. I kept the old one though; I never wanted to forget who I really was, underneath the veneer of upper-class Englishness, and who knew if I might not become Arkadios again in the future?

So my Greek passport was duly renewed whenever that became necessary, via a contact in Athens, and I did use it again, of course, when I came back to see my parents before they died, and afterwards for their funerals, and I have it with me now. But you know that bit, of course."

He heaved himself off the bed with some difficulty and made his way slowly round to the well, bringing a cup of water which he offered to Stephanidou whilst drinking none himself. As the latter drank thankfully Kadi laughed gently. "This has been fun, hasn't it? All the little hints which I gave and which you took, thirstily drinking in every drop to try to make sense of it all; and now you have a part of it, but not the whole. My temper, my parents and the heavy weight they had borne for me, my wanting to kill the Turk with an iron bar, my brother's support for me which warranted a reward (I missed that one, thought Stephanidou with some irritation). All these you still have, but how do they fit together to solve the puzzle for you?"

He finished with a dry laugh and Stephanidou was crestfallen; so Kadi had been playing him, laughing at his efforts to try to solve the cold case of Eleni Christou and Nikos Osman Nikolaides. But the old man patted him on the shoulder gently and spoke seriously now. "Don't be hurt, I wasn't trying to make fun of you, just giving myself a little light amusement. You were a gift from the gods, you see; I needed to put things right before I go, and you were exactly the right person to help me. You'll benefit by it, I'd bet my life on that if I didn't owe it elsewhere, and not just with the British authorities but the Greek also. There is a case to be solved, but it's not what you think and I'll explain it to you, on Friday, which is the day appointed."

"Today, however", he continued as he settled himself on one of the chairs, "it is time to tell more of Magdalena, the love of my life. There we were, if you remember, at the dinner, standing in the corridor appraising each other, and I hadn't got a clue what to say, so I just went with the banal, the mundane; I invited her to have a drink with me, and she accepted. I took her to the bar and gave her champagne, and I could tell that she was impressed; I gathered later that she didn't drink, well, not before that night, but she took to it very easily. That was a part of her attraction, you know; her total innocence juxtaposed with her appetites, waiting to be stimulated, and I was the one to stimulate them. The dinner was over, and the guests were on the hunt for the game, the fair game that was the sisterhood of hostesses. The bar around us was descending into Bacchanalia, and my girl did look rather alarmed, so I invited her to my room. So obvious as to be cringe-worthy, I'm afraid, but she accepted with honesty and a kind of dignity."

"There was no artifice about her; when I kissed her for the first time she tasted of soap and toothpaste, no perfumes, cheap or expensive, like the other women I'd known. That first night, it sounds so stupid, but I almost couldn't bring myself to touch her, apart from that kiss. Even before I found out that she was a virgin, the prospect of despoiling her made me feel like a brute; I wanted to put her on a pedestal and worship her, love her and spoil her and keep her untouched, unsoiled. But then I thought that, if I hadn't got her another of the beasts here would have, and they wouldn't have hesitated. She was a student, looking for a sponsor to pay her fees, as she told me on the following day when we got to know each a little other better, and she would have accepted any reasonable man, I felt; something which put me on my guard against her at times in the future, which I now bitterly regret because I know that she was pure, and innocent, and good. She'd just had bad advice, to come to work at this dinner, which in her innocence and need she'd taken."

"Anyway, I initially suggested that she service me orally, you understand? Apologies for the indelicacy. Well, she backed off as though I was a monster, and I was irritated, I thought she was taking the innocent act a bit too far; so I was sharp with her, and she burst into the most genuine tears possible. No doubt about it, when I questioned her further, she hadn't got a clue what I was proposing and had no other sexual experience apart from a bit of teenage foreplay. I was delighted, of course, I couldn't believe the incredible gift that had been sent to me and I didn't want to rush things in case I scared her off. I cradled her in my arms, under the covers, and soothed her by stroking her hair, talking nonsense to her, as though she were my little lost baby in need of comfort. She slept then, poor darling, she must have been worn out with fending off advances from those pigs all evening."

"I looked at her as she slept, marvelling at her beauty and youth. It felt unhealthily odd though to contemplate her innocence that reminded me of little Bibi, and to realise that she was about the age that my darling daughter would have been, had she been spared. How would I have felt about some man over thirty years her senior playing around with her? I'd have killed him. No, that was too uncivilized; I'd have asked him some pointed questions, to which I wouldn't have liked the answers, and then I'd have killed him. But I didn't feel that I was playing around, trifling with her feelings. This was to be no one-nighter, with cash given in exchange for pleasure the following morning; I intended it to be more, even though so far I'd done no more than kiss and caress her. I kissed her again, then, my sleeping beauty, and she awoke with that momentary puzzlement at where she was which can occur upon awakening in an unfamiliar place; but then she saw me, and remembered, and her smile was like the sunshine."

"So I took her, I made her a woman, although not all at once; I was so controlled with her that first night, you have no idea, I've never needed such control. I was gentle, and patient, and undemanding, and it paid me in dividends, although that's not how I thought of it, you understand. I made love to her, slowly, gently and with infinite patience, showing her how and going at her pace; and she unfolded in my arms like a flower, a bud bursting into fullness. She was indeed a virgin, keen yet nervous despite herself at the point of no return; she even bled, but having crossed into womanhood she abandoned herself to the act and I could have wept at the pleasure she showed. It was everything my wedding-night with Eleni ought to have been, had it occurred instead of the horrific events which took its place, and my joy was infinite."

Stephanidou duly noted the reference to 'horrific events', but *Control, control, Stephano*, he told himself with irony, *he'll get there, he's promised as much and I trust him to deliver*. "I wanted to wrap her up in the bedding and carry her off", Kadi continued, away to my apartment at the top of the building, closest to the sky and the stars and with a view of the river, keeping her there away from the prying eyes of the world and enjoying our mutual love. For I did love her; I ought to have taken her and married her as soon as possible after that night, for I'm sure she would have taken me for her husband as she took me for her lover, with total love and lack of artifice."

"But I did not, for that same resemblance to my first love, Eleni, which had attracted me to her as soon as I saw her, by a trick of fate also put me on my guard against her, reminding me also of the manipulative deceptiveness of that same first love. And of the second, Aphrodite, whose sensuality my new, true love showed every sign of matching. So I switched with Magdalena between trust and distrust, over-controlling her in the smallest things, testing her obedience through the vilest ordeals, and punishing her mercilessly when she showed natural signs of repugnance and wished to have some control over her own life."

"Eleni had been selfish, you see, out for herself; but that's for later, I have other things to tell before I address her case. Aphrodite was certainly selfish, self-serving; I knew this, and still I loved her, although less and less, little by little, as I came to know her. She dropped the man she was engaged to when she met me, left the function where we met with me, then finished with him by text the next morning, from my place. By text, can you believe it? Then, when she sensed that I was not so keen to marry her, she tried to secure me by other means. She didn't ask my consent to us having a child, just stopped taking her pills and let it happen; and then of course I fell in love with the child, so her ruse worked. Ironically, though, because I loved the child more than I did her, and she sensed that; she knew, when I was ready to marry her, that it was for the sake of our little girl. But poor little Bibi died, suddenly, and the marriage never did happen; and life and reality caught up with Aphrodite then. She became a mother in every sense, living for the child, finally loving someone else better than she did herself; and when the baby was taken from her she couldn't go back to that old self, she had nowhere to go, so she followed her child to the grave. Poor Aphrodite. I know I could have done more for her, but I was so shattered myself; and ultimately I don't think I could have changed the outcome."

"So when little Magdalena came along, totally unselfish and in love with me, I took total advantage. I didn't mean to, I adored her, I loved her so much, but I just couldn't tell her so. She was my three-in-one, you see; the physical beauty, the uncanny resemblance to Eleni, joined with the raw sensuality of Aphrodite, which I awoke in her, my little virgin bride. Added to which, there was innocence, like that of my little daughter, Bibi, which I suppose is where the unselfishness came from; it made me feel uneasy, as I've told you, Magdalena being about the age which Bibi would have been, had she survived. I did speak to her about that once, and how I thought her father would want to kill me for it; but she said, 'Oh, my father doesn't believe in killing, he's a committed Christian'. He was from some dedicated sect or other, she did tell me but I've forgotten the name now. Well, that didn't really comfort me; not because I was afraid of him, when you've done the things I've done you don't fear physical violence (which phrase Stephanidou noted). But I felt that any father worth his salt ought to want to protect his children. And as to her father, well, I knew I was old enough to be her father, I was older than her actual father, even he could tell by just looking at me."

"Because I did meet her parents, just once, and that was enough for all of us. Magdalena's graduation, it was, and she didn't know what to do about who should be there for her. The parents had supported her through her first year, but then they'd stopped, because they wanted her to leave and marry some young man who she didn't love. Well, that was when, through financial necessity, she went to work at the dinner and met me; so her parents were to blame for what happened to a great extent. I mean, what kind of parents leave their child to depend upon the kindness of strangers to get them through life? Anyway, Magdalena felt she owed it to them to invite them, because of their year of supporting her, but she wanted me there and knew that they and I wouldn't get on with each other."

"So she didn't invite them, but decided to tell them afterwards, about her graduation and about me, I suppose; however, there was some mix-up over the tickets for the ceremony, they didn't arrive and Magdalena had to go into the office and raise merry hell, because they swore they'd been sent. That may be, she told them, but they haven't arrived, so they're obviously lost in the post and I need duplicates. Well, after some argument she got one ticket out of them, for me, which was all she wanted; but in the event it turned out that they hadn't updated their computer and the original tickets had been sent to her parents' home. They, not having heard from their daughter in some time, decided to come to the graduation and find her that way. We didn't know they were there until it was over and Magdalena came racing over to me, her face shining and her gown flying out behind her; I held my arms open to her and she leapt into them, and that's when the father pounced."

"I was ready to stay with her and support her, obviously, but she gave me her stern face – she did have one, occasionally – so I retired, not too far away that I couldn't get to her fast if the father turned nasty, but enough to give them privacy to speak. Not that they needed it; the father didn't trouble to lower his voice, and people started looking, eventually. I took the opportunity to study the parents while the father chewed Magdalena out. The mother was a nonentity, just stood there and let her husband talk for her; or at any rate, spew out his views and venom, which naturally she would make her own. I wondered briefly what she might have been like, before she married him, then turned my attention to him. A classic bully, used to getting his own way and demanding it, if it was not given freely; I'd met his type before, too many times. I liked my own way, but preferred to think that I went about getting it somewhat more subtly. I had to exert all my control, because I wanted badly to knock him down, for the way he was treating his daughter; instead I fixed him with a penetrating stare as he continued to rant at Magdalena. I put all my dislike of him into that stare, my view of him as a bad parent and how much I despised him for that, and it certainly had an effect on him. I held him with my eyes and he couldn't look away, I stared him out and he crumbled; he finally made one horrible remark to Magdalena, disowning her, and then departed at speed, with the mother in tow."

"So that left Magdalena with just me to look after her, a man old enough to be her father; old enough to be her grandfather, even. I met a woman once who was a grandmother at thirty-two, you know. She'd had a baby at sixteen and, like mother like daughter, the child went on to do the same thing. So I was far too old for Magdalena, I knew, but I wasn't messing about with her; I wanted her for the rest of my life, if she'd have me, and I was sure she would. She'd said she'd do anything for me, said it more than once, frequently, and I used to get the urge to test her, to see if she really meant what she said. It was like one of those old stories, the tale of patient Griselda, you've heard of it? Well, Boccaccio put it in his *Decameron* and the Italian Petrarch took it and used it, and Chaucer got it from him and put it in his *Canterbury Tales;* you can look those up if you're interested. A king marries a peasant girl, the poorest of the poor but respectable, and demands total obedience from her. Well, she gives it, in her love for him, but he has a curious need to push the boundaries, to see how far he can go before she cracks and says No. Terrible things he does, takes away her children at birth and makes out that he's had them killed; then sends her back to her father in nothing but a petticoat, telling her that he's going to marry someone more suitable, a princess, and brings Griselda back to organise the wedding. And all the time she accepts his behaviour, can you believe it? He sticks with her though, and brings back the children, who've been raised elsewhere, so it ends happily, if you think a traumatised wife and children who've been made that way by a crazy man can ever be happy."

"Well, of course there wasn't the fairytale ending with little Magdalena. I made her do terrible things, things I'm sure even Griselda would have turned and said No to, but Magdalena did them, until I pushed her too far and she turned against me. I wanted to protect her, but to control her also, as I hadn't been able to control the others, my two almost-wives and my daughter, all of whom ended up dead. It was as though my total control of her would mean that she couldn't get away, couldn't be taken away, from me; but she did, and she was, and it was I who drove her away. But I blamed her, and punished her, and now I have to punish myself."

He was clearly deeply affected by what he was saying, and stopped for some moments to collect himself. Then, with a look at Stephanidou which the latter clearly interpreted as shame, he continued, in a low voice hardly much above whisper. "I shared her with my brother; little Iannis had wanted Eleni, well, all the young men had wanted her, but as James he'd wanted Magdalena also. I'd made sure that I got to her first, however. I hadn't intended it, it just happened one evening. James had dropped by unexpectedly with a business matter that needed urgent attention, and it just so happened to be a Friday and Magdalena was due to arrive for the weekend. When she did, she was in a reckless mood; wearing her coat with nothing underneath, and just grabbed me as soon as she was through the front door and dragged me into the bedroom, ripping my clothes off as she went. She could be very unexpected and spontaneous, that was a part of her charm. Well, despite James being in the lounge I had very little choice but to go with the flow, so we ended up in a fast and furious coupling; and when we'd finished, there was James standing in the doorway. I still don't know how long he'd been there, and he'd never tell me, but I'd walked in on him and a girl more than once when we shared a flat and I suppose he thought it was time to even the score a little. Well, he diffused the situation with humour, and Magdalena saw the funny side and they obviously hit it off, which was when I had the idea."

"I suppose it was because he'd wanted Eleni, and because I owed him so much on her account (And I'm looking forward to hearing exactly what, thought Stephanidou; he was impatient to get to that part of Kadi's story, but sympathetic to the man's need to recount the rest of his tale, shameful as this part of it was). I sent James to get us a bottle of wine and asked her while he was away", Kadi was saying. "Well, I had to do a bit of getting around her, but I could always do that and anyway, she wasn't totally averse to the idea, I could tell. Neither was James, when we put the idea to him on his return, and so we proceeded. I'd never been into anything too different, too out-there sexually, if you know what I mean, but it was a distinct turn-on to watch her with someone else. That someone else being my brother, who resembled me not a little, produced quite a strange effect; it was as though it was I who was with her, but at the same time removed from myself and watching from the sidelines. I could tell that they enjoyed each other very much, these two people who I loved best in the world; I was so proud of my little Magdalena for making James so happy, she'd made me feel so much better about all that I owed to him, and I loved her the more for it."

"So that night wasn't a test as such, but it did have a bearing on the things I asked her to do thereafter, and of which I was then and am now thoroughly ashamed. I'd changed, you see, over the years; the young man who had wanted to live life correctly had been corrupted, slowly and surely. On a personal level, whenever I'd told a woman that I loved her it had been a signal for them to take advantage of me, knowing they could wrap me around their little fingers. Eleni had done it, most shamefully and shamelessly, and paid the ultimate price; while Aphrodite, much more honest than Eleni, had still tried to bind me through her early pregnancy and child. I'd have married her too, over-ridden my doubts and made her my wife for the sake of our child; my little Bibi, taken far too young, and Aphrodite taken herself, taking her own life possibly, when the baby was gone and I was too unhappy myself to give her the support she needed. That left Gabrielle, with whom there was never any pretence of love; my uncle had contracted her, in essence, to make a man of me, and she'd carried out the task given. Not without huge enjoyment for both of us, I'm sure of that, and she'd always have a special place in my affections, but she'd never tried to take advantage of me because she knew I wasn't head over heels in love with her and therefore exploitable. So my most successful relationship with a woman was with she who had been contracted to me for sexual purposes; and here was little Magdalena, ready to sell her sexual services to me in a similar way, and I made the mistake of valuing her at the level of Gabrielle, when she was far, far above her in every way."

"She loved me, and that rendered her vulnerable; she tried to fight me, when I requested something which she found unacceptable, but I could always talk her round. I remembered the way she'd fought back at her father at her graduation, and won out; what made the difference? Was it love? Her parents had given her little, and earned little in return. Whereas I, what had I done, I wondered, to deserve the love of this darling little child-woman? Because I knew that I had, with certainty, she made no bones about it in her engagingly candid way. I had bought her time, and her sexuality, for as long as I paid her expenses. But I hadn't bought her love, that hadn't been in the contract; it had happened for other reasons, and eventually I felt ashamed that I had taken advantage of her feelings for me. I knew that I loved her too, far more than those who had gone before; I just couldn't tell her because I'd learned that to do so would render me vulnerable to whatever hidden agenda and designs a woman might have upon me."

He was rambling somewhat now, and being repetitive also, in a faint and hoarse voice, but Stephanidou hadn't the heart to tell him so. Aside from which, Kadi might take offence if he did, and refuse to explain exactly what had happened with Eleni Christou and Nikos Osman Nikolaides. So he offered Kadi some water from the rose-patterned tea cup; but it was waved away, albeit politely, as the old man changed track momentarily.

"On a business level, I'd wanted to bring things back to an honest way of working when I took over at my uncle's death, but that hadn't proved practical. His methods of doing things were too well entrenched, they'd been going on for too long and so much that had been achieved was sitting on a foundation of dishonesty. To try to change things now was likely to bring the whole edifice crashing down, which happened eventually, but not through my trying to proceed more honestly. So I carried on with things as they were, which is how I came to use Magdalena in facilitating certain business dealings. I'd met her not long after I'd seen Gabrielle again, you see, which had linked them in my mind in some way. So, when I remembered how Gabrielle used to help matters on for my uncle with recalcitrant business associates, it occurred to me that Magdalena might be useful in the same way."

"It was madness, of course; she was as sensual as Gabrielle, but in an innocent way. She wasn't at ease with sharing her favours, but of course she had done so with James, partly to please me and partly because he was like me to some extent, I suppose. She'd been in a mad mood that night, and we all do mad things sometimes, do we not? Plus, the way she'd come to me worked against her; she'd been on the lookout for a sponsor for her studies, to sell herself, in effect, and I'd bought her. But at the time I interpreted things wrongly, and devalued her in my opinion, and used her in ways in which I ought never to have used her."

"It was her three-in-oneness, I suppose, that did it. I wanted to protect the innocent, Bibi-like part of her, and to enjoy the sensual Aphrodite-like part, because she was created for love-making; but the Eleni part I wanted to punish. There was love there also, of course; sometimes I'd look at her and see Eleni and remember how much I'd loved her, but inevitably this was followed by the memory of how she'd tried to take advantage of my love and use me. Then the desire to revenge myself would creep in, and using Magdalena as a Gabrielle-figure with other men would satisfy both that desire and the need to test her love for me."

"I'd used other women for this purpose, of course, those

who were happy to do these things if they were well-paid for their services, and I didn't want anyone else to fully take my Magdalena, unless I wanted it, as with my brother. But then there was a man to be, shall we say, persuaded? One who I knew to be impotent, but who liked to be mildly-disciplined by a woman to achieve such satisfaction as he was capable of. So that was the first time, and she wasn't happy about it, but she did it for my sake and achieved the result I wanted because the man was so pleased with her; and after that it wasn't difficult to do it again, whenever there was an impotent, older man to be persuaded, or sweetened, or thanked; and there are plenty of those around, in the world of big-money business."

"Your face well-expresses what you think of me for this, and I don't blame you; I'd feel the same, if I were the honest young man I had been." Stephanidou at this tried to change his expression and hide his feelings of disgust, but found it difficult, and Kadi continued. "It wasn't good behaviour by a long chalk, but I was in control, which pleased me; and compared to when I was jealous on a personal level, and felt out of control of events, believe me, it was very mild. Take my brother, for example; she'd been with him under my control, and I was fine with that. But there was another time when I allowed them to be together; I had to go away on business, very last-minute it was and Magdalena faced the weekend spent in her poky student digs. So I suggested that she spend Saturday evening with James, and they were both agreeable. I gave my chauffeur instructions to take her over to James's place and to collect her later, and I gave specific times for this; but she tried to stay overnight, past the time I'd set for her to go home."

"Thinking about it much later, and rationally, why wouldn't she? That place she was sharing with a bunch of students was damp and dingy, why would she want to go back there when she could be in my brother's warm apartment? Which meant his warm arms and warm bed, which is where she was already, obviously, but only because I'd allowed her to be there, and for as long as I decreed. James sent her home, of course, but I found out and I was furious. Not jealous, you understand, I'd given her to him of my own free will, but angry because she'd tried to take control, and I couldn't have that. So I punished her, physically as well as mentally on this occasion; I'd been in Amsterdam, so it wasn't difficult to get a little cane, which I used on her. Nothing heavy, just a few light strokes on her rear end, but she wasn't expecting it and was pained and ashamed. I also forced her to wear a gold chain at all times, with a letter 'H' suspended from it; for Whore, Hooker, Harlot and so forth; derogatory English words to humiliate her."

"She was wearing it when we went to Milan, another time when I had to punish her, and this time I was jealous, as jealous as it was possible to be. I'd taken her with me, purely for pleasure; we'd been shopping, and sightseeing, and then I took her to see a local singer who I'd seen before, an excellent performer who I thought warranted better recognition than he'd received in his career, which was long, he being not much younger than I was. Well, he performed, with another man and a girl who I could tell was his off-stage partner also, and little Magdalena enjoyed it, and more. She could never hide what she was feeling in our early days and didn't see why she should; she was always so honest, although that changed with time. She learned to conceal things from me, not because she was naturally deceptive, far from it, but because I punished her so savagely when I was displeased."

"Well, as to this musician, I could see that she was attracted to him, and I was jealous; unreasonably, gut-wrenchingly, jealous. I checked out the room, furtively, and every woman there, I would have said, felt his attraction as he played and sang, totally immersed in the pleasure of what he was doing. He could have laid them end to end, right there and then, had he wanted; but his girl was there, a tambourine in her hands and a look on her face similar to the other women yet different in that it was the look of requited love, consummated love, pride in her man because he was hers, and not theirs."

"And among them sat my Magdalena, with that look of desire in her eyes, all unconscious of it though she might be. I'd awakened it, I was sure, that first night when I brought her into womanhood; something indefinable, of her going out of herself and abandoning her body to sensual pleasure. It had intensified since then, as she became familiar with the act of love; it was in her eyes, faintly, as she became aroused even before love-making began. Whenever I saw it there I wanted her, it had that effect upon me, and I wanted her now; but it wasn't there for me, but for him, and I was as jealous as it was possible to be. I tried to control it, to reason with myself; Kadi, look, every woman here is attracted to him, why should she be any different? But that was to place her with the common herd of womanhood, and I'd put her on a pedestal above that and wanted to keep her there."

"The musician finished his set, and came and sat with us, he and his girl and the other man, the harmonica-player, and I kept a surreptitious watch as he spoke to Magdalena. No doubt about it, she was attracted, and he was attractive, although in a manner very different to my own. I remembered seeing some street musicians in Madrid once; they arrived in the square and threw down the lid of an old wooden packing case, on which one of them danced Flamenco while the others played. One of them had somehow fashioned some kind of double-bass out of the rest of the packing case, a stick and some strings; and the notes he teased from that weird instrument had to be heard to be believed. If I'd practised for years on a Stradivarius I could never have made such beautiful sounds, but this chap in Milan was the same as the Madrid musician. He had music in his fingertips, and only needed a guitar to draw it out, and people responded to his talent."

"I had a talent too, we all have, but some talents are more attractive than others, and with music people perceive the talent required to conjure up the sounds. My particular talent is for making money, which has an attraction, certainly, but I fear it's the end product which does the attracting. So when my Magdalena saw this guitar man she saw a raw talent for giving pleasure, and when she saw me for the first time at that dinner what did she see? A walking wallet, I thought bitterly; she went there to find money, and if I hadn't got to her first she'd have found someone else and she'd have taken them, if the price had been right. I felt myself giving in to my jealousy; I was losing control, although I managed to hold on until we were in the car back to the hotel. Then I lost it totally, and I was poisonous to her; psychologically-violent, you understand, as I'd been with Eleni, and she was terrified by the time I'd finished."

He looked up at Stephanidou at this point, taking the latter off-guard by fixing him with an expression which somehow combined a challenge with the sardonic grin with which the Lieutenant had become familiar. He knows I've picked up on that, Stephanidou thought, shocked despite what he already knew about what Kadi was doing; he referred to being psychologically-violent to Eleni and expected me to react to it. He's been playing me, toying with me all this time, feeding me bits of information and getting amusement from my thinking that he's slipped up, but he did tell me so, to be fair. He looked down at the ground, not knowing what else to do, and his host continued;

"But it wasn't totally spent, my anger, my jealousy, so although I soothed her and allayed her fears I kept bringing the matter up again over the next week; I couldn't help myself, although I tried hard. Trying to control my anger, I'd noticed over the years, could have the effect of elongating and intensifying it. It was like opening a bottle of fizz which is over-exhuberant and forcing the cork back in; the liquid forces its way out around the edges bit by bit, rather than just spending itself in one huge explosion. So over the next few days, in Naples, and even back in the UK, I took it out on her. In Naples I told her the story of an aristocratic composer, Gesualdo, who'd murdered his wife and her lover because she was a total nymphomaniac who'd seen off two husbands before him. I compared Magdalena to her and watched her little face crumple as she tried to keep control."

"Back at home I acted as though things were as normal, then on my way out of the door one morning I casually suggested that I'd find another way to punish her, leaving her in mental torment until I returned a few days later. She was desperate by then, the poor girl must have had a hell of a time, but she'd worked out a way to deflect my anger and, as a side-effect of which she was unaware, she aroused the pity and protective feelings which I always wanted to give to the Bibi-like part of her. So I let it go, and she was hysterical, poor girl, with the nervous tension she'd been living in. So I soothed her and held her while she slept, and felt thoroughly ashamed of myself."

He stopped at this point, looking away into space as though collecting his thoughts, and Stephanidou waited for him to resume. His own thoughts as he waited concerned Kadi's use of language, which the Lieutenant realised did something strange when speaking of Magdalena. Kadi would slide unconsciously between English and Greek, but the former apparently when speaking of positive things which he associated with her, and the latter whenever he had confused her with her doppelgänger Eleni and all the negative associations attached to her. However, at this point Kadi recommenced his tale, and Stephanidou his role as audience.

"So my treatment of her see-sawed between my love-bombing her, as they say nowadays, and testing, punishing and abusing her. I'd lavish everything on her, jewellery, clothes, holidays, the best restaurants, you name it and I gave it to her. And she never asked for any of it, only the financial support to get her through university debt-free, and she didn't ask for that for nothing. We had drawn up a legal contract, my money for her time and body, and that may sound crude, and mercenary, but at least it was honest; she wasn't looking for a free ride, my innocent little girl. And our relationship was severely damaged by the abusive things things I did to her, both on the personal and the business front."

"And that, I think, needs to be the end for the day", Kadi concluded. His face had reflected so many emotions while he told his tale, shame, rage, love, grief, and now it seemed to hang on his cheekbones, drained as it appeared to be of all emotion now. Stephanidou agreed, albeit reluctantly; as far as he was concerned he'd stay all night, so that they could get on to the truth about Eleni and Osman. But he'd agreed to wait until Friday for that particular information, and so involved was he in Kadi's life-story now that he needed to hear it all. So he said his goodbyes for the day and made his way down the hill.

18: HOLY THURSDAY

Stephanidou arrived at the ruin very early the following day; he was eager to get to the answers he so desperately wanted, and which lay near the end of the story, planned by Kadi for Friday. Today was the penultimate chapter, however, so he didn't have too long to wait, he told himself. Kadi was waiting for him, recumbent upon his bed in the same position as that in which Stephanidou had left him on the previous evening; which gave the impression of his not having moved since then. He smiled when he saw his audience, who was sure that the old man knew of his visitor's impatience and was amused by it. Kadi made no comment, however, other than his usual greeting, then waited until Stephanidou was seated and the recording machine running and recommenced his tale:

"I thought I had it all at that time, despite the cracks which were appearing in my relationship with Magdalena. Despite her objections to what I made her do with other men she always accepted my wishes eventually, and I thought she always would. A mistake on my part; hubris, our ancestors called it, as you well know, and it hasn't gone away. The gods play with us, and they were playing with me, I believe. Kadi thinks he's got it all, in total control of his empire and his woman; time to take him down a peg or two. Oh yes, time for a little *peripeteia,* swiftly followed by some *anagnorisis* in what was to become my personal Greek tragedy."

"I think the one big factor which finally broke myself and Magdalena was when I gave her to a so-called prince, from the Middle East, a contemptible sub-human as it turned out. I knew he was impotent, like the others, but what he wanted was unacceptable. He held a gun to her head, not loaded as it happens, but she didn't know that and the poor girl lost control of her bladder, despite the drugs. I'd got her taking cocaine, you see, when she did these things, and that's something else to my discredit. I'd tried the stuff myself, but never took to it. I think we've established by now that I prefer to be in control as far as possible, and drug-taking is a road in totally the opposite direction. But I could tell that it would be a useful tool to help Magdalena get through these ordeals, although I didn't consider the wider implications of getting her onto drugs."

"Anyway, she was heavily humiliated by her inadvertent loss of bladder control, which was what the Arab wanted of course. He made her undress, caressing her with his free hand before he pulled her head back by her hair, hard, with one hand while attending to himself with the other, all the while abusing her verbally in the crudest terms. I know, because I filmed it, the first time, and she took a lot of soothing and sorting out afterwards; but I got what I wanted from him that time, and the next. There wasn't supposed to be a next time, but I was up against it as it happens. I thought I was in real trouble when those Middle-Eastern contracts came up for renewal and the competition tried to pull a flanker, the rivals lined up against me and tried to put me out of the game for good. I stood to lose massively, so I had to get the Prince on-side; even though I despised him I needed him to come through for me then, and all the usual perks weren't enough, even when substantially increased. So I had to throw Magdalena to him again; I didn't want to, but he'd requested her especially. She wasn't happy, and I felt guilty as Hell, but what was I to do? She took so much persuading, because obviously she didn't want to go anywhere near him ever again."

"I forced her into it, though, and I'm sure that was when I lost her, that night for sure. I had my chauffeur deliver her to him and bring her back, and she must have broken down in the car with him whilst returning. Of course, that oily little shit Shine would have been straight in there, consoling her and stealing her right out from under me. I delayed going home myself, I was so nervous for her that I took the girl who was my driver that evening into the drinks party I was attending, as a distraction so that the other men would talk to her and not realise that I wasn't totally on the ball. I drank more than usual, as well, and when I got home Magdalena was offhand, which was to be expected, but I couldn't tell much more than that."

"It was only from the next day onwards that I realised it was worse than I had thought; she'd always been an open book to me, she was very honest anyway, but I could read her easily, something in her eyes and general demeanour always gave her thoughts away. Now the book was closed, slammed shut like a door; she behaved much as she usually did, but there was an air of falseness about her, she was acting a part for my benefit. And the eyes, it was like an opaque blind had descended, I couldn't see through any more. I tried hard to get things back to the way they'd been, but it was no use; I'd lost her."

"The so-called prince got his just desserts a few years later, I heard. He was out flying his falcon in the desert, just he with his souped-up four-by-four and his bird handler and other attendants in another vehicle, because he'd got some visitor with him that he wanted to impress. Well, he took the vehicle too fast over the dunes and hit an uneven patch he wasn't expecting, shifting sands, you know? Well, the thing went right up into the air, they said, crashed down on the roof and exploded, a fireball. They said it must have been fast, he and the other couldn't have known much about it; a pity, I would have liked the bastard to suffer, as Magdalena had suffered, as I had suffered."

"Because I did suffer; I found out what was going on between her and the chauffeur in the worst and most ironic manner, given how I'd filmed her with various men, the better to control those men. It must have been about six months after that bad business when it happened. I was checking the security cameras in her apartment, because both our apartments were full of them, it would be madness to go without, in such a well-off area in such a city. Checking remotely, you understand; the wonders of modern technology, and I liked it, giving me control of things even at a distance. A *deus ex machina,* perhaps, the god in the machine sorting things out, but not necessarily for the best."

"Well, there seemed to be a problem with the cameras in Magdalena's apartment, going off and on intermittently, and I found out why; clearly she and Shine had been very careful for some time, switching the cameras off, but they'd gotten careless or I would never had found the footage of them together, in her bedroom, doing things which she'd only ever done there with me before. I'm sure you get the picture? Of course, as I did, over an hour of pictures, moving pictures of moving bodies; I won't go into the details."

He paused here, his eyes clouded over and looking back into that dark time; there was pain in his voice as he continued. "Her apartment, her bedroom, her bed, where I'd been with her so many times, but now it was her, but with someone else; Him. Shine. The chauffeur. I watched it, numb, and then the red rage rose slowly in me and took over; I was shaking with the intensity of it. Bitch. Cheating Bitch. Tramp. Whore. It was Eleni and the Turk all over again, and had it been real rather than film they would have been just as dead." Stephanidou's eyes narrowed at this point, but he restrained the urge to interrupt; Kadi had promised to tell, in his own time, and Stephanidou would just have to continue to play the waiting game, as Kadi was playing his own game.

"I went through so many emotions", Kadi continued; Rage, anger, jealousy, then shame, grief, heartbreak. Red mist competed with rain as the tears ran down my face; I realised that I was crying, uncontrollably, and I tried to get a hold of myself but it was no use. I remembered my father; Control, control, Kadi didn't work that time, and why would it? She broke my heart as only the death of my daughter had broken it before, but of course this was a different kind of heartbreak. My emotions competed, and rage won out; I stormed out, from my apartment to hers, to deal with her. Only a ten minute walk, and I still don't remember how I got there. I do remember being at the door to the block and thinking, What if he's there with her now? I wasn't afraid of him, he might be taller and heavier-set but I could handle myself easily and had done so in many situations over the years".

"I went to tap the numbers into the pad for access, and nothing; memory white-out. I rang for security to let me in, and the man came; Christophe, I knew him and he knew me, so opened the door obligingly. 'I'm sorry, Christophe, I've done this a thousand times but today, a total blank.' I shrugged and he smiled; 'No trouble, sir, happens to us all sometimes, we live and die by numbers these days, don't we?' We exchanged smiles, man to man, and I said, deliberately casual, 'By the way, has my chauffeur been looking for me here? I seem to be having one of those days and I appear to have lost him also'. 'No sir, I've not seen him and I've been on since nine this morning'."

"That recalled me to the fact that it was afternoon by now; I'd totally lost track of time. I thanked Christophe and took the lift, relieved; deal with her first, then I'd have time for the boyfriend. I remembered that he'd had a few of the women I'd had, over the years; the short-term, couple-of-monthers. I'd spend some time with them, take them to dinner and take them to bed, stay over with them, and then one day I'd glaze over in their company and know that they'd joined the host of similar women who'd come before and who would come after. So I'd take them to dinner and give them the speech, 'Darling, it's been wonderful but I

162

think we've gone as far as we can and it's not fair of me to keep you hanging on when someone else could be finding you just as wonderful … '. Something like that, and a handsome present, a piece of decent jewellery and a discreet envelope of currency, the kiss-off, and a call to Shine to take them home, wherever that might be."

"Well, they might cry directly in the back of the car, or look stunned, or wounded, or whatever, but he'd work out that I'd finished with them and turn on his oily charm to ease his own way into their panties. I didn't really care, I was done with them and if his rather obvious consolation made them feel better, why not? For one thing it would keep them from harassing me with wounded telephone calls, not that they could get through these days, I didn't need the grief and had efficient call-guard systems in place."

"But this wasn't one of those affairs; Magdalena was supposed to be the love of my life, and I of hers. My blood was seriously over-heated by the time the lift got to her floor; as it went steadily upwards I thought of *Othello;* 'Oh, that the slave had forty thousand lives!/One is too poor, too weak for my revenge'. That was for him; but first she must be dealt with; 'Arise, black vengeance, from the hollow hell!/Yield up, O love, thy crown and hearted throne/To tyrannous hate!'. And I did hate her, then."

"She was surprised to see me; was she expecting him? But in fact I rarely called on her at that time of day. I thought her wary, and with good reason; but she played along with my request that she undress, and let me fix on her a collar and chain as she knelt on the bed; a toy we had used sometimes, you're a man of the world, you understand. Well. she wasn't expecting what came after, as I played the footage of her with lover-boy and forced her to watch. I'd had to watch it already, but now took a masochistic delight in seeing it again alongside a sadistic one in her humiliation. She couldn't defend herself, the evidence was there before her, so she stayed silent when it finished after what seemed like an age. I didn't, though; I really let her have it, verbally; the things I said to her, called her, made what I'd said to Eleni pale into insignificance." The hairs on the back of Stephanidou's neck stood up at this, and a shock went through him, though he tried his best to hide it. What he'd said to Eleni; he had confronted her, then, at some time, but it hadn't come up in the initial investigation. Stephanidou was sure by now that Kadi had played some part in the death of Eleni Christou, possibly the whole of it. But the man had dropped so many hints, by design, as he'd now confessed, and Stephanidou would just have to wait for the details.

"She fought me, verbally", Kadi continued; "told me it was my fault, because of the prince, because of how I'd treated her, and she was right. I couldn't accept it, though, it was all too much and my mind was exploding; the red mist came down and the pain in my hand told me that it too had exploded, across her face. I'd hit her; I hadn't realised I'd done it, the first time, it was like the paper-knife and the iron bar again, I'd done it automatically. But then I did something I'd never done before, and thankfully never since; I hit her again, this time in full consciousness of what I was doing, and I'm not proud of it. Her face was already bloodied and bruised from the first blow, and now the collar around her neck cut into her and arrested her flight across the bed and she just lay there very still. Had I killed again?" (So he did then, Stephanidou thought with triumph; I knew it!).

"No": Kadi breathed a sigh, of relief it sounded like; he was back there and living it all again. "She was still alive, still breathing, and just barely conscious; I could feel her pulse when I removed the jewelled collar from her neck and replaced it with the 'H' pendant, which she'd removed earlier to facilitate the collar. I didn't want to touch her, the feel of her flesh made mine creep, but I couldn't avoid it and I was glad to know that she was still alive. Not for her,

I'm ashamed to say, but for me; I've never killed a woman and I didn't intend to start then". Stephanidou felt somewhat deflated at this; so he hadn't killed Eleni then? Patience, Stephano, he told himself, give him time and all will become clear.

"It was as though I was in a trance then, Kadi continued. I opened the wardrobe which contained all the clothes I'd given her over the years, which had adorned her beauty. Now I ripped them apart, savagely, with my bare hands, and threw them on the bed beside her. I opened the wall safe, the repository of all the jewels I'd gifted her with, none of them as bright as her eyes, as lustrous as her hair, as shining as her skin, I'd thought when she'd put them on. Now I stuffed them into my pockets in handfuls; let her and lover-boy live on love, I thought vindictively. I remember looking at her now-unconscious form one last time, before I took out my phone and actually called Shine."

"I sounded so matter-of-fact when I requested him to come to the apartment to meet me, and equally so when he arrived. I confronted him, and he didn't attempt to fight, or to deny it. It was as though he knew they'd have to get caught at some point, and accepted that this was it. I dismissed him, and gave him the Bentley as severance pay; far too much, but I didn't want it. He'd been with her inside it, in the back, where I sat, and how could I do so ever again now that I knew this? I told him, in the crudest possible terms, to take it and her and get out; then I turned and left him standing there."

"I don't remember leaving the apartment block; I do remember somehow getting myself to one of the waterside cafés down the street from it. I don't know how I didn't get mugged; I must have looked terrible, there was blood on my knuckles and thousands of pounds worth of jewellery in my pockets; but the waiter refrained from comment and brought me whisky, which I drained in one gulp and asked for another. Then I just sat, staring into the road outside and sipping the whisky. I couldn't see the Bentley parked in the road anywhere nearby, because it would be in the underground car park; but *he* (I couldn't bring myself to even think his name at this point) would have to turn up the road in this direction to leave, so I'd see him go past."

"I did; but I couldn't tell whether or not she was with him. Was she? Or had he left her, deserted her when she needed help, taken the car which I'd given him and abandoned her to whatever fate had in store for her? Or was she lying down on the back seat? The latter, I hoped, given the state I'd left her in. I wasn't proud of having hit her, I'd never hit a woman in my life before then" (Not even Eleni? wondered Stephanidou). "My terrible temper, you see; all my life I'd tried to control it, as I controlled everything else around me, but I just couldn't master it. It had mastered me then, and I have no excuse; except that she was the love of my life and I was heart-broken at her infidelity. So it was most likely that she was in the car, but what if she wasn't? What if she were still lying, broken and bloodied, where I'd left her on the bed? I couldn't stay away, I had to go back, but I dreaded doing so."

"I paid for my whisky, over-paid probably, but what did I care about money? The receptionist, Christophe's relief I suppose, kept his face impassive as I entered the lobby, called the lift for me very respectfully, and most likely had a good time speculating with the other staff over the happenings in the penthouse that day, the owner coming in and out looking dazed, with blood on his knuckles, and potentially the mistress being carried out by the chauffeur, bloodied and beaten. Well, it wouldn't take them long to work that one out, and then they'd have a good laugh, at my expense. I didn't really care what they thought, even the laughter, I'd conquered that one, but I did care about *her,* even now, even after what had happened."

"I let myself into the apartment, and just stood in the lobby, listening. So quiet it was; I forced myself to go through the place, to the bedroom. The ripped clothes were there, in a pile, and the bloodied sheets, but their former occupant was gone. As was the duvet, I registered; he must have wrapped her in it, and while I was insanely jealous of him with her in his arms I was also glad that he hadn't abandoned her, and was taking care of her. Relieved, I sat down on the edge of the bed, and then started shaking, trembling, I couldn't stop myself; my life, I felt, was over."

He stopped speaking at this point, overcome with emotion in remembrance of the time, trembling and shaking with emotion as he must have done back then. Despite himself and his own agenda, Stephanidou felt pity in the extreme for him. To give his host some dignity, and time to recover himself, the Lieutenant took himself to the well, filling the rose cup and taking it back, offering it to Kadi. For once his host did not refuse, although he did not drink more than a small sip, with which he moistened his mouth and then spat out onto the ground, delicately turning his face away from Stephanidou to do so. The rest he poured into the cupped palm of his free hand and splashed it over his face and hair, gasping at the coldness of it. Stephanidou took the cup and returned to the well, refreshing himself also and returning to find Kadi looking more calm; the old man didn't meet his guest's eyes but, in control of himself again now, waited until the Lieutenant had reseated himself and then continued in a quiet voice:

"I don't know how long I sat there, but eventually I realised that I had to do something, although I didn't know what. So I phoned Imelda; my loyal PA, who made so many decisions for me, who knew the business so well and saved me the trouble of a thousand small things that all put together made up a very large chunk of potential trouble if not attended to. Imelda would know what to do, because I didn't. She and I had a history, and I hadn't been totally honest with little Magdalena about that. Once, when she was trying to find out if I'd got any other women, I'd told her that there was nothing between Imelda and myself, which was true at the time, but historically not so. We'd had a thing years ago, when her bastard of a husband buggered off back to Bergen, or wherever it was he came from. She'd been much younger then, with two young children to provide for all by herself, in the total absence of any maintenance from him."

"I didn't know all this initially, of course, just that she'd come to work for me as a temp when my PA of the time was on maternity leave. I'd been impressed by her efficiency and initiative and so, when Patricia elected to stay at home with her new baby, I asked Imelda to stay on, and she'd jumped at the chance. I paid well, far better than what she was getting as a temp, but even so she found it a struggle to make ends meet; which is why one day when I returned to the office unexpectedly early I found her crying her eyes out over the desk."

"I was shocked, it was so atypical of her, usually so calm and controlled and co-ordinated. She tried to talk the whole thing down, she was a bit under the weather, her time of the month, the children were playing her up; but I could tell there was more. So I insisted we finish work there and then and took her for an early dinner. She warmed up and opened up after a few glasses of wine, and I got the whole story. Well, she was valuable to me, so I increased her salary, but in such a way that she paid no tax on the increase; I was trying to help her and her family, not the bloody Inland Revenue. She was so grateful, and I liked her; she was an honest person, working hard and trying to do her best for her family. She reminded me, in a womanly way, of the kind of person I'd wanted to be, had circumstances not got in the way."

"At some point we found ourselves in bed together, and it was good for a time. The children got used to Uncle Edward and I liked seeing them, being around the house with them and playing with them. It felt like the normal, married-with-two-children relationship which I'd wanted when I was young, and I even considered asking Imelda to make it permanent. I didn't, however; it wouldn't have been fair to her. I wasn't in love with her, the way I'd been with Eleni and Aphrodite, not with the white-hot passion I'd felt for them; it was a cosier, friendlier, everyday relationship, and for many people that might be enough, but not for me. I didn't expect to meet anyone else for whom I'd feel as I had for Eleni and Aphrodite, but you never knew with these things, and as it happened I met Magdalena, the love of my life."

"But if I'd married Imelda and then met someone else whilst with her? Divorce, and losing not only someone very dear to me but also my business partner, because that was what she felt like. So we kept things as they were, and the sexual relationship ended eventually, by mutual consent; we remained close though, working together as always and with a relationship as good as it had ever been. Imelda was one of those special people who could accept when the dynamic of a relationship has changed; she was totally loyal and I'd trust her with my life."

"So, not knowing what to do next, I phoned her; 'Please come and collect me, Imelda, from Bankside; park downstairs and come up, would you?' She made no demur and arrived soon afterwards, while I was still sitting on the bed feeling lost and staring at my feet without seeing them. I heard her come in and walk through the place looking for me, when I failed to respond to her tentative enquiry as she entered. 'Edward?' I felt rather than saw her as she reached the bedroom door; she stopped, and I knew without looking that she was taking it all in, the heap of torn clothes and bloodied bedclothes, the picture torn off the wall to show the empty safe door hanging open. 'Oh Edward … '; she didn't say, 'What have you done?' but it was hanging in the air between us. Others might have thought that the place had been burgled, but Imelda knew me and knew that this mess was of my making."

"I found it difficult to speak, but when I could manage it all I said was, 'I think I need to go home; would you take me, please?' That became her immediate focus and she swung into action, helping me out of there with her arm around my shoulders, down to her car in the basement to drive me the short distance to my own apartment. I felt like a sleepwalker, although I noticed that she made sure the door was locked securely behind us. She must have felt my pockets bulging with jewellery as she helped me into the lift and down and out to the car, but she said nothing, just belted me into the passenger seat and drove for the few minutes it took to get to Thameside."

"When she got me back into my place she ran me a hot bath, zombie that I was, undressed me and bathed me as though I were one of her children; and I, obedient as one, allowed her to do so. She dried me off like one too, and helped me put on underwear and dressing gown; then she prepared for me hot soup and bread, and stood over me while I gulped it down mechanically. Then she made me take a sleeping tablet, and put me to bed; she sat with her arms around me, holding me close as my living trance finally broke and I cried like a baby over my broken love. When the storm of tears had abated she put on a pair of silk pyjamas which she found in a drawer, got into bed with me, and held me like her child, soothing me until I slept. She was still there when I awoke, watching over me while I slept, which I must have done for about fifteen or sixteen hours, as I calculate, because it had been mid-afternoon when she came to me and now it was morning, seven or eight o' clock, I thought."

"I won't go into the details of my life at that time; it was no life. Before Magdalena, I'd lived for work, the business, the joy of controlling it all, the other people involved, and succeeding where they failed. Now, since I'd had this great love, it wasn't enough any more, and I lost interest. I went through the motions, bolstered by Imelda and my brother James, but it wasn't the same. When someone had to be sweetened, or rewarded, or coerced, there were other women I could use for the purpose, but it always reminded me of my lost little girl and how I'd abused her love with my infernal tests of it. I'd thought that I'd lost her when Shine consoled her over the prince, but in truth I'd lost her long before, the first time I gave her to another."

"Whenever that had happened, however, nothing went well after she'd gone. It took a few years, but gradually the rot set in. I was losing control, deals went bad, the whole edifice was beginning to crumble, despite the valiant efforts of James and Imelda to plaster over the cracks. And then, of course, the police got involved; I hadn't had my finger on the pulse, and they got the thin end of their wedge into one of the cracks, applied pressure, and hit me with accusations of corruption, bribery, fraud and blackmail. The competition smelled blood and the insects began coming out from the woodwork, and then it was downhill all the way. I fought, but I was finished."

"My solicitors did their best, but the outlook wasn't good; the tax authorities had been sniffing around for some time, and there was plenty of ammunition for them to use against me. It looked as though I couldn't avoid a custodial sentence, but my people were working to make that as short as possible; and then some total bastard came on line with a blackmail accusation. There was footage of him with Magdalena, which he claimed I was using to blackmail him. Well, of course I was, why else would I have recorded the bloody thing? The fact was though that his wife had left him by now, and he was estranged from his children, so he didn't care what was disclosed about him because he'd little left to lose; so the problem for me was that the authorities could use this film to get me an even longer prison sentence."

"It was getting worse and worse, and then I was

informed that they'd got hold of Magdalena and were pressuring her to be a witness for the prosecution. She was on a drugs charge, apparently, and they were offering her a deal if she would testify against me; which she'd agreed to do. I'd lost track of her after she'd gone, I'd tried to put her out of my mind for the sake of my sanity, but I'd seen her in the last six months. Our encounter hadn't been a good one; I'd been approached by an associate to finance a project of his, a pornographic film, of all things. I wasn't keen, but I did owe him a favour, and I was always scrupulous about paying my debts, so I agreed. Well, he invited me to visit the set, as they laughingly called the store-room where they were filming the thing, and I wasn't keen; but he was so grateful for my help, pathetically so, and I realised that I had been his last option and he'd now owe me another favour. So I went, really just to emphasise that he was in my debt in every sense; what I hadn't banked on was that Magdalena would be there."

"They'd started when I arrived, and it was a jolt to see her there. It turned out that her current boyfriend was playing a starring role, and it sickened me to see her there, watching him doing such intimate things publicly, and with another woman. I watched her covertly; I couldn't see her too well because the room was darkened to some extent, but I thought she looked older, coarser than when she'd been with me. I hid my feelings though, I'd become very good at that, in public anyway; but while I looked on impassively my head was racing. Merton, the man who was making the thing and who had been so grateful to me, hadn't told me that she would be there. Either he thought that I might withdraw my money if I knew she was part of it, or he was trying to discomfort me. Either way, he'd tried to conceal the truth from me, and I'd make him pay, in the fullness of time."

"Fortunately I'd taken a girl with me, so I didn't look like Magdalena's grieving ex-partner, more like someone who was indifferent to her by now and more interested in younger and more novel women. The girl was nothing to me, in fact; she was blonde, and glamorous, a trophy date I'd adorned with some of Magdalena's old jewellery and paid to accompany me. She'd sleep with me later, if I wanted it, and seeing Magdalena again I did want it; to blot out her memory and revenge myself, if that makes sense. It wouldn't be an issue for the girl, she was in the business and used to all sorts; as apparently was Magdalena."

"I was asked by Merton if I wanted to go and talk to her when they finished, but I declined. There was obviously some foolhardy malice towards me in him, I decided then, but I would let my anger cool and serve up my revenge cold, at a later date. Magdalena clearly hadn't known that I was there, and barely registered me as I gave her the once-over with my eyes in passing her on my way out. She didn't look well, and was clearly off her head on something, cocaine probably; I could tell from her unfocused eyes and dilated pupils. I felt guilty then, because it was I who had got her onto the stuff in the first place, to ease her encounters with the men who she assisted me to sweeten, or bribe, or blackmail. I hardened my heart towards her, though, and thought poisonous things about her, not wanting to accept my guilt; but she was in my head with a vengeance and I gave in to the temptation to find out everything that had happened to her since our acrimonious parting."

It didn't make good reading. Shine was dead, apparently, killed in a road traffic accident. No-one had informed me, however, no doubt because our acrimonious parting was common knowledge. I'd put the word around to block his attempts to start a private chauffeur business which he'd proposed to start, with the Bentley I'd given him, can you believe that? I'd wanted to be rid of it, but I wasn't having him prospering with it; let him sell it and do what he could on the proceeds. Before his death, however, it appeared that he'd abused Magdalena, which I cannot deny I had done also, but he was far worse. He kept her living with him for some time, in a cheap flat over a shop close to where I'd lived when first in the country, but then put her on the game in the fullest sense, pimp that he was. After his death, and good riddance to him, she'd moved in with one of her regulars, and from there she'd gone on to work as an escort with an agency owned by an old business acquaintance of mine, Danny Martini. After some time doing that she'd met and moved in with the star of the porn shoot, a black Londoner whose entire household of hangers-on had been arrested in a dawn raid and were now all up on drug charges. Which, of course, was how she was about to re-enter my life again, as a witness against me. More importantly, though, it appeared that she'd given birth to a child well within a year of my having discarded her; but more of that later."

"So I was put on trial, and Magdalena came to give evidence against me. I saw her as she came in; I said she'd clearly been on drugs on the porn set, but at least now she wasn't, because it would have been madness to come into court that state. Her clothes were cheap and tarty-looking; the prosecution hadn't done a very good job of making her look like a respectable witness. I noticed she had the 'H' pendant around her neck; a message to me, I thought. 'Look Teddy (her name for me), you made me wear this to proclaim me a Harlot and a whore, and now I'm officially one, so don't be surprised that I've sold myself, to the other side, against you'. Reason told me that of course she would, I'd hurt her deeply and why wouldn't she take her revenge on me? I would have, had our roles been reversed, I thought. I was beyond reason, however; Traitorous bitch, tart, whore, all those things and more I aimed against her in my mind, and vowed that I wouldn't forget what she was doing."

"But what she was doing in actuality was not what I'd

expected, as became gradually clear, and I was as delighted as it was possible to be in the circumstances. It was unbelievable, such nerve she had. She'd got herself into the court by telling them she'd testify against me, and then she went hostile and blew their blackmail charge out of the water. She said that Shine had got hold of the security camera footage of her willingly going with other men for the pleasure of it, and that she'd seen it in his possession; so the blackmailer was either Shine, or whoever had got hold of the film after his death. She screwed the prosecution, as I said to my counsel when she'd been taken down for contempt of court. He grinned at me, I remember, as he noted, 'Well, I guess that's what she does for a living'. I shot him a look and he shut up, fast; just because he was defending me didn't mean that he couldn't make an enemy of me, which would have been a very bad idea, even if I was going inside for a stretch. Which I was, only not for as long as the prosecution hoped, courtesy of little Magdalena, all grown up now and helping me, at some cost to herself."

"I won't bore you with the details of my life behind bars", he continued wearily, "except to say that I had an easier ride than most. I might no longer have had the clout which I'd had on the outside, but on the inside I was top of the pile. I'd always looked after the little people, you see, the ones who did the dirty work, legal or illegal, and a good proportion of those who did the latter were now my co-residents, and they remembered. So now that we were all together in misfortune, so to speak, they showed their gratitude with a pleasing deference and looked after me in their turn. As concerns the prison staff, those who did the difficult work that the rest of society would rather not, and got precious little thanks for it, well, there were those among them who were always ready to make up the deficit in their wage-packet if I needed something, and I paid handsomely. So much so that the word went around, and those who had kept to the straight and narrow initially

175

finally came around to the way of thinking of their less-scrupulous colleagues, and I was surrounded by a coterie of guards making sure that I had every comfort that it was possible to provide for me; and it was via this means that I had my final meeting with Magdalena."

"I'd made an offer, when both she and I were incarcerated, to supply her with drugs, given that she clearly had some dependence upon them; however, I wasn't surprised when she declined, politely. She'd apparently decided to get off them, although as a known user she would have been subject to regular drug tests, which would have made continued usage hazardous and spoiled any chance of her getting an early release for good behaviour. She did get the early release though, but not as either of us would have wanted."

"Before that, though, she asked of me a boon; instead of the supply of drugs which I'd offered, she wanted me to put care measures in place for her young child. A daughter, of whom I'd heard when I enquired into her doings after we'd parted, and seemingly the offspring of my brother James, Magdalena thought. Shine it seemed had told her some story of his having had a vasectomy some years ago, which I doubted but was able to verify through contacts in the medical service. Therefore, as she'd never become pregnant in all the time she was with me, and as her pregnancy now showed her to be capable, she'd naturally assumed that the fault, if it could be called that, lay with me. I knew differently, however, given my painfully short time as father to my little Bibi; so there was at least some chance that Magdalena's child was also mine. But it wouldn't have mattered if her father had been someone else completely. I remembered how Aphrodite had been far from my ideal of a mother for my child, but I still loved the daughter she gave me, and the same stood for Magdalena's feelings for her daughter, no matter how the child had come to her."

"So I understood her anxiety on behalf of her child,

given how I'd suffered when my own was so cruelly taken from me; so, for the sake of little Bibi I now undertook to make little Katie as financially and emotionally secure as was possible whilst her mother was in prison. Even if James was her father, he was my brother and I would happily look after her for the love I owed to him, not to mention my debt of gratitude for his support and assistance down the years. He too was incarcerated at this time, on account of such of that support as Her Majesty's Constabulary and Inland Revenue took exception too, and I'd extended my influence to see that he didn't do his time too severely. But he was still far less fortunately-placed than I to see to the child, so I took it upon myself to have her cared for."

Kadi stopped and looked blank here, the his face began working, struggling for control before he mastered his emotion and continued. "I thought I'd got everything covered, but the gods hadn't finished with me yet. It came to my ears after some time that she was suffering from terminal cancer, and was to be given a compassionate discharge for the last few months of her life. I thought I'd go mad when I heard this; the ending of our relationship, the way it had ended, none of that mattered any more. I made it clear that I didn't want to be disturbed, and just sat in my cell for a whole day and a night, thinking back over all she'd been to me, and I to her. I wanted to see her, but it didn't seem possible. That was unbearable, so I called in a whole heap of favours, and paid out an extortionate amount of money, and via those means I saw her again, for the last time."

"They did it one night", Kadi said faintly; the cumulative strain of retelling and mentally reliving his life was telling on him now. Stephanidou offered the rose cup, but the old man shook his head and waved it away, even though his throat was clearly dry and his voice rasping as he continued. "She was so close to death, and it was a wonder that she hadn't died before our meeting; it must have been very painful for her, physically, but she didn't falter, and then for one short hour I had my Baby in my arms again, and nothing she'd done mattered to me any more; Shine and the other men … ."He sighed, but then his eyes flashed suddenly and his voice rose, strong again:

"I don't give a damn about the others!" He was agitated now; "I tell you, if she was here now I'd have her down the hill to the priest and marry her before her feet could touch the ground". Then he grew quieter. "But she can't come to me, that's beyond my control and I have to accept it." He paused, for what seemed like an age, and then looked up at Stephanidou. "But I can go to her; and you're wondering why I haven't gone already? Yes, it would be so easy like that, it could have been so easy; I might have done it when I was inside had I wanted, nothing simpler. There were weapons to be had, but I never liked mess, someone with my obsessive-compulsiveness, you understand, so there were always drugs. I smuggled a woman in very easily, drugs for an overdose would be child's play."

He looked again at the Lieutenant, who was looking back at him searchingly. "I last saw her in prison, you understand. She was dying, there was a system in place but our relationship fell outside the authorised bounds of it. That's the main problem with authorised systems, they have boundaries which exclude so many things, relationships not sanctioned by the Church or State being one of these, and what to do then? Either accept and be frustrated, or decline and do it your own way, and I've tended to do the latter since I found that acceptance and honesty never got me anywhere. But I digress; we'd never been married, and never even lived together really, my having kept her in a separate apartment and visited her most nights and weekends. Even this long-term relationship, however, was over some years before her death, and she'd lived with other men since, so letting me out to see her for the last time, chained and under guard, was a no-no. But I had to see her, so she had to come to me, and it was arranged; there's always a guard, someone in authority ready to take a bung, but I don't have to tell you about that, do I?" Stephanidou nodded bitterly in assent, No, he didn't need any education on that score.

But Kadi had continued, quietly and almost to himself now. "They got her there and back in a van, a laundry service bringing fresh items and removing soiled ones. She was so weak, poor little mite, they had practically to carry her in, the guard and the woman who came with her. Her old cell mate it was, apparently, and she took a risk, but said that she did it for love of Magdalena. Well, I understood that, no-one better, and I could have loved the woman for that, but I made sure she didn't go without afterwards. But my Magdalena got there with assistance, and I didn't care that she looked so ill, I almost welcomed it. Her hair was gone, and with it her resemblance to Eleni; her sensuality had gone, and with it her resemblance to Aphrodite. Because we made love briefly, if you could call it that, as much as she could in her condition, you understand, for she was past such pleasures. It was something we had to do again, though, a reclaiming of each other, becoming one flesh, man and wife, as it were, as much as we could. Her innocence had gone too, although that was my fault and I take full responsibility; so her likeness to my little Bibi had gone too. All three gone, and their ghosts laid at last, and what remained was pure Magdalena; worn-out and tired now from too much experience of the wrong kind, but so humble and apologetic. She was made of love, loving and loved, because I loved her too, but I made such a mess of it. I'd made her my sexual toy, as Torvald had of Nora in *A Doll's House,* if you know Ibsen's work, although he'd married her and given her three children. And we had no children for her to controversially leave behind, but I'd let her go and now I was the one who wanted to tear himself in little pieces."

The tears were running down his face now, and he put his head down and cried, his chest heaving with the effort of trying to restrain the force which pushed great gasps from his mouth as the tears fell from his eyes. Stephanidou remembered how he too had wept in this same place on the day when they had met, and he felt a pain in his chest, sorrow for these lives which had gone so tragically wrong. He waited patiently and in pity for the storm of weeping to be over, looking away up towards the sky over the hilltop to give the old man some dignity. When the gasps subsided and Kadi had regained control, he looked up into the far distance and spoke again, more calmly now.

"It would have been easy to end it when I first returned here and go to her, or even without returning, but that's not what I did. She gave me seven years of my life back when she testified for me, plus another two-and-a-half months of her life, because she harmed herself then and they put her away for that extra time for contempt of court. So I owe her that time and I can't go to her until my debt is paid. I could have passed some of it in prison, but that would have been too easy; three meals a day, a bed, clothing, showers and a solid roof over my head? Too much luxury which I don't deserve. They're outraged that I left, they think I evaded justice; do you?"

His voice was rising again and he stood, albeit with difficulty and an obvious gathering his remaining strength to do so. He indicated his emaciated body with his arms and then flung them wide to encompass the dereliction amongst which he lived. "I'm not exactly living it up on the Costa del Crime, am I? I chose to come back here, to come home and do it like this, meting out to myself the justice which I believe I deserve. I live like the Magdalen in the wilderness, but with no angels to feed me with celestial food. I eke out my existence, eating and drinking enough to keep me going, but only just, and I decrease the amount a little at regular periods. I live amongst these stones most of the time. I lived inside my old family house in the village when I first came back here, very simply, but still it was too comfortable for me. So now I only go there when the weather is bad, in the winter, but only because I might otherwise die too soon, before the appointed day has arrived."

"Do you think I want to live like this?" He struck the bedstead in frustration. "I wear these rags, I bathe in the sea and I wash with water from the well to keep away disease and stay alive. When I think of my Italian tailoring, the best that Milan had to offer; my penthouse apartment, sumptuously furnished; the restaurants I frequented, food and wine of the very best; I hate the way I live now, I tell you! But I hated the other way too, latterly, because there was no-one to share it with, no-one I cared for. I lay on this filthy, mouldering mattress and I want my comfortable bed, my silken sheets and my eiderdown pillows, with my beautiful Magdalena in my arms! But were she in them again, even here", and he struck the bedstead again, "I tell you it would be the only bed in this world in which I'd want to be!"

His eyes flashed fire and he was shouting now, declaiming wildly, and his voice echoed around the basin of the village below flanked by the cliffs on either side above. Stephanidou felt fear then, as well as pity for this flawed and tormented wreck of a man, who had done such fearful things despite trying to live a good life and whose mind was nearly gone. He felt similarly for the girl, this Magdalena whom he'd never met, but who had apparently and innocently paid the price for her predecessors. He knew he was witnessing tragedy, in this ruined natural amphitheatre on a hillside on the edge of the Greek world.

But Kadi had subsided now, onto the bed he so despised, and continued in a quieter voice which Stephanidou had to crane forward to hear. "But I can never have her here again; never, never, never, never, never." Then he was quiet, exhausted from his effort, spent, played-out and controlled again. "I'm doing this because I owe it to her, I'm counting the days and I know exactly when my self-imposed sentence is to end. Then, and only then, will I pass over and find her, and peace with her, I hope." He rose, and there was calmness in his manner again, and something else which Stephanidou couldn't quite identify; a knowingness, he would have called it, although he would have found it hard to explain exactly what he meant by that.

"They let me out in half the time", Kadi continued steadily, "for good behaviour. The paid-off prison staff would have lied through their teeth for me anyway, but I behaved so well for the rest of my time inside that they didn't have to. My brother collected me on the day of my release, with a plan of action and a story ready for the authorities of my having gone off to stay with some old girlfriend for a few days. I did everything that he'd put in his story for when they came calling, because they would come calling when I failed to show for my parole officer. James took me back to his place, where I had a long bath and a clean shave, the first time I'd been beardless in many years. I then ate, drank and caught up with James and his doings before I put on the clothes he had ready for me; casual things, jeans and boots and thick shirt over T-shirt, pull-on wool hat and three-in-one jacket so that I could remove the fleece layer when it got warm. Then I made a phone call, which was expected by means of James's good offices, and we said our goodbyes and hugged while we waited. It would be a few years before we saw each other again, because they'd certainly be watching him and he couldn't risk leading them to me. Then I received a text and James closed the door behind me with a last embrace before I made my way down to the car parked over the road in the rapidly-falling dark of evening."

"Imelda; the only untruth in James's story, because we weren't going to spend a few days together at all. She had been totally loyal whilst we'd been inside, because James had gone down too, insider trading for me, you know? Anyway, Imelda had done whatever was needed for us both, and I'd taken steps to see that she would never be in want again. Now she was performing her last task for me; I hadn't told her that I was leaving, and that we'd never meet again, and she was too wise to ask. When the police questioned her later she'd be able to tell them truthfully that I'd requested a lift into Kent but hadn't told her where I was going. Ostensibly visiting her sister in Hythe, she pulled into the car park of the motorway services near there to drop me off; the lorry was there, waiting as pre-arranged. We'd spoken on the way, but now she embraced me and kissed me, and I her; 'Thank you, Edward, goodbye and good luck'. I wished her the same to her; 'Have a good life, Imelda, thank you for everything'. There were tears in her eyes, and in mine, I felt, so I went as quickly as possible and didn't look back; I'd do that later, when I was as safe as I could be.

The old man stopped speaking here, but declined to avail himself of the cup of water which Stephanidou offered. "I'm afraid you'll have to excuse me for today; that's all I'm able to manage." He looked exhausted, no mocking smiles or tantalising phrases in evidence now, just a man who'd given every bit of energy to his story and was in need of rest. "Do come early tomorrow, he managed, there's still much to tell and you need to hear it all, if it is to be of any help to you." Stephanidou realised now that the afternoon was drawing in, the sun very close to the horizon; it had been a long day and had clearly taken a toll on the storyteller. He didn't like leaving him like this and said so; but Kadi waved a hand dismissively. "The bed's in the shade and it's getting cooler now, I'll be fine when I've slept for a while." So, having done as requested, Stephanidou returned to the station-house; he felt that he'd returned after a very long time away from the simplicity of the village.

He was feeling pretty tired himself, but wanted to go through the tape of the day to pick out the clues, or hints, which Kadi had thrown out deliberately; he wasn't sure that he needed to do this now, as the old man had promised to explain all, but any report which he filed needed to be exact, he told himself, so no detail ought to be omitted. The machine needed charging however and, although he could have plugged it into the mains and used it that way, Stephanidou took the need for charging as an excuse to give himself a break. So he plugged it in, then took a shower and his dinner from Sofia before returning and looking at it; but he was so tired by now that he lay on the bed and drifted into a deep sleep until the early hours of the morning. Then, still lying on the bed, he played the thing back at a low volume and noted down those things of interest which Kadi's voice re-told him, to add to his list;

> Iron bar/Psychologically-violent to Eleni/I'd never hit a woman in my life before/
> Had I killed again?/It made what I'd said to Eleni pale into insignificance/
> It was Eleni and the Turk all over again, and had it been real rather than film they would have been just as dead.

Stephanidou thought about Kadi then, with a mixture of emotions; disgust, mainly, for the way he'd treated Magdalena, the love of his life, he'd claimed. Yet had shared her with his brother and given to any number of impotent men for their perverted pleasure. What kind of a man did that? One whose life has gone so wrong that he's become warped and twisted and beyond decent behaviour, perhaps? Because Stephanidou also remembered the things he'd been told by Father Lambros about the young Kadi, the decent man who only wanted to live an honest life working and raising a family; and he liked the vestiges of that young man which were still apparent in the old man he'd become.

Pity he felt too, for how the one could have turned into the other; and fear also, for what was still to be disclosed; although he was impatient to know these as yet untold things, to satisfy the policeman's need to solve a case, potentially. Still musing the complexities of the man living as a hermit (the reasons for which were still part of his untold story), Stephanidou fell asleep once more.

19: GOOD FRIDAY: APOCALYPSE

The following morning was Good Friday, and Stephanidou was showered and up the hill to the ruined house and ruined man before the sun had moved too far above the horizon. He'd made his own coffee, and eaten cold food which a disapproving Sofia had supplied at his request the previous evening, because he wanted as much time as possible for the day's disclosures, from which he expected much. Kadi, sitting up on his bed this morning, although looking tired, was nevertheless refreshed to some extent by sleep and welcomed his guest without wasting too much time before he spoke quietly.

"So here I am, returned to my roots and telling everything to you, hopefully for your benefit." He looked at Stephanidou steadily, and the Lieutenant returned his gaze, although he was the first to break eye contact. "There is an unspoken question which I can read in your eyes", Kadi told him, "and I think you ought to ask me before I answer you". Stephanidou looked up, hesitantly, and then said what he'd been itching to say for so long. "I believe that you had something, a great deal, to do with the death of Eleni Christou and the disappearance of Nikos Osman Nikolaides. I can't for the life of me work out quite how, but I'm convinced that I'm correct, am I not? Because you've been dropping hints all through your story to that effect, controlling how much information you provide me with. So I would be grateful if you would finish it for me now."

Kadi smiled thinly. "It has been entertaining, hasn't it? Possibly more for me than for you, because I have all the answers; and now that you've asked, I'll answer. Yes, I killed Osman, for he is dead also, but not in the way that you think and not for the reasons you think either. I suppose I killed her too, though not directly; I didn't push her over the cliff. I didn't intend for either of them to die, it was purely circumstantial." He sighed, looking back through time; "Well, you've waited all this time, so now you should hear the conclusion; or the beginning, as it was, from my point of view". He settled back on his mattress now, and Stephanidou moved to sit on the ground facing him; his back was aching already from trying to keep his balance on the broken chair, but he was going nowhere as Kadi commenced the final chapter of his story.

"I couldn't believe how lucky I was; I felt like the luckiest man on the island, and the happiest. It wasn't exactly an arranged marriage, although that was sometimes the case back then, but our respective parents approved; if either of them had not then it would not have happened. Equally, there was no coercion; the young man and woman had the right to refuse, but there was no refusal in our case. We had known each other since childhood, and I'd always known that she was the one for me. She was so unusual in appearance, strikingly different from the norm in this part of the world where dark hair and eyes are most usual. But men of many different races had passed through these islands over the centuries, for bad as well as for good and from the North as well as the South, and it was obvious that someone from the former region had left behind his genetic inheritance in her white-blonde hair and blue eyes. A recessive gene it was called, as I learned later when educating myself in England, showing itself only occasionally through the years. Something special, I had called it when young, making my wife-to-be a prize that many young men desired but that I had won."

He was speaking completely in Greek now, with a look in his eyes that Stephanidou hadn't seen there before; he was back in the past, in the throes of young love, first love, which his guest recognised with a pang as Kadi continued. "She was a good catch for a fisherman, as so many of the men of our village told me, with their hackneyed attempts at humour; but I agreed with them. We were poor, but respectable and respected in the community. My father and his forefathers for centuries, it seems, had lived off of the sea, and I had no issue with continuing the tradition. I was happy with the life which seemed to pan out before me with work, wife, and hopefully children at some point. A simple and traditional life, and I wanted no more. Happy is the man who doesn't want too much, for he won't be disappointed; I didn't know who had said that, but I believed it then and was content in my belief."

"Even the fact that Eleni had chosen me seemed meant to be, when I considered the matter. I'd thought myself lucky, but was she after all my just reward for not asking too much of life? I'd never wanted any other girl and never attempted any improper behaviour even with Eleni, being happy to wait for our marriage and not nervous of what that entailed, physically. I endured all the usual ribbing from my peers, but I was confident that I could make her a good husband. I'd done my National Service on the mainland, along with other young men of my age, and I knew of their night-time visits to back-street establishments not mentioned to their families when they returned home. I'd never made such visits myself, although I didn't condemn those who did. Each to his own needs, and if this rendered the young men in question more confident of their abilities with their future wives, then so be it. I preferred to wait for marriage, however; I expected my bride to be pure for me, and I felt it correct for me to do the same for her. It was in my nature to like things well-ordered, organised and tidy, and this applied to my marriage also."

"I knew what the sexual act looked like. Living in a rural community I'd seen the beasts of the fields, the ram with the ewes, the stallions with the mares and so forth. But something else also; I remember being ten years old, no more, and Lambros, the bad boy, coming to me. Everyone used to say, If you want trouble, find Lambros; but he found me, that day, after school, on the way home. 'Want to see something really good?' 'Like what?' I was interested, he usually came up with the goods, delivered what he promised, and I couldn't help my curiosity. He just winked at me, waved his arm in the direction of the beach; 'Come and see'."

"I went, intrigued. Much of our coastline is made up of cliffs; the few beaches which we have are located at points where these break up and give way to gravel tracks, leading down to small, pebbled areas, called beaches for technical reasons because they sit between the land and the sea. Such a one is our local beach, you've been there, it's accessed via a very slight slope which makes it more accessible than those reached by steeper tracks. However it is bordered on both sides by cliffs, and more cliffs. The upshot being that there aren't many beaches on our island, and those we have aren't of the best, too little sand and too many pebbles."

"You know this, by now, of course"; Kadi remembered his audience and came back into the present momentarily, before going back to his youth. "They made good places to play, though, and to swim from, easily, for the children of the island. There weren't many tourists either, not back then, the industry being in its infancy and our island being off the beaten track with the aforementioned dearth of beaches. But there were some, and this couple had found their way here; American, Australian, or British? I didn't know, but they stood out, obviously, plus the girl had deep red hair of an unusual shade, seen here even less than Eleni's blondness; although now I suspect that it was dyed, it was so red. They'd rented a room with Chrysoulla, who had space now that her daughters were married, and spent the few days they'd been here in exploring the land or swimming off the beach, with the bushes at the back of it to

189

which now Lambros ushered me, his finger to his lips to warn me to keep quiet."

"The couple were out swimming when we arrived, playing around and splashing each other for quite some time." I dug Lambros in the ribs; 'Is this all you brought me here to see?' But he shushed me as quietly as he could; 'Wait and see'. Sure enough, not too long afterwards they headed back to the shore and, as they came out of the water, I realised that they were completely naked. I'd seen a naked man before, with my father and brother in our small house it wasn't difficult, but the woman; my mother's privacy at home was strictly respected, so I'd never seen one undressed, like this. Years later, confronted with Botticelli's *Birth of Venus* in the Uffizi, I remembered this woman, unknown and yet so known, from her exit from the waves and what happened thereafter. Because, as they lay on their scant towels, and dried their unclothed selves in the sun, they began to play in a different way. Touching, and stroking, fondling, hugging, then kissing and more intimate things yet, laughing softly with pleasure as they enjoyed each other; and all totally unaware of the presence of the two little peeping-Toms in the bushes behind them."

"I was fascinated yet disgusted at the same time; so different was it from the acts I'd witnessed from the beasts in the fields, and it felt so wrong to be watching like this, yet I couldn't drag my eyes away. As the lovers separated after what I now know to be the climax of their act, Lambros dug me in the ribs; 'Good, huh?' he mouthed, but I turned and left, as quickly and quietly as I could manage. At a safe distance, I realised that he'd followed me; 'What's wrong with you?' I glared at him; 'We shouldn't have been there, we shouldn't have watched, it was a private thing'. He shrugged; 'Then they should keep it for when they're in bed at Chrysoulla's, if they do it out in the open they should expect to be seen by anyone who's passing. They were at it yesterday and I saw them by accident; their own fault.

They're breaking the law, anyway, they're lucky I don't report them'."

"He did have a point; they were outraging the hospitality of the island, as well as the law. Just to sunbathe nude was an offence then, and even now is offensive, never mind making love, so they were far more in the wrong than Lambros and I. Yet I still felt bad about what I'd done and, when I saw the couple walking through the village with their arms around each other later that evening, I turned aside from the square and down a side street so that I didn't have to pass them."

"I liked to do things correctly; I don't know why, it was just the way I was, and it stood me in good stead, I thought. Life seemed to me to be a contract; if I behaved in the required way I'd be rewarded with what I saw as my just desserts, and so far it had worked for me. At school I did the work required, without demur, and was rewarded with good marks and praise from the teacher. If others didn't do the work, being lazy or uninterested or whatever, then they got bad marks and censure, which also seemed right to me. At home, if my parents asked me to do something, I also did it without question. They had given me birth, raised me, fed and clothed me and were training me for the means to make my own living when I was old enough; of course I owed them my obedience, because that was how our family contract worked. Not to mention that they loved me, and I loved them in return."

"I was a true child of Apollo, in the main, a lover of order, and was known for my honesty; 'If Kadi tells you he's done something, or not done something, it's the truth'. That's what they said about me around the village, even around the wider community of the island. So watching the American couple had not felt right to me, and rankled for some time after they had left the island, making their way elsewhere, another island, or the Turkish mainland. But eventually I forgave myself; I'd been led into an erroneous action by Lambros, a true child of Dionysus, chaotic, the opposite of myself. But I reasoned that I was only ten, after all, and if I'd known what Lambros had in store for me I'd have refused; probably. We're all curious when we're young, but from there on in I kept my curiosity tightly controlled."

"Such control was not easy for me, because if I was known for correctness and honesty, I was also known for a hot temper and a tendency to flare up suddenly when provoked; a Dionysian element within me and at odds with the rest of my nature. 'Control, control, Kadi'; it was the constant mantra of my father, Arkadios, and my mother, Androulla, as I was growing, and later of my younger brother Iannis, although he used it more in fun, to tease me when he thought I might be on the verge of an outbreak. It didn't always do the trick, however, this pre-emptive warning, and I still had to work hard on self-control despite my parents' numerous chidings. I wanted to be controlled and correct, a pattern of conformity; it was in my DNA, I decided later, when I discovered the existence of such a thing."

"Which was why I was so circumspect in my dealings with Eleni, both before and after our engagement. It wasn't strictly necessary to have an engagement party any more, times having changed, but with my desire for correctness and respect for tradition it was taken for granted by all concerned that I would wish for one. Further, in our out-of-the-way island community, such gatherings formed the backbone of both social cohesion and entertainment. We didn't have a cinema, or the discos which were rapidly becoming popular in the wider western world, or any of the trappings of modern-day life taken as a given by cities like London, Paris and New York. Life continued at its old, slow, traditional pace, and I for one liked it that way. So when Eleni suddenly said, 'Let's get engaged, and have an engagement ceremony, please, and let's do it soon, I don't want to wait'; the ceremony was quickly arranged and duly took place on the following Sunday afternoon."

"We were a poor community, so there were no expensive preparations required; just some cakes, which the women all baked between them, and wine, which was easily arranged. We didn't have such gatherings often, as I've said, so the community was happy to get together at short notice. The blessings of both sets of parents were given, then Eleni and I wore gold rings on our right hands, donated by her mother and my father, as there was no money for new ones. I, bursting with pride, was allowed to escort her back to her home, with her parents walking behind us, when the celebrations were coming to an end. I was to stay for the evening meal, so while Eleni and her mother busied themselves preparing food, her father brought ouzo to the veranda and we sat, drinking it long with ice and water in the traditional manner, making men's talk and responding to the greetings and congratulations of passers-by."

"One of these latter changed the planned course of the evening, however. 'Is Kyria Anna there, Kyrie Christi? I think Mama's about to have the baby!' This from Thekla, the oldest daughter of the house next door, in a hurry and a panic. Christis rose, to go for his wife Anna, but she'd heard already, with the extra-sensitive hearing of the wife and mother grown accustomed over the years to hearing anything and everything said in her house, and appeared at the door, her sleeves rolled up from the kitchen. 'Holy Virgin', crossing herself, 'I'd have sworn she wasn't due for another month, at least'; and she was off next door without taking a pause. 'You'd better go and find Petros', over her shoulder to her husband, who duly made me his apologies and disappeared in the direction of the kafenion to find his neighbour, who was about to become a father again, slightly sooner than expected."

"Which left me alone with Eleni, who appeared from the kitchen drying her hands on a dishcloth and looking perturbed, which I took as worry both for the neighbour and for herself at some time in the future, bride as she was soon to be. 'I'm sure Kyria Maroulla will be fine', I reassured her, 'she's had four already and never any problems. I'm sure there'll be more warning when it's ours', I added by way of reassurance for her own future birthings. She frowned; 'Babies come when they wish, they take little heed of our need or convenience'. 'Well, at least there's no chance of that yet'; I spoke with some unease, because I wanted to reassure her, but I wasn't happy speaking of such an intimate subject out here near the street, with people passing and able to hear us. I thought she must agree with me, because she turned to go inside; then in the doorway she turned and beckoned, 'Come inside with me'. I wasn't sure, it didn't seem proper for us to be alone in private; at least out here we were bound by the propriety of a public place. But she looked exasperated, 'Oh do come in!' So I put aside my misgivings and went."

"She looked at me; 'You're so … *correct,* Kadi'; her exasperation turned into amusement once she had me safely inside. 'So what if we speak outside of having children? It's what life is about. And being alone inside together? It wasn't planned this way, my parents weren't expecting to have to leave us. Anyway, we're engaged now and people will take a far less strict view. Everyone knows you won't take advantage of me and then leave me'. She laughed as she walked purposefully over to me, waving her be-ringed right hand before her face, extending it before her as she reached me to pull my face towards her and kissing me on the lips. I was stimulated, but shocked to my correct core. We'd only ever kissed twice before, after the ceremony today and before that, chastely and briefly, at my instigation when I asked her to marry me; and even then I'd spoken to her father before I spoke to her, to be sure that I had his approval. Now here was Eleni taking the initiative, presumably emboldened by our engagement. I noticed that there were roses in her cheeks, more so than usual; she looked utterly divine and I was sorely tempted, but I kept my control, albeit with difficulty."

She pulled me down onto a bench beside her. 'You think I'm being forward?' I nodded; 'But adorable also'. She took my hand and put it to her face, stroking her cheek with it; 'We're engaged, Kadi, and we want each other'. She looked at me questioningly at this last and I nodded again; I couldn't speak, I was totally under her spell. 'Well, we don't have to wait now; many don't, what do you think?' Her look was meaningful and I was further shocked, if that was possible. 'Eleni, I think you're excited by the engagement and you've been drinking wine, which is why you're saying this. It wouldn't be right. And there might be consequences'. I jerked my head in the direction of the house next door, where Kyria Maroulla was presumably in the throes of childbirth. 'And if there are?' She looked at me challengingly. 'It wouldn't be the first time, even in this village. Nobody minds; it's a good sign, a promise of fertility, the couple will have children. Imagine getting married and then finding that you can't have them. They just bring the wedding forward, that's all'."

"I just looked at her, speechless; I couldn't take in what she was saying as she continued. 'Kadi, I could come to you; when I'm supposed to be in bed, I could climb out of the window, I used to do it as a little child; I could meet you somewhere quiet, we could be together, properly'. She was caressing me meaningfully as she said this, and I had to summon all my control, she was so inviting. At last I found my voice; 'I want you too, Eleni, you know I do, but I just couldn't, not before we've been properly married. I know others do, but I can't; I'm sorry, but I'm not made that way. I love you but I respect you also and I won't do anything like that with you until you're my wife, in the eyes of the Church and society'. She looked back at me, blue eyes pleading, and was about to speak, but another voice interposed; 'Eleni!'"

"It was her father, Christis; who knew how long he'd been standing in the doorway, listening? Quite some time, I gathered, from what followed, but for now I just sat as turned to stone. He lowered his voice; 'Kyria Maroulla has just had a boy, healthy it seems, thanks be to God, and your mother needs your help, you'd better go to her'. Eleni rose and went, all obedience to her father now, and obviously bothered by the thought of what he might have to say to her later. He moved aside to let her through the door, but didn't look at her or otherwise pay her any attention; his gaze was fixed on me. I opened my mouth, 'Kyrie Christis', but he waved me to silence; 'No need to speak, Kadi, I heard everything and I praise you for your self-control. It's what I would expect from you, it's one of the reasons I consented to you speaking to her when you asked my permission and, God be praised, the foolish girl made the right choice. But is she the right choice for you? I have my doubts now. Other men would be trying to persuade her, but it's the other way around here'."

"He looked troubled, deeply so, not as a man ought to look who has just seen his daughter betrothed to an honest man. I sought to reassure him with the things I'd said to Eleni herself, plus my own ideas; 'She's young and in love, it's just excitement from the ceremony, she's had some wine to drink, found herself the centre of attention and was emboldened by that. Besides, she may look like a woman of the cold North, with her fair hair and eyes, but she's of the South, this island, and the climate breeds people as hot as its summers and passionate too. She's ready to be married, perhaps we should do it soon? She'll settle when she has a child to care for'."

"I was excited at the thought of Eleni's passion, and for once out of step with correctness, in mentioning it to her father; but Chrystis was a realist and, perhaps, rendered indulgent by my diplomatic excuse of his daughter's behaviour. So he just listened, nodding, as he poured us fresh glasses of ouzo, then indicated that I should sit again and passed me a glass whilst holding his out to me by way of a toast, which I returned as he expounded his view of the nature of womanhood."

"'She's a good girl really, a bit flighty sometimes, but maybe they're all like that when they're young. Why shouldn't they enjoy their time in the limelight, while they're pretty, and slim, before they're wrinkled with housework and thickened from childbirth? Her mother was a beauty, but she settled and she's been the best wife a man can have; but this one, with the hair and eyes ... well, she looks different, and she's been treated as something special by everyone, all her life, even by me. So I suppose I ought to expect her to step out of line on occasion. She'll settle, as you say, and you'll know how to control her, you're the best man on the island for the job'. He nodded as he spoke, to himself, he was reassuring himself that his daughter's display of immodesty was purely circumstantial and unlikely to be repeated."

"I agreed with him, both outwardly and inwardly, and asked him not to be too hard on her when he spoke to her later; as we both knew he would, because he couldn't do otherwise. He was still lost in contemplation of Eleni, however, and voiced his thoughts to me, man to man, father-in-law to son-in-law only for want of another ceremony. 'You know other men wanted her?' Yes, I knew; every young man in the village had wanted her, even my young brother Iannis, far her junior, had sighed over her. 'The Turk even asked me for her', Christis continued, 'but of course I couldn't; he's a good young man, no question, but ...'. He shrugged by way of an ending to his speech, and I understood the unspoken end of his sentence."

"I hadn't known, though, that this young man had also wanted Eleni enough to ask for her, and I considered the matter in the ensuing silence as we both sipped our ouzo.

The Turk; old prejudices die hard, the longer-standing the longer the death-throes, and the Ottoman empire had cast a long shadow. Nikos Osman Nikolaides, called Osman to his face and the Turk behind his back. His father, as a headstrong young man, had flown in the face of both his parents and convention and married a Turkish girl. There were still some of them living here at that time, and the communities didn't really mix, but somehow he and the young woman had become aware of each other and found a way to be together, and finally married. She'd converted to the Orthodox Church, which didn't please her parents, who had disowned her and not long after moved back to their own land, leaving her somewhat isolated within the community she'd chosen. People were polite to her, as the wife of a Greek, but there was no-one close, she wasn't an insider in the women's world here."

"Her son was teased at school too, which is where the nickname originated, from schoolboys looking for a fight, children being what they are. And, although I personally never levelled it against him, feeling it wrong to stigmatise him for what was not his fault, neither did I ever take to task those who did. He was a pleasant young man, more so than you'd expect from the rough time he'd suffered at school and from the fact that his mother had died when he was still very young. So it was just him and his father, although he made regular trips to the Turkish coast to visit his mother's people there. But for most of the time he worked very hard at learning the trade of motor mechanic, which gained him a measure of acceptance from the community because increasingly there were buses and cars and vans on the island and someone had to fix them when they went wrong. So he was accepted as a useful member of the community, but when he became of marriageable age he found that fathers were not so keen to give him their daughters for a wife."

"So he'd asked for Eleni, and been refused, and who

knew how many other fathers had refused him as well as Christis? I didn't, and decided that it didn't bother me; Eleni had chosen me, we were engaged and our wedding would not be long in coming. Neither were Kyria Anna and Eleni, returning with tidings of the new arrival next door. The doctor, who lived here in the village but worked at the hospital in Ayios Andreas during the week, was fortunately at home, it being Sunday. So he had come and pronounced the infant fine, but Anna had brought it, in the way the women used to. I approved; the modern world from outside was intruding too much into the old ways, I felt. I liked them, the traditions, so simple, so manageable, within my control. So I went with Christis to congratulate Petros on his new son, and to take ouzo with him, before I made my way home, having excused myself from the evening meal because Anna had other work to concern her now. I thought back over the events of the day, the engagement ceremony, the unexpected birth, Eleni's eagerness and the following interview with her father. Later I was grateful for that interview, because he knew it wasn't my doing when it all went wrong."

20: GOOD FRIDAY: CONFESSION

Kadi stopped here, his eyes glazed over, looking off, into the distance, into the distant past. Stephanidou moved over and offered him the rose cup; the old man took it gratefully, yet took only a minute sip, moving it around his mouth, to moisten it, before expelling the water onto the ground. Then he continued speaking, and Stephanidou listening, as the sun slowly moved across the sky.

"It was late evening, a week after the engagement ceremony, and I made my way up the hill via the track; little-used by anyone now except the goats and their herder, and myself. Behind me I could hear the music from the kafenion. Stelios, the son of the grocer, had returned that day from his National Service and everyone wanted to see him, shake his hand, and stand him an ouzo; they'd go on until late tonight. I'd been there with my father and brother, but we and the other fishermen had to go out tonight, so we had to eat and then prepare the boat."

"I'd left my father and brother outside our house, promising to see them soon, because before work, stargazing was my mission. I loved to look up to the heavens whenever I got the chance, from as high a point of the land as I could reach, which in my case was the cliffs at the top of this hill and at a good distance from the village. Tonight the sky was clear with a half-moon, meaning enough light to see where I was going in the rapidly-descending darkness, but not enough to spoil my view of the heavens. I found it calming to observe the stars and contemplate the order which the ancients had tried to impose on them; it was so in keeping with my nature."

"I didn't know much about astronomy, just what I had gleaned from school and the people I lived amongst about how the Greeks had named the planets and stars for gods, or the humans with whom they were supposed to have interacted, usually to the detriment of the latter. I particularly liked the constellations Ursa Major and Ursa Minor, known generally as the Great Bear and Little Bear, and the myth of Callisto and Arcas, her son by Zeus, who were supposed to have been turned into these. My own name, Arkadios, was derived from them, for I had been named for my father and his forefathers, all the way down from one of our ancestors. He had apparently come from the region of Arcadia, in the central Peloponnese, of which Arcas was king, before he was reunited with his mother in the heavens."

"Arcadia was thought of in ancient times as a harmonious, natural area, which is perhaps why I like order and harmony in my life. Yet it was also supposed to be the home of Pan, thought to be the son of Dionysus, a god of wine, sex, fertility and general chaos, the polar opposite of harmony, which may be why I have such a sudden and hot temper. Perhaps this polarity of nature came from my ancestor who, despite living in the most congenial of places, apparently yearned for the sea, of which there was none in the land-locked Arcadia. So he took himself to the coast, and sailed the sea, and eventually his seed found its way to our island, so far from his original home. I mused on these ideas as I climbed; pagan mythology informing family history, I knew, but part of my culture and of great interest to me."

"I couldn't be long; my father and Iannis would be down at the harbour soon, readying the boat for our night-fishing trip, and I was expected to be there to go with them in less than an hour. I could of course watch the stars from the boat, whilst we sat and waited during the small hours, but it wasn't the same as being just myself alone in the night on the hillside. My path uphill passed by the ruin of what had once been a dwelling, and which had been my mother's home in her youth. Now, however, her parents were both dead and she, an only child, married to a man without the means to repair and restore it to what it had once been, a family home. So it had fallen into decay, but it was our property nevertheless, and I liked to pass by as frequently as my working life would allow and make sure that it didn't totally turn into rubble."

"Although I wasn't very successful", Kadi interrupted himself, nodding at the enquiry on Stephanidou's face. "It was indeed this very house; I had hopes of one day restoring it", he continued, "and bringing my wife here to raise our children. Eleni's father had wanted to build her a house, but he lacked the means, like many in our village. One day, as an only child, she would inherit his house, but that was a long way off and, as we would be living in my parents' home after marriage, sleeping in my room but sharing the rest of the house, I was keen to begin soon on bringing my mother's childhood home back to life. I took any opportunity therefore to check on the place. Small boys played there sometimes, clambering over the breaking-down walls, but it was too far out of the village and off the beaten track to gain their attention very often. I could see it now, in the half-moon light, overgrown and ramshackle with pieces of broken brick, peeled plaster and fallen fence posts spread around the ground outside."

"Something was different though; noises, swift and unpleasant, which I couldn't identify; a strayed sheep or goat perhaps, rummaging through the rubble? Or a wild dog, doing likewise, scavenging for what it could find? No, I was sure it was neither of those; a rat, or more than one, perhaps? I hated them, vermin to be eradicated, and I did so whenever I was able. I peered around in the pale light, finding the weapon I wanted in a heavy metal bar, a fallen fence support, most likely, or a water pipe, part of the collapsed plumbing. Whatever it had been it was now to be the means of killing a rat, and I approached the crumbling walls as quietly as possible. I noticed as I did so that a few clouds were gathering above, and if I wasn't fast I'd lose the stars for tonight."

"At that moment the moon was covered by a cloud, the brick walls turned to darkness as I climbed stealthily over them; then the cloud moved away, the moon threw out its pale and dim light once more, and I froze with horror at what it revealed. A man and a woman, the source of the strange noises, like the couple I'd seen on the beach but so unlike them. More like the beasts I'd seen in the fields, an animal coupling, direct and brutal it seemed, from the noises which emanated from the woman. No sounds of pleasure here, I thought, more like wails of despair; and it hit me like a brick wall that I was witnessing a rape. Here, on my island, in my community, on my property? I couldn't believe it, but there it was before me. Anger enveloped me, the red cloud of rage descended, justifiably, and I felt the iron bar in my hand. I watched as it descended, almost in slow motion and as if of its own volition. The man fell away as it caught him; the back of his head collapsed and the blood spurted as he cried out, briefly and terribly. Then his body hit the scrub like a sack of gravel, and he was still and silent on the ground."

A sound, almost of relief, burst from Stephanidou at this point, but Kadi continued regardless. "What his fall revealed to me horrified me even more; the woman, desperately trying to cover herself, her white-blonde hair tumbling around her shoulders and breasts and her bare legs exposed up to the groin, all revealed by her dress being pulled off of her shoulders at one end and up around her waist at the other. Her eyes, crazed with fear, met mine, similarly crazed but with disbelief; 'Eleni?' My Eleni? It was she, but she didn't react as I expected, if my thoughts were ordered enough to know what I expected; I certainly hadn't expected any of this."

"'Kadi, what have you done?' She scrabbled desperately through the dirt, to the supine man, and the moon reappeared once more to show his face, as she turned him; The Turk, Osman. Eleni was shaking him now, trying in vain to waken him; 'Niko, Niko', over and over, and I noticed, even through my shock, that she used his Greek name that no-one else used, except his father. Her voice raised little by little to a scream, which was cut off by my taking her head in my hands and covering her mouth. 'Eleni, try to calm yourself, keep quiet, no-one must know what has happened here'."

"What had happened here? She wasn't behaving like a woman rescued in the middle of the act of rape; why was she so concerned for her attacker? I looked at him, as the moon came out from behind yet another cloud; they were coming thick and fast now, no chance of any stars, I thought irrelevantly. I removed one hand from Eleni's mouth and put it to the back of the man's head; I felt the stickiness, I saw in the dim light the dark pool spreading out from it. I put my hand inside his opened shirt and felt for a heartbeat; there was none. He would not rise again. There was a silence that seemed to go on forever, but it could have only been a few seconds, while Eleni looked at me, uncomprehending, then at the lifeless body; Then she screamed, despite my remaining hand, although in a fearful whisper of a scream. 'What have you done, what have you done?' Over and over, as she scrabbled down in the dirt and tried to wake him, shaking him, talking to him, imploring him to 'Wake up, wake up, Niko mou'; not understanding that the bloody hole in his head meant that he'd never wake up again."

"And then she did understand; she was up and all over me, as I stood, uncomprehending in my turn and trying to take in the enormity of what I'd done. Cursing and swearing at me, words I wouldn't have believed she'd known, then hitting me, thumping my chest, slapping my face, and I not trying to defend myself until she scratched my face and drew blood. Then I grabbed her wrists and wrestled her to her knees; she fought back but her strength was no match for mine, so she eventually stopped fighting and knelt there, sobbing as though her heart would break. I let go one of her wrists and turned her face up to mine; 'What the hell is going on here? He was …' I wanted to say 'raping' but I couldn't, so '… assaulting you, I saw him, why are you crying for him?'"

"She looked at me as fear, desperation and then despair passed over her face in rapid succession. 'No, it wasn't rape'; I noticed that she could say the word where I couldn't, but I listened as she went on. 'I wanted it, I love him, he's been my lover for some time now'. I couldn't take in the enormity of what she was saying; 'But you're engaged to me, Eleni, we're to be married'. Resignation took her now; 'No, Kadi, we're not, we never were. I let them think I wanted it, I let them go ahead with the arrangements; it diverted attention from Niko and I'."

"What to say to her? I couldn't think straight; 'But why?' Her voice trembled; 'They'd never have let me marry him; a half-Turk, can you imagine? He asked for me, but my father said No. He approved of you, though, so I let them think I wanted you too'. I interrupted her; 'But when the wedding day came?' She was bitter then; 'I wouldn't have been here, we were going to leave by night; tonight'. Defiance came into her face here; 'He's been over there' (and she pointed towards the Turkish mainland) 'and arranged it; one of his family, or a friend, has brought a boat so we could go over there, he'd have married me there'. I just stared at her; 'But how? You're both Orthodox Church, it's a different religion'. It was totally irrelevant, and not the most important thing, given that I'd just killed her potential husband, but it was all so much for me to grasp. 'Kadi'; she hesitated again, then, 'I'm carrying his child. We'd have found a way, we'd both have converted, if that was the only way, it wouldn't have been a problem, just to be with him, married to him, without all the sneaking around'."

"It all became clear to me at the same moment as the red cloud began to descend again. So much for my honesty and trying to do the right thing; good old Kadi, he'll make a good cover, to hell with his feelings. My voice was tight with attempted control as I spoke again; 'You were using me as a smokescreen, to cover your shame with him?' She was defiant again; 'There is no shame; I love him, I loved him, we wanted to be together but it was impossible here. I needed time while Niko found a way; you asked me to marry you and I used the opportunity to gain time. You wanted me, but you'd have got over it when I'd gone'. Her mood was strange now, unnatural; she appeared proud of her power of attraction over me and confident of her ability to wield that power. The most generous interpretation I could put on it was that she was in shock, from love-making turned to killing and confrontation within moments."

"My anger was growing, though; I was dangerous, but she didn't realise it. 'But there will be shame now'; I sounded oddly calm, given how angry I was. 'He can't marry you now, but you're carrying his child and it will become obvious at some point. How will you explain that?' Her answer took my breath away with its shamelessness. 'You can marry me, Kadi, I know you want me. We'll say it's your child, and after it's born I'll be a real wife to you'. She sounded calm now, and calculating, with hope in her tone and badly-covered desperation; the shock must have loosened her wits, I thought. 'You want me to marry you, after you've been with that misbegotten Turk? Be father to his bastard? Cover your shame with my respectable name? It's not going to happen, how can you even think so?' I wasn't proud of the things I said then, but my pride was wounded and I was deeply hurt."

"She turned hostile then, as her desperation grew. She

threatened me with the fact that I'd committed murder: 'I'll report you, you'll be shot'. I recoiled from her as from a snake, but I wasn't afraid of her threats; I knew I'd have the community behind me and against her, once the people of the village knew what she'd been up to, and with whom. I told her so in no uncertain terms, including that I'd be seen as justified in stopping what I'd thought of as rape. That when they found out that it was in fact a local slut giving away her reputation and that of the village to a Turk, of all people, they'd help me cover the killing. No body equals no murder. It would be thought in the larger community that, having had his way with a local girl who was no better than a whore, he'd left quietly by boat, under cover of darkness, like a thief in the night, to avoid answering for his conduct to her father and male relatives. Of these latter there were quite a few, this being a small island and intermarriage between local families common; to these she would of course be left to answer for her own conduct, and she could expect no mercy for the shame she'd brought on their name. She might as well leave for Athens now and find a brothel to work from, or maybe Turkey, it being that much closer and given that she obviously liked Turkish cock. She'd do well, being so unusual, a blonde Greek whore, she'd make a good living at it until her looks faded and she was left to starve in the gutter."

"And so on and so forth; I was crude and cruel, merciless and mean, in my righteous indignation and my broken faith. I would have said Love, because I had thought I loved her for so long. I'd never wanted anything in return but her love, and she had never given me any indication that this was not forthcoming. But now, her coldly-calculating manner, her plans to use me to cover her guilt, because she thought she could, had killed any last vestiges of love. I had dreamed of marrying her, enjoying the first fruits of love with her, my virgin bride; a virgin myself, I'd saved myself for her, thought of us discovering the act together and creating children of our love. Now I was being offered what? No virgin, her first fruits given to another and his bastard in her belly, tolerating my embraces and keeping my house as a thanks for saving her face and a way of paying rent? Chaotic, incorrect, intolerable and totally unacceptable."

"Now I just wanted revenge, and I spared no effort to let her know how miserable her existence was about to become. She sat immobile as I poured forth my venom, shaking with anger, or fear, or hate, or all of those plus other feelings which I couldn't discern. Eventually she hauled herself to her feet and, not looking at me, half-walked and half-ran into the dark, back down the hill towards the village or up it towards the cliffs I didn't know, immersed as I was in my own outpouring of hate. I didn't follow; left alone with the body of her late lover I focussed on more immediate problems than her. Let her do her worst, I'd deal with it later. I sat and put my head in my hands, trying to work out what to do."

"My decent side, the part of me that wanted always to do the right thing, said that I should go to the police and tell them what had happened, but I had my doubts. Despite what I'd said to Eleni, I was far from confident of being supported by the community, of being seen as having killed accidentally. If I told them the truth, that I thought I was saving a woman from rape? They wouldn't believe me, because of course they knew that Eleni was my fiancée; they'd say that I'd killed Osman in a jealous rage when I found out that he was seeing her behind my back. My honesty was well-known, but so was my hot temper, and this latter would condemn me; I'd be convicted of murder and face the firing squad."

"So the honest way was closed to me, and I had a body to dispose of. I dragged him into the scrub and covered him as well as I could, doing my best not to get any of the blood on myself or my clothes. Fortunately this place was well away from the village and the main road; Eleni and Osman had chosen their trysting place well, I thought inconsequentially. No-one was likely to have found them here, it was just their bad luck that her supposed husband-to-be had been passing while they were there."

"I returned home as quickly as possible; I was becoming increasingly worried about my own predicament. I'd lost all sense of time and wondered if my father and Iannis were waiting impatiently for me at the harbour by now. No-one was around as I entered the village; the square was empty, although the music and voices still drifted across from the kafenion. The men were all still celebrating the return of young Stelios, the women back at home with the younger children."

"My mother, Androulla, met me at the door; she knew that something was wrong as soon as she saw me, wise woman that she was. I slumped into a chair, my head in my hands, and just told her the facts. She was a severely practical woman, with no hysteria about her, who calmly met whatever situation presented itself and dealt with it. Her face hardened as she listened to my tale of Eleni's treachery, and then she took charge with no comment, cleaning the scratch on my face which Eleni had inflicted with her nails. It would arouse no suspicions, it wasn't unusual for manual workers such as we were to cut or graze our faces and limbs. Then she brought me ouzo and food, which latter I waved away, but 'Eat, Kadi; you need your strength', she ordered me. Her tone implied no disobedience, so I ate mechanically, unaware of what I ate, while she went to the harbour."

"As I said, there was no fuss or drama about my mother; she was a straightforward soul, always correct, and when I considered her I knew from whom I got my desire to be exactly like that. People obeyed her because it was unthinkable to do otherwise and my father, a wise man, did likewise. In public, she deferred to his will, as she was expected to, but within the house he respected her opinions and frequently acted upon them. He later told me that, when she arrived at the harbour side that night, she had given him minimal information and instructions which he and Iannis had obeyed, without question."

"Left alone, trying unsuccessfully to eat, I saw the scenes of the evening playing repeatedly before my eyes. I couldn't help myself, I considered the love-making I'd interrupted, although there had been very little of love to it, to my eyes and ears; lust, more like. I tried to block it out and sleep, sitting there at the table, closing my eyes, but sleep wouldn't come. What did come was the person of Lambros, bursting in through the kitchen door as though he owned the place and, when no-one was to be found there, into the dining area beyond. He looked surprised to see me; 'What are you doing here?' 'I live here', I told him drily, 'I'm eating before I go out with my father and Iannis. What are *you* doing here?'"

"He grinned sheepishly; 'I thought maybe your mother had a few left-overs from your dinner she might want finishing up'. Honestly, ever since that day when she gave him pourgouri and yoghourt he'd been turning up at the house around meal-times, looking for more. And, as my mother continued to feed the motherless one, as she called him, he continued to come. 'You can have this, I told him, I'm not that hungry, I've a headache'; and I pushed my plate over. He didn't need telling twice, it disappeared into his face in a few mouthfuls, and then he walked down the road with me to the harbour. We met my mother coming in the other direction; she gave me a meaningful look, which would have meant nothing to Lambros, but all she said was, 'Hurry up, your father's waiting'."

"On the boat, which I boarded in full view of Lambros and the other fishermen, some of whom greeted me, I descended to the cabin and told my father the whole story. Iannis drove the boat and kept watch, for fish but also for any of the other boats coming too close. The engine noise would cover our talk anyway, but a stiff breeze had sprung up also, ruffling the waters and making more noise, so no voices would carry on the still air. This was good; we didn't need to take any chances. When we'd gone out far enough and the other boats, having dispersed in different directions, were out of our sight, we cut our lights and turned back towards the shore slowly; a risk, but a necessary one."

"The moon still appeared periodically from behind the clouds which had now gathered, giving us the mixed blessing of some light to guide us, but also making us visible. At a certain point we cut the engine and rowed ashore to the beach, where I disembarked and was off stealthily up the track, making my way quickly and quietly to the ruined house where Osman lay. I didn't look back, but I knew that my father and Iannis would be rowing back out again, before putting the engine and lights back on and going far enough out to look convincing in terms of fishing whilst watching the beach for our signal."

"When I reached the ruin my mother was already there, hiding in the shadows and as unlike my mother as she could have been. She wore black, which was usual with her since her father's death, but tonight it was a shirt and trousers belonging to my brother Iannis, and a pair of his boots, I judged with the minimal night vision I had. She was a small and slender woman, yet muscular from hard work, with no spare flesh on her. My father's clothes would have been too large, but my brother's fitted her fairly well. She took my hand, 'Come, we need to be quick and quiet'."

"She had worked already, fast and efficiently. The body she had found where I'd hidden it and already got it partially into a sack she'd brought, after wrapping it in other cloths, tarpaulins or sheets, such as are used to spread under the trees during the olive harvest. She hadn't flinched from the work, it seemed; she'd wrapped a thick cloth around his blood-matted head in the same way that she used to

211

bandage the cuts that Iannis and I received frequently from playing too roughly when we were young. I suppose she had prepared more than one body for burial when medical facilities on the island were sparse, some years ago. At her bidding I helped fasten the sack and, when it was ready, she inspected the ground where Osman had lain; she moved then to the well at the back of the house, bringing water in a rusty old bucket and pouring it to dilute and wash away the blood. Three trips she made, until satisfied with her handiwork; then she touched my shoulder gently to rouse me for the next task."

"I sat dumb on the ground as she did all this. It was dark now, the moon almost totally concealed by the clouds which had gathered in the heavens, and late, so few if any people would be around. The men had been at the kafenion, I remembered, welcoming young Stelios home; how long ago it seemed since I had been there with them, happy and carefree and leaving them to go look at the stars. Now I was an automaton, still emotionally confused and dazed by the events of the evening. I ought to have been out on the calm sea, waiting for the fish, yet I was on my way to conceal a murder, myself the murderer, and dispose of the evidence, the body."

"My mother waved me to the end of our load which housed the legs and feet while, not hesitating to take the end covering the bloodied head herself, she took the lead as we carried our grizzly cargo in the direction of the beach, taking care to use what cover presented itself. It was fortunate that the clouds had become even thicker now, totally covering the moon and its unwelcome light. It was hard labour, for Nikos Osman had been a large man, tall, broad and big-boned; but we managed, and deposited him at one end of the beach, at the shoreline and behind some boulders which had sat there ever since I could remember. He was well-hidden there, and any blood was washed away by the waters of the Aegean. The wine-dark sea, I thought irrelevantly, remembering Homer's *Odyssey* from my schooldays. My mother scrabbled around, finding a number of smaller rocks from around the boulders and pushing these into the sack, the better to keep it and its morbid contents beneath the sea. I did the same, helping her to carry some much larger and heavier ones between us; we'd need my father and brother to help carry the load, which was now too heavy for just the two of us."

"There was a temporary lull in the proceedings then, which I did not welcome; the work I'd been doing, even given its morbid and clandestine nature, had kept me busy and stopped me from thinking too much. Now, while I waited in the bushes, unwelcome thoughts came rushing into my mind. I exerted every ounce of control I could muster to push them aside and focus on my mother, crouched beside me, flashing a torch intermittently in the direction of the sea. We seemed to be there forever, until the slow splash of oars signalled the presence of a boat; my father and Iannis. They knew what to do with no words exchanged; my resourceful mother it seemed had indeed masterminded the whole operation."

"The boat was loaded with its doleful cargo, including the iron bar to be thrown overboard at a good distance from the sack. My father took me by the shoulders and enfolded me in his arms, then nodded reassuringly. My brother touched and squeezed my arm; they understood and would support me no matter what. As they climbed back into the boat I followed; my mother would make her way home, keeping to the shadows, and at this time of night should encounter no-one. Apparently she was successful, for nothing was said afterwards by anyone. She'd be there, I reflected once back on the sea, taking the clothes she'd been wearing to check for blood and to launder then first thing in the morning; which wasn't that far off now. I'm sure she didn't get any sleep, making sure nothing had been overlooked in covering up my crime, but I did; worn out, emotionally and physically, I finally succumbed to much-needed sleep there on the boat, and my father let me sleep until he had to wake me to complete our grizzly task."

"He had run the boat due south, as far from land and fishing waters as he could without arousing too much curiosity, although he hadn't seen any other boats. Then, when he had awoken me, we put our unorthodox cargo, my unfortunate handiwork, overboard; he sank like a stone, while we all crossed ourselves and my father said a prayer. Then we headed away, back towards the land and as far as we could get from the site of the burial, heaving the iron bar overboard at a certain point."

"We duly tried to fish as normal, but normal was the last thing this night could be called. We were all quiet with our individual thoughts and, for me, these centred now on Eleni; What would she do? Had she done it already? Needless to say, we didn't catch any fish, and when the sun was beginning to rise above the horizon we headed back towards the harbour. Luck was with us; about halfway there my father thought he saw something, and sure enough there was a shoal of sardines; we stopped, and got a good catch, enough to convince anyone that our entire night had been spent as usual."

"We were the last boat back to the harbour; as we approached we could see them, all the other fishermen, standing around on the rough harbour-side. They all turned, as one, to look at us; at me, I thought self-consciously. My father tried to act naturally, with a bright air; 'Sardines, out by the Cape, a good catch, thanks be to God, how did you all miss them?' Old Spyros, who was closest to us, gave a weak smile by way of an answer, but then his face became serious again. They know, I thought then in rising panic, she's told them; but then I saw the thing on the ground, shapeless and covered roughly with a tarpaulin, maybe five to six feet long?"

"Osman, I thought then, they've found him already, how

could that be, we weighted him well. But then Christis, Eleni's father, staggered over to me; his face was as pale as the whitewash we used to freshen our house each spring and his eyes were staring and ghastly as he put a hand on my shoulder. I bent mechanically and lifted a corner of the tarpaulin; I saw the tumbled and damp white-blonde hair, dappled with mud and blood. I let the tarpaulin drop with a cry, and staggered backwards, into my father's arms. I felt him sit me down somewhere; I put my head in my hands and wept; for Eleni, for Osman and for my well-ordered life, which had slipped suddenly out of my control and turned to chaos."

21: GOOD FRIDAY: CONCLUSION

Stephanidou didn't interrupt the story, but waited silently for more. He felt sympathy now for the old man, and did not doubt that the tale he was telling was true. Kadi took some time, looking into the sky, and then recommenced:

"They had found her at the far end of the beach, not far from where her lover had lain awaiting his burial at sea; had she been there already, when we brought him? She had been noticed by one of the fishing boats returning as the dawn rose, it seems, something out of harmony with the familiar, unchanging line of the land which they had known for all of their lives. They had gone to investigate because items did float ashore occasionally, having fallen from passing ships further out to sea, and these could turn out to be useful or not. On one occasion there had been a dead cow, I remember; it must have fallen from a livestock transporter and drowned. It was bloated and stinking, we'd had to douse it in petrol and burn it where it lay, and the smell had lingered for some days in the still summer air. But now they found the lifeless body of a local girl to be recovered and brought back for a post-mortem to discover the cause of death."

"It was all anyone could talk about; had she been swimming, and drowned? Or fallen from the cliffs above? Both unlikely; Eleni had been playing on the cliffs and swimming in the sea since a small child and, like the others of the village, knew the land and the sea like the back of her hand. In any case, why would she be swimming, fully-clothed, or walking the cliffs, at night? Her parents could testify that she'd gone to bed early, was safely shut in her bedroom for the night when they retired to their own. No-one could work it out, so they had to wait for the autopsy and in the meantime extended their concern and pity to her family; and as her fiancé I came in for a share of this."

"My emotional reaction when I came in with the other boats had been noted, and was taken for the heartbreak of a man in love, which impression I naturally did nothing to dispel. I had felt emotional, of course, traumatised, with everything that had happened in the space of a few short hours, and I was grieving for my lost illusions. I still remember the scene at the harbour when I came in and found Eleni lying there, dead; I'd witnessed the heartbroken wails of her mother and the grief of her father which seemed to have aged them by twenty years in the space of minutes. But I had my family with me, and if they looked uneasy they were also firm in their belief; I was to be protected at all costs."

"When we eventually got back to our house my mother took herself off to the kitchen to prepare food, as she usually did for her returning menfolk, but today she did it automatically, out of habit, for her thoughts were elsewhere. When the meal came none of us could eat much, trying to take in this new twist in the developing tragedy. I didn't believe that Eleni had drowned herself; she would have had to go back to the main road towards the village to reach the track leading to the beach, and there was a possibility that someone might have seen her. Of course, that theory depended on her being in a state of mind to consider such a thing, and I didn't believe that to have been the case; she had been clearly distraught when she staggered away from me. Nevertheless, I still thought that it had to be the cliffs, and there was a chance that, in her traumatised state, she may have fallen over the edge accidentally; but I was sure that she had done it deliberately, and that I had goaded her into it."

"I couldn't be totally sure, though, so I'd just have to wait with everyone else for the results of the post-mortem. I tried to order my thoughts but it was impossible; there was too much to take in and I just couldn't control any of it. I'd been overtaken by chaotic events and my ordered world thrown into disorder. The thoughts went round and round in my head; all I'd wanted was to marry and raise a family, supporting them by my honest toil. I'd thought I was saving a woman from rape, and now I was a murderer, with the woman's death on my conscience also and my family dragged in as accessories after the fact. Could I have done things differently? If I hadn't passed the derelict house at just that time I wouldn't have been in this position; however, I'd have been left looking like a fool when Eleni and Osman eloped. Would I have preferred that to being a murderer? The thought was intolerable, and irrelevant anyway; what had happened had happened and nothing could change that."

"I still couldn't take it all in; I was living in a waking nightmare, I thought, and then, bizarrely, that I must be dreaming. I had to go to the Christou family house, where Eleni had been taken until she could be moved to the hospital mortuary in the main town, to make sure that it was true. I didn't really want to but I had to, and it would have looked in keeping for me, as the dead girl's fiancé, to go to her family. I looked terrible, but so did Eleni's father. I didn't see her mother, who was prostrate with grief; she was lying down, Maroulla from next door watching over her, but Christis was there, with the body lying covered on the table. He just looked at me, his face dragged down with sorrow and a maze of lines and wrinkles that hadn't seemed to be there before, and shook his head; he seemed to be ageing before my eyes. I lifted a corner of the cover, and saw once again the mass of white-blonde hair, spotted with mud and blood, and dropped it again; it was true."

"I tried to go about my business as usual in the days that

followed, although I felt as though I was sleepwalking. Fortunately the community interpreted this as to be expected from a bereaved fiancé, but things changed when the results of the post-mortem became known. Eleni's injuries were consistent with her having fallen from the cliffs, but the presence of a foetus in her womb, about two months old, was also discovered; and then the tongues really started wagging, and fingers pointing in the direction of our house. Christis, himself shattered by this latest blow, nonetheless made it know within the community that he knew with absolute certainty that I was not responsible, based on what he had witnessed between Eleni and I on the evening after our engagement. The shame he brought on his family in so doing must have crushed him, and could have been avoided had he kept quiet; yet he didn't flinch from telling the truth, for my sake. He also pointed out that, even had Eleni been expecting my child, there would have been no cause for her to kill herself. We were engaged to be married and, if we had got carried away and anticipated the wedding, well, these things had happened before and would happen again. The fecundity of the bride was a good omen, and all that was needed was to bring the wedding forward. He convinced the majority, although there were still a few doubters, but I could live with those, if with gritted teeth; how I would have liked him for a father-in-law!"

"The news of Osman having gone missing also broke around this time. He'd gone to Turkey recently, ostensibly to visit his mother's family, so his father had had no reason to worry. However, when his absence went on for longer than expected, enquiries were made. It was found that he had left his Turkish family, announcing his intention to return to the island, on the day on which I'd discovered him with Eleni. It would seem that he'd arrived and gone to meet her before even going home to his father, because no-one else appeared aware of his return. As there was no commercial ferry between the island and the Turkish mainland he'd most likely got one of his relatives to bring him over, and they would have returned without knowing anything about subsequent events until Osman's absence was noted and questions asked. No-one admitted to having brought him back here though, which I thought must mean that they'd been sworn to secrecy and now, like me and my family, were keeping their guilty secret rather than potentially having to admit their part in helping a half-Turkish man elope with a Greek girl. It wasn't a perfect explanation, but no-one was telling the truth and I wasn't asking."

"Such items of news as Eleni's pregnancy and presumed suicide and Osman's disappearance were unusual, unheard-of even, on a small island and in a small community like ours, even singly. So, with both events coming together, naturally people started putting them together and coming up with something very close to the truth. It had been noted that Eleni had become secretive recently, although that had been put down to her impending marriage by everyone, including myself. It was known by her closest friends that Osman had asked her father for her, and been refused; and she had seemed somewhat to regret that fact when she'd told them. Come to think of it, they said, Osman had seemed to be nearby quite frequently whenever Eleni was around, and when they'd teased her about it she hadn't seemed irritated by his attentions. Quite the opposite, in fact; there even seemed to be something in the air between Eleni and Osman, the friends had felt, with that indefinable sense that women have about such things."

"Whatever the actual truth of the matter, the gossips said, the facts couldn't be denied. A young woman, pregnant outside of marriage and not by her intended husband, had died by falling from the cliffs, while a young man who had been rejected as an unsuitable suitor by her father had left the island not long before and not returned, his whereabouts remaining unknown. These facts seemed to point in one direction; that of a forbidden relationship, a girl deserted by the father of her unborn child and her suicide because of this. Shocking, and spoken about only in hushed tones to spare the feelings of the girl's family, hitherto respected within the community and untouched by scandal."

"It became clear to me now, I thought, why Eleni had suddenly wanted an engagement ceremony and why she had offered herself to me in the evening afterwards. Her father must have been thinking the same thing too, but I wasn't going to raise the subject with him; better leave him alone to cope with what he had to, rather than reminding him by my presence of the extent of Eleni's bad behaviour and rub salt into his wounds. It could only be that she wasn't as sure as she had said of Osman; he'd been away when we became engaged, had she been worried that he might not return? Was her offer to me a form of insurance, to dupe me into thinking the child was mine? Because I was sure that had he not returned, she would have gone ahead and married me, and then had an apparently premature baby after a pretence of virginity on the wedding night. I tried to feel some pity for her despite her devious behaviour, because she'd paid for it with her life; but it was difficult, given how she had injured me."

"The police were asking questions, of course, because they couldn't rule out foul play, given Eleni's condition and the sensitive issue of male honour in these parts. But I had a watertight alibi; I'd left the kafenion with my father and brother, and only they knew that I'd gone up the hill before returning home. Lambros had found me there, eating my dinner, before accompanying me to the harbour where he and the other fishermen had seen me going out in the boat with my father and Iannis; who would of course tell no-one of the brief period when I'd been alone. When we returned the following morning, my return and reaction to Eleni's death had been seen by almost the entire village. Christis was also questioned, as her father, but he had been at the kafenion all evening, along with most of the male population of the village, welcoming young Stelios home. So, as there was no-one else who would have wanted to harm Eleni, except perhaps the mysteriously missing Osman, the police ruled out foul play and closed their enquiries. Suicide could not be proved definitely, however, so the verdict was left undetermined."

"I tried to cope with it all in the best way I knew; by trying to continue the well-ordered and controlled life which I'd lived before this disaster had happened. So I got up each day, worked with my father on the boat, ate my meals and attended church; but things could never be the same. For one thing, I avoided the kafenion now; the men felt awkward with me, unsure what to say; it was difficult for them to make conversation about the news, the political situation, local events, as they had before. So I made it easy for them by not putting them into that position, taking coffee on the veranda at our house with my father, who had been affected in a similar way, by association; as had my brother."

"Iannis was still a schoolboy by day, although a fisherman by night when there was night fishing to be had; he was learning the trade as others had before him. Now, he began to dislike school, having been obliged to knock down several boys whose parents were of the persuasion that I had been responsible for Eleni's pregnancy. The physical side of this didn't worry him, for he was muscular if wiry of build, and well-able to take care of himself. The boys who taunted him were called fools for doing so, because it was guaranteed that Iannis would always get the best of the fight."

"But it bothered him that he had to take up arms to defend my honour, as it were, because it ought to have been obvious to anyone with a brain, in his opinion, that I was not guilty; my previous reputation for honesty spoke for itself. As to his private knowledge of my responsibility for the death of Osman, he kept his opinion to himself, but it must have bothered him along with his own involvement in the aftermath. He started missing school sometimes, going to the harbour and spending time on our boat, mending nets and doing other general tasks required; and my father didn't rebuke him for this, understanding as he did the reasons for the boy's behaviour."

My mother, on the other hand, let him know in no uncertain terms what she thought of his absences, as well as venting her anger over the dishonest behaviour that had been forced on our honest family through peevish outbursts previously unheard-of in her. She kept these for inside our house though; she was self-sufficient to a fault and had never needed close friends on whom to unburden herself. She had been well-respected in the village, and the other women knew better than to annoy her by a thoughtless remark. Now they were even more guarded than in the past, and, although this didn't bother her of itself, the reason for their behaviour did. She knew they gossiped about us behind her back, and couldn't take them to task over this in case she inadvertently revealed something which ought to stay secret. So we would be treated to muttered outbursts as she served food, or went about her household tasks. I assumed that she was trying to spare my feelings over events, so these outbursts were unintelligible in the main; but the ending was audible and always the same, 'That no-good girl, God rest her', grudgingly-spoken and accompanied by the sign of the cross."

"There seemed no way back to life as it had been, for either myself or my family; and it was my father who took steps to improve matters. One day he received a letter; a rare occurrence in the normal run of things, but this one had a foreign postmark and stamp. He took it onto the terrace, to read with his coffee, and it was clear that he wanted to be alone. I went to the boat to prepare to put to sea later, and when he arrived we did so, just he and I, this being a school day and Iannis having chosen to attend. When we were far out, and alone, with the nets and lines in place, he spoke to me, at some length."

"'Kadi, we need to do something about this situation'. I agreed with him, but what could we do? 'Perhaps a change of scene would do you good', he suggested, 'get away from all these bad things for a time?' In fact, I'd been thinking the same thing myself; this was my home and I loved it, but things were not as they had been and elsewhere I wouldn't be tormented on a daily basis by reminders. So, 'Yes', I told him, 'but where would I go?' He took a deep breath; 'I wrote to your Uncle Michalis recently, and he's written back'."

"My father had clearly been giving the matter deep thought, because he'd been out of touch with his older brother for some years, since the latter went to England, bored with life here and seeking excitement, as well as to make his fortune. He'd succeeded too, it seemed, and had tried to send back financial assistance for his brother's family here. But my father was proud and wouldn't take it, stating that he was able to support us himself, with goodness and honesty if with little money. Uncle Michalis was offended, even though he must have understood my father's pride, and they'd been out of touch since. So my father must have been deeply concerned to approach his brother again, especially to ask for the assistance he'd previously declined. He'd asked my uncle to let me go to him in England, to take me into his business in London and let me work for him; and Uncle Michalis had agreed."

"I considered the idea; it would get me away from the island and put me at a distance from the bad memories, give me something to do not related to Eleni and the life here in any way. It didn't have to be a permanent move, I could always come back if I didn't like it. Overall, though, it might remove some pressure from my family; once I wasn't here, a walking reminder of events they were trying to forget, they might be able to return to some sort of normality. This decided it for me; the opportunity for my family and I to assume control of our lives once more, albeit in different places. I told my father that I was willing, and preparations were put in place for me to depart for England."

"And the rest you know", Kadi concluded wearily. He took a small sip of water from the cup at his side, but spat it onto the ground almost immediately before continuing wearily. "So you see, even though I didn't push Eleni over the cliff, I certainly goaded her into throwing herself over, which I'm sure is what happened. She knew the lay of the land here like the back of her hand, since childhood, and even in what must have been her distress and distraction she'd know to stay well clear, had she wanted to live. I do regret it, and the way I treated her; my temper, you see. The red rage descended and I was powerless to stop myself. I've worked on it since, of course, and learned greater self-control; but I still fell victim to the temper on extreme occasions, at times when I was sorely tried, as I've told you. I also remember being taught the fear of being laughed at, as a child; If you don't behave, people will laugh at you. Well, I behaved well and they would still have laughed at me, and I couldn't have that, which would have happened if Eleni had run off with Osman and left me standing there like a fool, so what else could I have done?"

"Could I have done things differently? I've often asked myself that, and I fear that I couldn't. If she had come to me honestly, say, in the event of finding that Osman had indeed deserted her, and confessed what had happened and begged my help? I'm afraid I couldn't have done what she needed; marry her and raise his child as my own? There are men who might have been able to do it, but I'm afraid I'm not one of them. I might have tried to help her in another way, but I can't see how I would have done that, given the situation. I've never pretended to be a hero, just an honest man who wanted to live his life correctly, and look how that turned out. But Eleni didn't do things honestly, maybe because she sensed that I'd refuse; she deceived me, and the best case scenario was that I'd be left looking like a fool when she eloped with him, because I'm sure she would have done so even if she had been married to me by the time he returned."

"Because what if he'd been further delayed on the Turkish mainland? She'd have had to marry me at some point, if I was to believe that the child was mine, and then run away with him when he eventually returned. And what would I have done, had that happened? Take the role of Menelaus and rouse our so-called fishing fleet to go and stake out the coast of Turkey to get Eleni back and kill her Paris-figure? I wouldn't have taken Helen back had I been Menelaus, and as Edward I discarded Magdalena when she was unfaithful. It was a different thing back in ancient times, I suppose; a woman was property, like a house, or a horse, and the point was to reclaim what had been stolen, whatever condition it was in. Not for me, though."

"Mind you, I never thought a great deal of Menelaus, always thought him a bit of a wimp who couldn't be bothered to do what he clearly had to. I'm sure it was his brother, Agamemnon, who made him go to Troy and get her back, for the sake of macho pride and honour. Menelaus would have said, 'Leave it, brother, she's not worth it', but Agamemnon would have forced him into it. Then Menelaus got stranded in Egypt, they say, on his way back from Troy, and why? Because he neglected to make offerings to the gods; not just the correct offerings, but any offerings at all! I mean, any ancient Greek worth his salt knew how the thing worked, but not him; he just mooched around Egypt whingeing about having no wind to take his ships back to sea but did nothing to get the gods to send him that wind."

"Not like his brother; Agamemnon did exactly what he had to do, he'd had no wind to get them to Troy, but he did just what the gods required of him, sacrificed his own daughter, of all things, but he got the wind, although it got him in deep trouble with his wife, and cost him his life at her hands and those of her lover when he eventually got home. Which, however, neatly makes the point about women being no more than property back then, and at the disposal of their menfolk. Only much later did the whole man-woman relationship come to be more about feelings, both his and hers; so when Eleni gave not just her body but her heart to another it was a double injury. She loved him, she cared for him, and why therefore would I want her? Having her going through the motions, all the while knowing she was thinking of him? That's what was going on with Magdalena, latterly, although it took me a while to find out, and I was physically sick when I did. I thought that I'd gone 'English', pretending that I didn't care what people thought of me, but I cared like hell. She had made me look foolish, in the way that Eleni would have, and I couldn't bear that; no man could, could you?"

Stephanidou had never considered the matter, he'd never really been in a position to consider it, until he'd met Elpida and known she was the one for him. He frowned, because now that he was forcibly separated from her who knew how she was feeling? Would she meet someone else and prefer him? Would Stephanidou get a letter, or an e-mail, or, God forbid (he forgot his new-found atheism in using the casual everyday expression) a text like the one Aphrodite had sent to Marston when she dropped him so casually for Kadi? He suddenly felt depressed, more so than usual, but Kadi gave him no time to consider the matter too deeply, as he continued:

"As to Osman, I'm sorry to have taken his life, although to be perfectly honest more so for myself than for him. He didn't behave well, and being with her like that, in a public place, they were breaking the law as surely as that couple on the beach when I was a boy. And when you cross that line you have to accept that things may happen which you don't want to happen, as I know from personal experience. From what you've told me, from the statement of the boatman who was waiting to take them away, it appears that they couldn't resist each other, after an absence of some weeks, or a month or more. Had they done so, they'd have been away and clear before I came up the hill and discovered them. So you see, they were really victims of their own lack of self-control, as was I; it all comes back to control, in the end."

His tone was matter-of-fact, disturbingly so given the occurrences he was relating, Stephanidou thought. But Kadi paused then, briefly, and then carried on, slowly and in a tone of more concern. "You speak to Father Lambros, don't you? He's the only one here now who's known me well as a boy, being more or less the same age as I. Odd, isn't it, that he was the bad boy of the village and I the good; we were polar opposites. 'If you want to go to the good, see Kadi, if to the bad, see Lambros'; that's what they said, they used to say it to their children, in our hearing even. Yet here we are, he a priest, a good one, highly respected, loved. He had a revelation, apparently, not long after I left the island, and went into the church. He's been to Jerusalem, and on retreat to Mount Athos, many times; he has a wife living, although you won't see her, she stays in the house, like a good, old-fashioned Greek wife. But she cares for him, she's devoted to him; they have three sons, strong men and good, a credit to them, living on the mainland because there's no work here, but they send money, like dutiful children, and they visit each year with their wives and children."

His voice turned bitter then: "Lambros is truly blessed, but what am I? Honest Kadi, who only wanted to do good, to marry the woman he loved, have children with her and work honestly to support them. Yet since the moment I found them together, Eleni and Osman, my whole life has been a lie! I thought I was doing good, saving a woman, but it took me to the bad! I am a convicted criminal on the run from so-called justice, with other crimes unknown to any but myself and the gods. I have never had a wife, not in the legal sense, anyway, and the only child I know for certain to be mine is dead. How did that happen? Whom the gods would destroy they first make mad; I can't remember who said that, I'm afraid, but maybe it's the answer. I always had a lot of time for the old, pagan gods; they're our Greek heritage, after all, and deserve due respect, I've always felt. But the Christian God is a jealous god, it's said, and won't tolerate us giving even the time of day to the others. A very selfish god, it seems to me; isn't it good manners to acknowledge them, just to lift our caps and say Good Day? I've always tried to do that, and presumably he knows it and has it in for me therefore. That's if you believe in religion, gods and that sort of thing, of course."

"Whatever the case, Poseidon at least clearly has some affection for me. Osman has never slipped his makeshift moorings and surfaced from the sea-bed to point the fatal finger of blame at me and my family. He did haunt me, though, and regularly; he appeared in my nightmares and shook his gory locks at me, because he could certainly say that I did it. I felt sorry for him, later, because it must be terrible to lose your life at so young an age, but of course he must have known very little about it. Eleni and their child died too, and I paid for that with Aphrodite and our baby; so perhaps there's your revengeful God at work, although I have to take issue with him. What did they do to deserve it? What did I do? I tried to do good, I tell you." He stopped briefly, hoarse with the effort of speaking, but started again, and now his thoughts had returned to Magdalena.

"Eventually I found the right woman, my Magdalena, and she was innocent, and sweet, and good, but I was past understanding innocence, and sweetness, and goodness, steeped as I was myself by then in lies and deceit and rottenness. She made one fatal error, she went to that dinner to find a wealthy sponsor, she made one little slip into *my* world, a world of people for sale, and I mistook her for one of them. She took bad advice, and through it she met me, and I ruined her, and she died, she paid with her life. If she'd never met me she might still be alive"; he paused here in his raving and squinted, as though thinking, then continued. "I should have married her, cared for her, maybe we'd have found out sooner about the cancer that took her and maybe I could have saved her; but I killed her instead and now I owe her a life; my life."

He stopped again, his voice and strength going, but he seemed to make a mighty effort, and continued. "I thought at first of starving myself to death, but that can happen too quickly. They say it can take as little as seven weeks without food, but will only take three to four days without water, and I didn't deserve to go that fast. I deserved to suffer, and for some years too, before I allowed myself the luxury of death. So I've been eating as little as possible, enough to keep me alive and, recently, in some pain. A slow starvation, like the slow suffering I inflicted upon her, my Magdalena. I have so many sins for which to atone, and I will do so, one by one, like the original Magdalen, in the desert at the end, like the Donatello sculpture in the Museo dell'Opera del Duomo in Florence; but unlike her legend, there will be no angels to nourish me, to drop manna from Heaven for me. I'll dole out what little I have, and suffer, until the last days arrive, at which time it will be easy to accelerate the process and finish it."

He spoke as though to himself now, unaware of the presence of Stephanidou, and repeated the ideas which seemed to obsess him. "I ought to have married her, made her my wife, despite what she said at the end; made a commitment, shown her how much she meant to me, opened up to her and shared my life with her. She deserved that much, and more; like motherhood. I wish I could have given her a child because, despite her damned parents having put her off the idea by trying to push her into it, I'm sure she would have liked to have one, with me, and she had one, eventually, possibly by James and possibly by me, but I'll never know for sure."

"Not taking her pills at first; it was so touching, and she was so sweet, when she confessed to me some years later, but of course I'd guessed long before. She wouldn't flush them down the toilet daily, but forget and then flush a whole card-load in one go, and of course they didn't all go. But I said nothing; I'd have liked to see her rounding out, slowly, while our child grew inside her, her stomach and breasts swelling, her face rounding slightly as she turned into a little madonna, my little madonna. I might have taken her, very gently, in the early days, but I wouldn't have risked it later. I can control myself, and I wouldn't have put her in danger, or the child."

"And then to see her with the child in her arms, nursing it, suckling it, giving it her breast, with me sitting beside her, with my arm around her, touching her, part of the process, father, mother and child. Our daughter, or our son; because every man wants a son to follow him. But I'd have been happy with whatever she'd given me, and possibly she has, but maybe James is the father. A daughter like her, hopefully, or if she'd had a son he ought to have been like her, for that matter, because I wouldn't want him to be like me; no more like me, please God."

"But of course it always seemed as though she couldn't conceive, not with me, anyway, so that could have been my fault, a problem that lay with me. But there was James, and I don't want to think about the others, but it never happened until too late. But if I'd married her, as I ought to have, I could have made sure she had tests, every test going, and treatment, if they'd found that it could have been fixed. At the very least they might have found the cancer much earlier, when it was treatable; and then maybe she would have lived, even if not for very much longer, but a few years at least, so that I could have done the right thing and made her some amends."

"But instead I condemned her to a life of misery; even when I was good to her I was bad to her also. I punished her for crimes that she didn't commit, the crimes of that other one, that Eleni, so long before. I couldn't leave them in the past, and I put them onto her and made her do such things that it makes me almost insane to think of them." His voice, almost a whisper which Stephanidou had to crane forward to hear, broke on the last phrase with a note of despair. But he mastered himself, with a visible effort. "Control, Kadi, control; it would do no good to lose your mind totally. I need to hold on because I have things to do that require me to be alive and conscious and cognisant of what I'm doing. I need to suffer and know that I'm suffering; I made her suffer, God knows. The violence when I totally lost control with her, when the red cloud of hate descended, like it did before, and then letting her go, to that greasy bastard and the others. Knowing she was in Hell and leaving her there, not lifting a finger to help her because of my damned pride."

He seemed to remember himself here, and the presence of Stephanidou. He collapsed back onto the bed, and his voice rasped. "So, my friend, what do you think? Is there a book to be written here, perhaps?" And he gave a dry laugh which ended in a hacking cough, but he refused the water which Stephanidou offered. When he'd recovered, he continued. "I have thought about this; maybe I could begin it like this." He collected himself for a moment and then intoned, in a storytelling-style:

"Once I killed a man; but over his lifeless trunk I climbed to the top of the tree, and then I had others to do my killing for me, had I wished it. But a lifeless trunk is an unstable foundation, fragile, rotting, dead wood; and it eventually collapsed, sending me back down, below ground level, but not far enough to reach the roots. I became the prey, the target, and the contract was out on me. They hit me, those in whose interest it was to do so; but they used one who showed me mercy, despite my having shown her none. So I returned to my roots, eventually, and I live on, although I do not wish to. It is not my wishes that matter any more, however, so I continue in this life, in payment of my debt, and will go only when that is paid."

"So I count the days, and watch the stars for my comfort; and when the time comes, the date specified in this contract I have made, only then will I move on. I can control this, as I tried to control all else, myself not excepted. Control, control, the story of my life, from the early days onwards. I think of those days, as I sit and watch the stars, and wonder if it could have been different; but maybe the answer lies there, in the stars which have always fascinated me. We are born under them, we are told that they carry our destiny, and if we believe that, which I do, then all was fixed at birth and it could have been no different, no matter how we may fight it. I'm where I was always destined to be, and no contract which I might have made could change that; I was never in control, no matter how hard I tried to be. Control, control, Kadi; the story of my life."

22: THE CONTRACT FULFILLED

Kadi closed his eyes and was silent, and Stephanidou sat, still mesmerised by the long tale which had unfolded before him. Then he shook himself out of his near-torpor and took the opportunity to go and refill the rose teacup, drinking the contents and repeating the action several times. He was very thirsty, and couldn't imagine how Kadi could go on, just moistening his mouth occasionally but swallowing nothing. Yet he refrained from offering the man water now; he knew it would be declined.

When he returned to his rickety seat, Kadi opened his eyes and continued in a quiet voice. "My brother Iannis died a few months ago; he had a weak heart, apparently, but we never knew. He went in his sleep, so it was very fast and possibly he never knew anything about it. I miss him though; we spent many years apart, on and off, but it was good to have him close so near the end. Nevertheless, I'm glad he went before me; I'd hate to think of him here all alone, and now it's a comfort for me to know how he ended."

"He brought me a wonderful comfort, did I tell you? My Magdalena told her own story, near her end; she recorded it onto tapes, and gave them to her old university professor, who had become a good friend to her and had taken her into her own home to care for her. My little girl had a gift for making people love her, I ought to know, and this woman was no exception. Well, this Laura gave the tapes to James, when they'd been transcribed, and he brought them out here to me. It was a miracle to be able to hear her voice again, and a comfort, if a bittersweet one. Her beautiful voice in my ears again; manna in my wilderness, and I listened, and cried, because the tale she told was unbearable to listen to, knowing the part I'd played in it."

"But it was a part of my penance to listen, and a profound pleasure to hear her voice, even though I can't see her, or hold her, as I so long to. But that's another part of the penance, and all my own fault. Her tale is told now, and has been published, and is doing very well, I believe; they've even translated it into several other languages. So the tapes weren't needed any more for that, and no-one else other than myself needs to hear her voice, so I deleted them. I'll be gone soon, to her hopefully."

"You have the recording of my own story, and it's evidence, of course, but perhaps it might be worthy of publication too? Or made public, at the very least, just as a voice, to give my side? I don't ask for forgiveness, of course, I have so many sins on my conscience to do penance for, and that's what I've been doing, because she deserves it. I tried never to care what other people thought, but I find that I do, in this, because I never meant to be bad. All I wanted was a simple life, and I tried to do good, at the beginning, but it went so wrong, at the end. And that's the point with human affairs, isn't it? They're rarely simple."

A low rumble from the direction of the Turkish mainland interrupted Kadi at this point; a storm was brewing, and a flash of sheet lightening lit up the darkening sky. He smiled. "A signal from the gods? Zeus letting me know it's time to move on? The end of my life; and my afterlife. Everyone who ever meant anything to me is there already, my parents, my brother, the others, so that's where I wish to be." He positively glowed with the idea, but then his forehead wrinkled in thought.

"Eleni will be there with her Osman, happy together at last. Aphrodite, though, she's bound to have found someone else there, it's in her nature and I don't hold that against her.

I shall have to apologise to them, and to little Magdalena, she's waiting for me, that I do know, we agreed before she went on ahead. And my little Bibi; will she be a baby still, or will she have grown, do you think? Do children grow after death? Does anyone, for that matter, or are they fixed as they were at the time of death? Or do souls exist in some other form which we can't possibly imagine here in the before-time? I should like Bibi to be a baby still, to put her in Magdalena's arms and see her Madonna-like smile at the baby; I wanted to give her a child, not at first, but by the time I came around to the idea, well … ."

"She had to leave the child she had behind, though, and those women who cared for Magdalena cared for her too, and raised her, and James played the paternal role and gave financial support as I couldn't be there to help. Katie, Magdalena called her, and a lovely child she is by all accounts. My niece? Or my daughter? I'll never be sure. It seemed better not to do the DNA thing, to leave it at her being either James's or mine but certainly of our blood. And she's alone now that he has gone and I won't be able to be there for her. He always meant to return to her, you see, but it wasn't to be. She has a half-brother, apparently, a child of James by some woman he had a relationship with some years ago, so maybe he'll be there for her. I hope so, but until she eventually joins us Magdalena will care for Bibi, Aphrodite will have to share. But will Bibi be a baby still? There's so much to find out, you see, and it's all there waiting for me to find out, along with the people I love; I shall die into life."

"What more is there to say? I tried to live an ordered life, but control was taken from me early on and it was hard work to get it back. Everyone likes to be in control of their own life, or to think they are, at any rate, and I more than most need to feel this. And, as death is a part of life, the final part, who wouldn't want to be in control of that also? But we know that ultimately we aren't; every night when we go to sleep we don't, we can't, know for sure that we will awaken in the morning. Or we can go to work in the morning as we do every day, like those unfortunate souls killed in road accidents, or aeroplanes, or terrorist attacks, and find that this is unlike every other day, and that Death is waiting for us."

"So we fear it, and don't think about it or discuss it, but we ought to. Sometimes it comes in a cruel form, mocking us, because we are also subject to the rules of our society, which dictates that we aren't allowed to help those in that situation by ending their suffering; Why is that? If an animal, a dog or a cat or whatever, is suffering, we don't hesitate to put an end to their misery. I knew once a woman who had a cat, had it for years and it was everything to her; but it got sick, it was suffering desperately, so although she loved it so much she called the vet, who came to her house and ended its suffering. But we don't allow human beings the same respect. Previously active people are left paralysed, needing others to care for them, to empty their bowels and bladder for them even, and where's the dignity in that? Personally I wouldn't hesitate if it was someone I loved needing assistance, I'd help them end their suffering and worry about the consequences later. But then I've already served time in prison, so I know what the worst outcome could be and, believe me, it would mean very little to me."

"I've often thought that suicide is the ultimate form of control, therefore; not to wait for Death to come for one, in a quicker or slower form, but to say 'I'm in control of my own death' and demonstrate the meaning of the words with the act. So I'm in control, total control, of the day of my death. Not too soon, she bought me seven years, two-and-a-half months and I owe her that much time; it's my new contract with her. I've researched the process, and I've been pacing it out, eking it out, only so much food and water, enough to keep me alive but to give me no pleasure."

His voice was a dry rasp now, yet surprisingly loud. Stephanidou hoped to God that the recording machine was picking it all up, but listened as closely as he could, the better to supply any parts which were missing when he transcribed the thing later. "Pleasure"; Kadi mused. I had so much in the past, at her expense, and it has to be paid for. So I've come into the wilderness, like the original Magdalen, to do penance, to expiate my sins for the time she gave me and then die. My own poor little Magdalena couldn't do this, but what did she have to repent of anyway? Her sins are forgiven, for she loved much; is that in the Bible? I can't remember, I'm afraid. I'm sorry, I'm not making much sense, I appear to be raving now, and repeating myself, but I'm feeling dizzy and faint and thirsty. No, no water, thank you, it will just prolong the process. It can't be long now. My stomach cramps frequently for lack of food, my mouth is dry for lack of water; not just corporeal, but spiritual refreshment I need. The body and blood of Christ, perhaps? I shall die back into life."

He paused, and closed his eyes and sighed. Stephanidou felt pity for the man, who he also thought was raving, but small wonder, given his by-now non-existent intake of water and food. Given his own recent disillusion with religion, Stephanidou thought that there was about as much chance of this island coming back to life as Kadi getting whatever it was that he wanted after death. But he kept this to himself as the man opened his eyes and spoke with renewed effort, subsided as he was on his mattress. Determined to finish his take, he seemed to regain his clarity and focus on the present now.

"Do forgive me, it's been a long day for you and it's probably time you went now, the evening is coming and you should eat and rest. It's getting dark also, and I have to watch the stars; I always watch the stars, I have a contract written up there and I have to keep it." There seemed little chance of stars, given the electric storm currently rumbling overhead, but Stephanidou said nothing and let his host continue. "So when you come in the morning it will be in your official capacity, you'll be wearing your uniform and I trust that you will discharge your duty honourably. So I'll say goodbye now as a friend; because I feel that a friendship of sorts has grown here, hasn't it? Quite, I'm so glad you agree, and I'm sure that you'll benefit from what has passed between us."

"You'll see me in the morning, I'll be here, I give you my word; where else would I go? I'll do myself no violence, I'm too weak to get up the hill and over the cliff, and I don't have the means to harm myself here; you can search me and my house to see." He opened his arms wide here, inviting Stephanidou to carry out a search, but the latter shook his head; "Thank you, but that won't be necessary." Kadi smiled; "You'll take my word? Thank you. So you'll come and I'll be here at your disposal and you'll do your duty, but not before morning; I have your word on that? Thank you; it's a gentlemen's agreement, our contract, and you are clearly a gentleman. I can tell, because I used to be one myself, once."

Stephanidou put out his hand, took that of the older man and shook it firmly. "Thank you", was all he said, but simply, and sincerely. Kadi nodded, then shook the Lieutenant's hand again, as firmly as he was able; then he lay back on his bed and closed his eyes, as though that gesture had drained his remaining energy. Stephanidou looked at his wasted form for a long moment, then turned and went back down the hill towards the village; halfway down he turned and looked back, but the old man was still supine on his bed. Stephanidou continued downwards, but turned off at the track to the beach, where he sat down on the rocks by the shore and looked out to sea meditatively for some time, watching the storm play overhead before returning to the station-house to shower and change.

He went then to see Father Lambros; he hadn't seen the

priest much in recent days, and apologised; 'My busy time of year', the good Father chuckled, 'no apology necessary'. But he became grave when Stephanidou explained what he needed, and agreed to accompany him up the hill on the following morning. Then the Lieutenant phoned the hospital in the town, to give them early warning that a doctor and ambulance might be needed out near the village in the morning. Then he went to the kafenion to eat, and thence to bed where his slumbers were only slightly disturbed by the ongoing electric storm which flashed intermittently in the sky overhead.

23: EASTER SATURDAY, EASTER SUNDAY

The next morning, Lieutenant Stephanidou was up early; he showered and put on a fresh uniform out of respect for what he knew he was going to find at the ruin on the hillside. When he emerged from the station-house he found Father Lambros waiting at the kafenion, so he gulped down a coffee and promised Sofia that he'd breakfast later. They set off then, in the beaten-up police car today, out of respect for the priest's age and girth. It took them only so far, however, steep hills having long since gone beyond its capabilities and the recent repairs by Costaki not proof against the uphill struggle; but the priest proved to be surprisingly spry on the last leg of their journey.

When they arrived at the ruin, Kadi was there, as he had promised he would be. He was dead, and cold, his eyes open to watch the stars as he had so loved to do. He lay on the outdoor bed, from which he had regularly observed the heavens above; he had gone to be one with them, and whoever they contained. His clouded eyes were open, and there was a gentle smile on his face; had Magdalena come to him at the end? As his guardian angel? Stephanidou knew she was supposed to wait until the third day, and let the soul wander the earth for two days beforehand, but he'd already been wandering so long, Stephanidou thought, so why would she make him wait any longer?

Then he realised that he didn't believe in any of this religious mumbo-jumbo any more, but inexplicably he felt tears well up in his own eyes. He moved away, up the hill,

241

waving his phone around as though trying to get a signal but in reality to avoid his emotion being witnessed by the Father. He actually got a signal, so called the hospital in Ayios Andreas and asked them to send what was needed. Unfortunately, they told him, the ambulance had broken down last night and was currently waiting to be fixed; the local mechanic it seemed could not be found. Annoyance took the place of sorrow, but there was work to be done and Stephanidou had to do it. Under control once more, he moved back down to the ruin, where Father Lambros had gently closed his old friend's eyes for the last time and was now saying the prayers for the dead.

It was unthinkable that they leave the body there, in the increasing heat of the day, until such time as the ambulance was fixed and arrived with them. Stephanidou took Kadi gently in his arms, the stage of rigour having passed relatively quickly, it appeared, and carried him to the car part-way down the hill. He placed him on the back seat and covered him with a blanket, which he had kept in the boot of the car; it was the first time Kadi had been covered when he slept since he had lived in the ruin on the hillside.

Stephanidou felt sorrow in his heart; in an odd sort of way he had grown close to this man, despite the games of control which the hermit had played with him. For he believed that Kadi had been a well-meaning soul whose life had gone wrong through one well-intentioned mistake, and Stephanidou felt an affinity with him based on their both having been honest men who had fallen through trying to do good. It could so easily have been him lying there; he remembered how he'd considered, if only momentarily, putting a bullet through his own head and ending it all. But this man had potentially given him a way back to life and, if in giving it he'd had a little fun at the expense of Stephanidou, the latter could forgive him for that.

When they reached the square Stephanidou left Father Lambros by the car, with Kadi in the back, whilst he went to the station-house to fetch the fold-up camp bed which he'd used when Socrates had come to stay. It wasn't ideal, but it was all they had; they'd have taken Kadi to his own house nearby, but it had been disused since his brother Iannis had died and seemed inappropriate, being in an unkempt condition. So the Lieutenant set up the camp bed in the church, at the front, before the Sanctuary yet not within it, because there was space there and it seemed the most appropriate location. Then he went outside and gently took Kadi from the back of the car, carrying him across the forecourt past the kafenion.

A few villagers had come over by this time, those sitting before the kafenion, old Sofia and Giorgos and Mandras, who happened to be passing. The priest having informed them of Kadi's overnight demise, he came into the church with Stephanidou, and they laid the body on the camp bed, covering it with a vestment which the priest brought out from somewhere. As they were finishing, all the others of the village, who knew by now what had happened because word travels fast in a small community where nothing much happens, came into the church to pay their respects. So they uncovered his face, and Kadi lay in state whilst his small community crossed themselves, said prayers for him, lit candles for him and gave him their last kisses. Then they covered him and left him in the care of God, but not before Stephanidou also had bent over and kissed the cold forehead.

It was well after dark by the time the ambulance finally arrived to take Kadi to the hospital morgue, so that his body was gone when the villagers came into the church before midnight to anticipate the resurrection of Christ and wait for Easter Sunday to break. There was just the empty camp bed and the vestment which the priest and the policeman had forgotten to remove, in their emotion at seeing Kadi being driven away. These were duly taken away, and when midnight came the candles were lit and the traditional hymn of *Christ is Risen* was sung before the congregation departed for their beds.

In the morning, Father Lambros performed the Easter Sunday service, and later in the day, when the heat of the sun (which was unusually fierce for this time of year) had abated, the village had an Easter celebration in the square. This was slightly muted on account of Kadi's death, but all felt that dying at Easter was a good omen for the departed in the afterlife and were happy for him on that account. All were there, and Stephanidou noted that old Georgina and her neighbour Panayiotis were sitting together and getting on very well indeed. Clearly the man had convinced the woman that he'd had nothing to do with her assumed homicide of the cat, which in all likelihood had wandered off and died of natural causes somewhere in the open ground, the Lieutenant believed. Giorgos kept the wine and ouzo flowing, and Sofia did them all proud with the food; slow-cooked lamb, after a selection of mezedes, tzatziki, saganaki cheese, skordalia, olives, sardines, keftedes of meat, cheese, tomatoes, kolokythakia and more too numerous to name, followed by galatoboureko and baklava.

Stephanidou had attended the church service out of respect for both the living and the dead, and now joined in the celebration for the same reason. Before, in his loss of faith, he'd have said 'No, it's not my belief'; but he'd learned now to respect others' ways of doing things, even if they were old and of the past and not for the future. So they ate, and drank, and even the curmudgeonly Costaki joined in, acting along with Stephanidou as an unpaid waiter to take food and drink to the elderly and save them the trouble of getting up and down. He even broke some plates in the traditional manner and danced, not too badly either; and while those whose dancing days were over sat and clapped their hands, old Mandras and Stelios were encouraged to get up and show Costaki how it ought really to be done, dancing as they hadn't for years, and even coaxing

Stephanidou into joining them.

The Lieutenant realised then that he'd been taking himself and life too seriously in the past and needed to lighten up in the future; because he felt now, for some reason, that he did have a future, although at present he couldn't say what it might be. He'd wait and see, within this, his community, which was talking and laughing, eating and drinking, dancing and alive now; and Stephanidou realised that it always had been, although in a quiet way, a muted way which he'd been incapable of recognising but would make sure to respect in the future.

In the meantime, at the end of the evening, when the need for sleep was beginning to be apparent in many, Costaki took and broke a pot full of water, a tradition which he'd seen practised in Australia by his Corfiot Greek neighbours and rather liked. As it shattered on the ground, and he exclaimed loudly, 'Christos Anesti! Christ is risen!', the rest of the community gave the traditional reply, 'Alithos Anesti! Truly He is risen!'; and Stephanidou was of their number. Alithos Anesti; Truly he is risen, which he hoped fervently for Kadi also, risen to the afterlife he had so hoped for. He didn't yet understand quite how, but he had got his faith back.

24: ABSOLUTION

The death was duly and officially noted, as was a report by Lieutenant Stephanidou of the events concerning this man, who the officer had identified as matching the photograph of Edward du Cain displayed on the Interpol site, even allowing for deterioration due to ageing and his neglected condition. He'd taken photographs of the dead face, and had the man's own confession, recorded as he told his tale, of his having lived as the man known as Edward du Cain, wanted in Great Britain for breaking his parole and absconding.

Further, he had confessed to the killing all those years ago of Nikos Osman Nikolaides and of disposing of the body, assisted by his father, mother and brother, all of whom had predeceased him. Stephanidou stressed the deceased's absolute belief that he was stopping the rape of a woman. It was only the circumstance of finding her to be his own betrothed that had caused him to panic and conceal the crime, thinking that he would be seen as having murdered the man in a rage at the injury to his own honour.

The woman, Eleni Christou, had subsequently killed herself, fearful of her future as the unmarried mother of a child and deprived of the father of that child. The family of that father, Nikos Osman Nikolaides, was informed. His Greek father had left the island some years ago and moved to the mainland. He'd re-married, apparently, but had died only last year, heart-broken at never knowing what had become of his son. The mother's family in Turkey consisted of a couple of nieces who'd never known the man, who would have been in his seventies now had he lived. They were traditional souls, and extremely pious; their deceased uncle had not been behaving well and had paid in an unfortunate manner for this. His killer was dead, as was the family of that man, who had assisted him in concealing the killing; but by all accounts he had paid through his exile from his home and through his self-punishment. They were content to let matters rest, and Kadi also.

He'd left a will, of sorts; more correctly a note making certain requests pertaining to the decent disposal of his remains and effects. The recording of his story which Stephanidou had made were police property, and evidence for the Lieutenant to use as he thought best. Kadi only asked that the contents be transcribed and made public, if that were possible, so that his voice and his confession might be heard, in order to set several records straight.

There was a postscript also, bequeathing his family house in the village to little Katie, daughter of Magdalena and his heir, as either his daughter or his niece. Kadi's parents were dead, as was his brother Iannis, so there was no-one else to lay claim to the place. Iannis had stayed there, prior to his demise six months ago, and it wasn't in too bad a condition apart from six months' worth of dust and the need for a thorough clean and several coats of paint. Katie also inherited the tumbledown ruin on the hill, where Kadi had spent his last years; what was left of the building was fit only to be demolished, but the land would belong to her to either build or farm on, whatever she decided. Given that she was not resident on the island, however, and far too young to deal with her inheritance, the property was left to the care of Father Lambros to manage as he saw fit, in consultation with Laura Hogarth and Celia O'Donnell, who cared for Katie *in loco parentis.*

In terms of his burial, Kadi hoped that he might be close to his family in the churchyard if Father Lambros could find a way to make this possible, the manner and timing of his death being under Kadi's own control and therefore potentially being seen as a suicide. This contention was borne out when Stephanidou and the priest checked over dates; they found it to be exactly seven years, two-and-a-half months to the day since Kadi had been released from prison and absconded back to his original home to serve out the sentence which he had passed upon himself. The two-and-a half months of her own life which Magdalena had served for contempt of court when she had turned hostile witness, and the seven years of his own life which she had saved him in so doing; all was repaid before he went to join her.

When they prepared him for burial, Kadi had written, they would find a pendant around his neck and a photograph over his heart; these should be returned to those places and buried with him. He referred them to a casket of ashes kept in his dwelling, those of his long-time partner Magdalena Mystry, which had been brought to him by his brother and were to be scattered into his coffin. They found these items as he had said, the photograph and the 'H' pendant, under a hair shirt which he wore, and which must have tormented him terribly. The photograph was of himself, albeit clearly of a prosperous period of his life some years ago, for he was well-dressed and impeccably groomed, a fitting match in appearance if not age for the much-younger white-blonde beauty on his arm. They showed the picture to Father Lambros, who declared her indeed almost the double of the Eleni Christou whom Kadi had loved so long ago.

The priest had argued in favour of his old friend's burial in the churchyard, and performed the rites at his funeral, which he declared totally appropriate and correct. Whatever he may have known and thought privately, he was insistent publicly that Kadi had not committed suicide. Rather, he had lived an ascetic existence, almost as a hermit, and had been fasting in emulation of Saint Simeon the Stylite and others of his ilk. When God had been pleased to take him, at Easter-time, no less, he'd been strictly observing the Great Lent fast, followed by that for Holy Week, and had he lived he would have partaken of the Easter Sunday feast with the rest of the community. The rest of the community had their private doubts about this latter claim, but if the good Father was able to square his conscience with God on this then they had no argument to make.

The traumatic events of Kadi's life had led him to his decision to live in this manner, Father Lambros said, and his memory required the understanding and compassion of the Church. The priest held the funeral as soon as possible, in case the authorities made any trouble; he felt that Kadi deserved to rest in the churchyard close to his parents and brother, back where he belonged after his troubled life. Exhumation was a complicated process, permission not necessarily easy to obtain, and a body once buried, he felt, has a greater chance of staying put. In the event, Kadi was allowed to remain where he was, lying peacefully in the bosom of his family with Magdalena's remains around him and her image over his heart. Lieutenant Stephanidou had been one of those who carried the coffin and placed it in the earth; they'd had to draft in Captain Petrides and the most able of the old men of the area to assist him, and Stephanidou was glad to be able to perform such a last service for this troubled man, who he hoped was now at rest.

25: TWO YEARS LATER

Captain Stephanos Stephanidou sat on the terrace of his comfortable house, on the hillside of a good area of Thessaloniki, and surveyed the scenery. Below him, the crowded cosmopolitan sprawl of the city, beyond it the azure of the Aegean and above them both the blue of the sky turning a deeper shade as the sun sank further towards the horizon. He glanced across to his wife, Elpida, sitting close by with their sleeping son in her arms; a smile passed between them as the infant made sounds of imminent awakening, and the mother rose and took him inside, the better to see to his needs, and to check on his older sister, asleep in her cot. She was a good wife, Stephanos thought, she was happy with hearth and home, which showed in the neatness of its aspect the care with which she tended it.

He was flourishing once more, which is why he had been in a position to marry Elpida at last. The resolution of the cases of Eleni Christou, Nikos Osman Nikolaides and Edward du Cain had brought him credit and the resurrection of his career, which he had thought finished. He'd heard additionally that his old boss had been retired somewhat early, although on a full pension. The man had been praised for his work, but it had been decided that the unorthodox methods he'd employed, and which had worked in the past, were not the way forward into the future of the force. Stephanidou had remembered his friend Socrates and his arguments regarding the past, present and future; a wise man, which is why he had been promoted as a direct result of that retirement.

Promotion for Stephanidou himself had followed, and a posting back to the city, although Thessaloniki rather than Athens. He didn't mind, the city was the city, although Thessaloniki had a more laid-back feel and was slightly further North, meaning the ferocity of the summer was tempered to some small degree, for which he was grateful. It was also closer than Athens to some of the more northerly islands which he wished to visit, when he took his summer holiday with his recently-acquired family. He had no problem in visiting these of his own volition; it had been the banishment against his will which had rankled with him, although he owned now that he had brought it upon his own head, in some measure. But he had found a way into the future, at the hands of one Arkadios Dukakis, and so much more. There were mysteries in these islands, the stories of old people which could when told be stranger than fiction, and he looked forward to hearing some of them, over a coffee at a kafenion. Or an ouzo; he raised his glass in silent remembrance of Kadi and looked up at the stars gradually appearing in the darkening sky as the old hermit had so loved to do.

He thought of the ancient figures of mythology, both the gods and the humans with whom they interacted, for the better, or more usually the worse, of the latter. Nowadays, whenever he cooked on the barbecue, which was often, this being Greece, with long hot summers and some mild days even in winter, he ritualistically burned a couple of pieces of meat as a sacrifice to Apollo, as due thanks to the deity for the restored order of his life. But, whenever he was off duty and went to a football match, or watched one on the television, or attended a wedding, or baptism, or other function of friends and family, he made a point of over-indulging, albeit only slightly, in the alcohol available. This as his homage to Dionysus, his acceptance of the need for a little chaos to break up the order occasionally. When his head protested on the mornings-after, Elpida took him to task; 'You know you shouldn't do it, what do you expect?' He liked her nagging him, because when she gave up and just accepted things he knew he would have to find a more extreme form of acknowledgement of the god, which he didn't want to do. So much chaos and no more suited him just fine.

As to Kadi, Stephanidou was rethinking his opinion on this strange man dying into life, to use the latter's own words, because he had personally witnessed the island experiencing a resurgence of life due to the media attention brought to it by the strange case of Kadi. Tourists of a certain type wanted to see the place where the international fugitive had evaded justice for some years, not to mention the mysterious case of Nikos Osman Nikolaides and Eleni Christou having finally been solved. There were always those ready to cash in by finding a supply to meet a demand, so boat trips had sprung up, from nearby Greek islands and the Turkish mainland. There was even talk of a hydrofoil service being organised, to speed things up. And of course, those tourists would wish to eat and drink whilst on the island, and correspondingly outlets had opened to fill this need.

There was talk of some second and third-generation returners coming back to run these businesses, and Costaki from Australia was apparently in the vanguard of this trend, being on the spot and apparently overflowing with ideas. He'd been filling the position of motor mechanic on the island since his wife had decamped to Rhodes. There wasn't too much for him to do but he was trained in the profession and it kept him busy and fed. Now apparently he was talking of renting out hire cars, organising tours by minibus, fishing trips with lunch provided, walking tours in the springtime when the wild flowers were in bloom; and the hire cars, minibuses and boats would need to be serviced regularly, by Costaki the mechanic, of course. His wife was prepared to compromise with him; Rhodes would be their home in the winter and during term-time for the children, but during the long summers they could come to the island to work at whatever business they took to, and give the children a change of scenery. All this of course depended upon there being a viable business for her to come to, which gave Costaki good motivation to work out carefully what he wanted to do and make a go of it.

Additionally, a botanist had hiked around the island for his holiday, logging the local flora and fauna and putting his diary into an online blog. This had been read by an eminent professor of archaeology, a hiker and amateur botanist in his turn. He had visited the island on the basis of what he'd read, because this island was in the news currently, and because he'd already been around many of the larger and better-known ones. Hiking around this island, somewhere near the West coast he'd found what appeared to be promising signs of ancient buildings; fortifications maybe, nothing major, and nothing that would be of note to the untrained eye, but this expert was sure that there was something there. So there was talk of funding being sought for an archaeological dig, which had put the island in the news again and which would bring in those who wanted to take part, who would need accommodation and all that went with it. It could amount to something or nothing, but for the present there were archaeological types coming and going and spending money and, should they find anything significant, that would promise well for future tourism to the island.

Stephanidou had actually returned already, during the previous summer, bringing Elpida and their baby daughter with him, because he felt the need to return to this place which had made such a significant difference to his life. He had contacted his successor, Lieutenant Solomides, an older man near the end of a far less auspicious career than that of Stephanidou and who was glad to find such an easy final posting. He was willing to arrange accommodation for

Captain Stephanidou and his family for a week, and this they duly moved into upon arrival. Stephanidou had been surprised to find that they were staying in the old home of the Dukakis family, which Kadi had left to the management of Father Lambros, and the priest had thought it fitting for Stephanidou to stay there for the duration of his visit.

Stephanidou had noted with approval some of the new life breathed into the island as soon as the ferry – a far more up-to-date vessel than that upon which he'd arrived the first time - approached Ayios Andreas. A couple of tavernas near the harbour, with the smell of freshly-cooked food issuing forth along with the sound of bouzouki music; clichéd but traditional, the latter, and it was what tourists expected. The kafenion had undergone a face-lift, fresh whitewash and blue for the shutters; the regulation old men were still there, possibly the same who had graced the place when Stephanidou had arrived like a lost soul into Hades, but he couldn't remember. They were playing tavli today; tourism was the order of the day, it would seem, but tavli had its place even in that, adding local colour for the tourists to make the subject of their photographs. And, if they were not of the smartphone generation, there were postcards of 'The Real Greece' on a stand outside the new souvenir shop and stamps for sale within. Mostly tourist rubbish for sale besides, but good for the economy of the place.

There were also signs of building work on the other side of the harbour, on a formerly scruffy plot of land between the end of the harbour and the beginning of the slope which moved gradually upwards to become the cliffs. It was thought that an imitation beach could be constructed there, as well as an extension to the one near the village of Palliohorio upon which Eleni Christou had washed up and from which it was now known that Nikos Osman Nikolaides had been taken to his watery grave. Not a great deal, compared to the bigger islands, but a good start for this place, and who knew how far it could go?

Father Lambros was optimistic on that score; he was seated at the kafenion when Stephanidou and his new family arrived in the village of Palliohorio, which was looking suitably prosperous in its own way. The enterprising Costaki, together with Giorgos and the approval of the Church in the person of Father Lambros, had opened an extension to the kafenion as a bar and café for the use of visitors, of whom a few were already in evidence. Most of the buildings around the square had been freshly painted, the streets tidied and flowers in old olive tins lined the kerbs. "You see", the good Father extended one hand in a sweeping gesture, "we are coming into the twenty-first century. The future will be good; not for me, I won't be around to see it, but better times are coming".

He had aged visibly since Stephanidou had seen him over a year ago, but was still in good humour. His wife had passed away six months ago, and he mourned her, but knew she had gone to a better place and expected to join her after not too long a parting. His own health had worsened, and he couldn't rise to greet the new Captain, but congratulated him on his professional elevation, as well as his new wife and daughter, from where he sat, with a view around the square.

He was glad that Stephanidou had come now, because he would be leaving soon. Two of his sons had returned to the village from their work on the mainland, and hoped to stay and be a part of the rebirth of the island; but for himself he was retiring, and about to retreat to Mount Athos for the remainder of his days. His replacement was here, and was summoned to meet the Captain. Father Demetrios was a pleasant young man, with a wife, a baby and another child on the way. By the time the children were old enough there would be schooling facilities on the island, he asserted. His wife Maria had been a teacher before they married, and she could take up the role again, if necessary.

This information was of great interest to Elpida, who had

loved the island, much to Stephanidou's surprise; so peaceful, so quiet, but with enough going on. The house which Kadi had left in the care of Father Lambros and in which they were staying met with her approval also. "I love it", she enthused, "it wouldn't take a great deal of renovation to be totally comfortable, but maybe no, leave it just as it is, a simple village house, painted and freshened up, new curtains and furniture and so forth. We can come here for the summers when the children are older, get them out of the city pollution and into some fresher air". "The children?" He smiled at her; "You're looking well into the future, we only have one so far". She gave him her special smile then, and placed one of his hands upon her stomach; "I wasn't sure until now, I was going to tell you later".

Another child! He was speechless with happiness; his future was shaping itself, although he would always now remember to show respect to the past also. He had certainly died back into life, along with his island. He thought of it as his now, given all that had happened to him here. So he met with Father Lambros and enquired whether the house might be for sale, with the priest leaving soon for the holy mountain? It might be indeed, the good Father replied, the guardians of young Katie had intimated recently that a sale would be acceptable, given that their ward was still young and had no plans to move to the island. The price which they were willing to accept was also acceptable to Stephanidou, who with his increased salary and some savings reckoned that he could afford it. The upshot was that, once the legal issues had been completed, Stephanidou would be the owner of a summer residence on the island on which he had both died and come back to life.

Which brought him back to Kadi, the catalyst for his current prosperity, and concerning whom Stephanidou still had a couple of calls to make. He left Elpida talking babies with Maria and made his way to the track which lead up onto the cliffs past Kadi's ruined retreat. There was now a sign, where the track left the main road, pointing the way up to 'Lovers' Leap' in English, German and Greek. Stephanidou noted that the apostrophe was in the wrong place in the English, surely, as only one lover had leapt. But he remembered with irony Kadi's comments about the English, amongst other races, not knowing their own language as well as foreign learners often did, and smiled ruefully.

He set off up the track, and soon arrived at the ruin; it was essentially the same, although trimmed and tidied to some extent now, with no sign of Kadi's rusting bedstead or the tattered awning. Beyond it, further up the incline, was a new structure of a temporary appearance, an outdoor bar with plastic chairs, tables and old olive cans sporting flowers forming a sort of boundary around it on the ground. Someone, probably the enterprising Costaki, had put up a sign which labelled it 'The Trysting Place'. Stephanidou considered both this sign, and that on the road below, to be in exceedingly poor taste, the whole thing in fact tacky and totally tasteless, he concluded. He reflected that good taste frequently flies out the window when prospective profit comes in the door, yet noted that someone had laid flowers within the ruins; a small sign of hope. He took a final look at the place where Kadi had breathed his last, and set off for the churchyard.

He had visited the grave as his final action before he left the island and returned to his former life. Now, he went there again and wished that his benefactor had found everything he had been seeking in his own death into life. The grave was more settled now, the grass and plants around it well-established and the original stark newness weathered and muted. It was in a shaded place, close to the family who'd gone before him, neatly kept at the orders of Father Lambros. There were flowers around the white cross, newly-placed just last month, and the inscription which Kadi had requested:

Arkadios Dukakis, 1950 – 20..
Et in Arcadia ego

BIBLIOGRAPHY

ONLINE SOURCES

https://www.academia.edu/32421926/The_Image_and_Lege nd_of_Mary_Magdalene_in_Italian_Renaissance_Painting_ by_Dawn_St._Clare_PhD Accessed 15 April 2019.

https://chaucer.fas.harvard.edu/pages/francis-petrarch-1304-1374-letters-old-age-xvii-3 Accessed 02 May 2018.

http://www.exploreforensics.co.uk/rigor-mortis-and-lividity.html Accessed 04 April 2019.

https://greekerthanthegreeks.com/2016/01/lost-in-translation-word-of-day-arcadia.html Accessed 10 February 2019.

https://www.nhs.uk/conditions/sudden-infant-death-syndrome-sids/ Accessed 01 March 2019.

https://www.nvphotographers.com/greek-wedding-traditions/ Accessed 17 February 2019.

https://oca.org/saints/lives/2000/09/01/102448-st-simeon-stylites-the-elder Accessed 02 May 2019.

http://orthochristian.com/95845.html   Accessed 24 April 2019.

https://www.purplemotes.net/2015/07/26/boccaccio-griselda-petrarch-chaucer/
Accessed 02 May 2019.

BIBLIOGRAPHY- continued

https://www.theoi.com/Heroine/Kallisto.html Accessed 02 February 2019.

https://www.uffizi.it/en/artworks/birth-of-venus Accessed 17 February 2019.

OPERATIC SOURCES

Puccini, Giacomo, *Tosca,* Libretto by Giuseppe Giacosa and Luigi Illica, 1900.

TEXTUAL SOURCES

Giovanni Boccaccio, The *Decameron,* Penguin Books Ltd, London, 1995.

Geoffrey Chaucer, 'The Clerk's Tale', in *The Canterbury Tales,* J. M. Dent, London, 1999, pp. 223 – 256.

The Epic of Gilgamesh, An English Version with an Introduction by N K Sandars, Penguin Books Ltd, London, 1972.

Euripides, *The Bacchae,* in *The Bacchae and Other Plays,* Penguin Books Ltd, London, 1973.

Homer, *The Odyssey,* Penguin Books Ltd, London, 1991.

Henrik Ibsen, *A Doll's House,* in *Four Major Plays,* Oxford University Press, Oxford & New York, 1998.

Thomas Mann, 'Death in Venice', in *Death in Venice & Other Stories,* Random House, London, 1998.

BIBLIOGRAPHY- continued

Francis Petrarch, *De Insigni Obedientia Et Fide Uxoria Griseldis in Waltherum*, Forgotten Books, London, 2018.

William Shakespeare, *Macbeth,* in Stanley Wells and Gary Taylor (eds.), *The Oxford Shakespeare: The Complete Works,* Clarendon Press, Oxford, 1988, pp. 975 – 999.

William Shakespeare, *Othello,* in Stanley Wells and Gary Taylor (eds.), *The Oxford Shakespeare: The Complete Works,* Clarendon Press, Oxford, 1988, pp. 819 – 853.

WORKS OF ART

Sandro Botticelli, *The Birth of Venus,* c. 1484–86, Tempera on canvas, 172.5 x 278.9cm, Galleria degli Uffizi, Florence.

Donatello (Donato di Niccolò di Betto Bardi), *Penitent Magdalene,* 1453 – 1455, Wood, 188cm, Museo dell'Opera del Duomo, Florence.

Nicolas Poussin, Et in Arcadia ego (Les Bergers d'Arcadie), 1637 – 1638, Oil on canvas, 87 x 120cm, Musée du Louvre, Paris.

ABOUT THE AUTHOR

Laura Lyndhurst was born and grew up in North London, England, before marrying and travelling with her husband in the course of his career.

When settled back in the UK she became a mature student and gained Bachelor's and Master's degrees in English and Literature before training and working as a teacher.

She started writing in the last couple of years in the peace and quiet of rural Lincolnshire, and published her debut novel, *Fairytales Don't Come True*, in May 2020. This book forms the first volume of the trilogy, *Criminal Conversation,* of which *Degenerate, Regenerate is* the second. The third volume, *All That We Are Heir To,* is in the process of being written.

Laura recently published her *October Poems,* to which *Thanksgiving Poems and Prose Pieces* is a follow-up. She has also recently written a psychological suspense story, *You Know What You Did,* which she hopes to publish in Spring 2021.

OTHER BOOKS BY THIS AUTHOR

Fairytales Don't Come True
(the prequel to *Degenerate, Regenerate,*
published May 2020)

…

October Poems
(published November 2020)

…

You Know What You Did
(due publication 2021)

…

Thanksgiving Poems & Prose Pieces
(published December 2020)

COMING WINTER 2021

The third volume of *Criminal Conversation,*

All That We Are Heir To

Printed in Great Britain
by Amazon

78408251R00154